PENGUIN BOOKS

THE MIDWICH CUCKOOS

John Wyndham Parkes Lucas Benyon Harris was born in 1903, the son of a barrister. He tried a number of careers including farming, law, commercial art and advertising, and started writing short stories, intended for sale, in 1925. From 1930 to 1939 he wrote stories of various kinds under different names, almost exclusively for American publications, while also writing detective novels. During the war he was in the civil service and then the army. In 1946 he went back to writing stories for publication in the USA and decided to try a modified form of science fiction, a form he called 'logical fantasy'. As John Wyndham he wrote *The Day of the Triffids* and *The Kraken Wakes* (both widely translated), *The Chrysalids*, *The Midwich Cuckoos* (filmed as *Village of the Damned*), *The Seeds of Time*, *Trouble with Lichen*, *The Outward Urge* (with 'Lucas Parkes'), and *Chocky*. He died in March 1969.

JOHN WYNDHAM

The Midwich Cuckoos

PENGUIN BOOKS

PENGUIN BOOKS

Penguin G
Penguin Group (Ca ... P 2Y3

Penguin Irelan ... td)
Penguin Grou ...

Penguin Books Ind ... India
Penguin G
(a division of Pearson New Zealand Ltd)
Penguin Books (South Africa) (Pty) Ltd, 24 Sturdee Avenue,
Rosebank, Johannesburg 2196, South Africa

Penguin Books Ltd, Registered Offices: 80 Strand, London WC2R ORL, England

www.penguin.com

First published by Michael Joseph 1957
First published in Penguin Books 1960
This edition published 2008

1

Printed in England by Clays Ltd, St Ives plc

ISBN: 978-0-141-03301-3

www.greenpenguin.co.uk

Penguin Books is committed to a sustainable future
for our business, our readers and our planet.
The book in your hands is made from paper
certified by the Forest Stewardship Council.

CONTENTS

Part One

Part Two

Part One

CHAPTER I

No Entry to Midwich

ONE of the luckiest accidents in my wife's life is that she happened to marry a man who was born on the 26th of September. But for that, we should both of us undoubtedly have been at home in Midwich on the night of the 26th–27th, with consequences which, I have never ceased to be thankful, she was spared.

Because it was my birthday, however, and also to some extent because I had the day before received and signed a contract with an American publisher, we set off on the morning of the 26th for London, and a mild celebration. Very pleasant, too. A few satisfactory calls, lobster and Chablis at Wheeler's, Ustinov's latest extravaganza, a little supper, and so back to the hotel where Janet enjoyed the bathroom with that fascination which other people's plumbing always arouses in her.

Next morning, a leisurely departure on the way back to Midwich. A pause in Trayne, which is our nearest shopping town, for a few groceries; then on along the main road, through the village of Stouch, then the right-hand turn on to the secondary road for – But, no. Half the road is blocked by a pole from which dangles a notice 'ROAD CLOSED', and in the gap beside it stands a policeman who holds up his hand. . . .

So I stop. The policeman advances to the offside of the car, I recognize him as a man from Trayne.

'Sorry, sir, but the road is closed.'

'You mean I'll have to go round by the Oppley Road?'

''Fraid that's closed, too, sir.'

'But – '

There is the sound of a horn behind.

' 'F you wouldn't mind backing off a bit to the left, sir.'

Rather bewildered, I do as he asks, and past us and past

him goes an army three-ton lorry with khaki-clad youths leaning over the sides.

'Revolution in Midwich?' I inquire.

'Manoeuvres,' he tells me. 'The road's impassable.'

'Not *both* roads surely? We live in Midwich, you know, Constable.'

'I know, sir. But there's no way there just now. 'F I was you, sir, I'd go back to Trayne till we get it clear. Can't have parking here, 'cause of getting things through.'

Janet opens the door on her side and picks up her shopping-bag.

'I'll walk on, and you come along when the road's clear,' she tells me.

The constable hesitates. Then he lowers his voice.

'Seein' as you live there, ma'am, I'll tell you – but it's confidential like. 'T isn't no use tryin', ma'am. Nobody can't get into Midwich, an' that's a fact.'

We stare at him.

'But why on earth not?' says Janet.

'That's just what they're tryin' to find out, ma'am. Now, 'f you was to go to the Eagle in Trayne, I'll see you're informed as soon as the road's clear.'

Janet and I looked at one another.

'Well,' she said to the constable, 'it seems very queer, but if you're quite *sure* we can't get through. . . .'

'I am that, ma'am. It's orders, too. We'll let you know, as soon as maybe.'

If one wanted to make a fuss, it was no good making it with him; the man was only doing his duty, and as amiably as possible.

'Very well,' I agreed. 'Gayford's my name, Richard Gayford. I'll tell the Eagle to take a message for me in case I'm not there when it comes.'

I backed the car further until we were on the main road, and, taking his word for it that the other Midwich road was similarly closed, turned back the way we had come. Once we were the other side of Stouch village I pulled off the road into a field gateway.

'This,' I said, 'has a very odd smell about it. Shall we cut across the fields, and see what's going on?'

'That policeman's manner was sort of queer, too. Let's,' Janet agreed, opening her door.

*

What made it the more odd was that Midwich was, almost notoriously, a place where things did not happen.

Janet and I had lived there just over a year then, and found this to be almost its leading feature. Indeed, had there been posts at the entrances to the village bearing a red triangle and below them a notice:

MIDWICH

DO NOT

DISTURB

they would have seemed not inappropriate. And why Midwich should have been singled out in preference to any one of a thousand other villages for the curious event of the 26th of September seems likely to remain a mystery for ever.

For consider the simple ordinariness of the place.

Midwich lies roughly eight miles west-north-west of Trayne. The main road westward out of Trayne runs through the neighbouring villages of Stouch and Oppley, from each of which secondary roads lead to Midwich. The village itself is therefore at the apex of a road triangle which has Oppley and Stouch at its lower corners; its only other highway being a lane which rolls in a Chestertonian fashion some five miles to reach Hickham which is three miles north.

At the heart of Midwich is a triangular Green ornamented by five fine elms and a white-railed pond. The war memorial stands in the churchward corner of the Green, and spaced out round the sides are the church itself, the vicarage, the inn, the smithy, the post office, Mrs Welt's shop, and a number of cottages. Altogether, the village comprises some sixty cottages and small houses, a village hall, Kyle Manor, and The Grange.

The church is mostly perp. and dec., but with a Norman west doorway and font. The vicarage is Georgian; The Grange Victorian; Kyle Manor has Tudor roots with numerous later graftings. The cottages show most of the styles which have existed between the two Elizabeths, but even more recent than the two latest County Council cottages are the utilitarian wings that were added to The Grange when the Ministry took it over for Research.

The existence of Midwich has never been convincingly accounted for. It was not in a strategic position to hold a market, not even across a packway of any importance. It appears, at some unknown time, simply to have occurred; the Domesday survey notes it as a hamlet, and it has continued as little more, for the railway age ignored it, as had the coach roads, and even the navigation canals.

So far as is known, it rests upon no desirable minerals: no official eye ever saw it as a likely site for an aerodrome, or a bombing-range, or a battle school; only the Ministry intruded, and the reconditioning of The Grange had little effect upon the village life. Midwich has – or rather, had – lived and drowsed upon its good soil in Arcadian undistinction for a thousand years; and there seemed, until the late evening of the 26th of September, no reason why it should not so to do for the next millennium, too.

This must not be taken, however, to mean that Midwich is altogether without history. It has had its moments. In 1931 it was the centre of an untraced outbreak of foot-and-mouth disease. And in 1916 an off-course Zeppelin unloaded a bomb which fell in a ploughed field and fortunately failed to explode. And before that it hit the headlines – well, anyway, the broadsheets – when Black Ned, a second-class highwayman, was shot on the steps of The Scythe and Stone Inn by Sweet Polly Parker, and although this gesture of reproof appears to have been of a more personal than social nature, she was, nevertheless, much lauded for it in the ballads of 1768.

Then, too, there was the sensational closure of the nearby St Accius' Abbey, and the redistribution of the brethren for reasons which have been a subject of intermittent local speculation ever since it took place, in 1493.

Other events include the stabling of Cromwell's horses in the church, and a visit by William Wordsworth, who was inspired by the Abbey ruins to the production of one of his more routine commendatory sonnets.

With these exceptions, however, recorded time seems to have flowed over Midwich without a ripple.

Nor would the inhabitants – save, perhaps, some of the youthful in their brief pre-marital restlessness – have it otherwise. Indeed, but for the Vicar and his wife, the Zellabys at Kyle Manor, the doctor, the district-nurse, ourselves, and, of course, the Researchers, they had most of them lived there for numerous generations in a placid continuity which had become a right.

During the day of the 26th of September there seems to have been no trace of a foreshadow. Possibly Mrs Brant, the blacksmith's wife, did feel a trace of uneasiness at the sight of nine magpies in one field, as she afterwards claimed; and Miss Ogle, the postmistress, may have been perturbed on the previous night by a dream of singularly large vampire bats; but, if so, it is unfortunate that Mrs Brant's omens and Miss Ogle's dreams should have been so frequent as to nullify their alarm value. No other evidence has been produced to suggest that on that Monday, until late in the evening, Midwich was anything but normal. Just, in fact, as it had appeared to be when Janet and I set off for London. And yet, on Tuesday the 27th. . . .

*

We locked the car, climbed the gate, and started over the field of stubble keeping well in to the hedge. At the end of that we came to another field of stubble and bore leftwards across it, slightly uphill. It was a big field with a good hedge on the far side, and we had to go further left to find a gate we could climb. Half-way across the pasture beyond brought us to the top of the rise, and we were able to look out across Midwich – not that much of it was visible for trees, but we could see a couple of wisps of greyish smoke lazily rising, and the church spire sticking up by the elms. Also, in the middle of the next field I could see four or five cows lying down, apparently asleep.

I am not a countryman, I only live there, but I remember thinking rather far back in my mind that there was something not quite right about that. Cows folded up, chewing cud, yes, commonly enough; but cows lying down fast asleep, well, no. But it did not do more at the time than give me a vague feeling of something out of true. We went on.

We climbed the fence of the field where the cows were and started across that, too.

A voice hallooed at us, away on the left. I looked round and made out a khaki-clad figure in the middle of the next field. He was calling something unintelligible, but the way he was waving his stick was without doubt a sign for us to go back. I stopped.

'Oh, come on, Richard. He's miles away,' said Janet impatiently, and began to run on ahead.

I still hesitated, looking at the figure who was now waving his stick more energetically than ever, and shouting more loudly, though no more intelligibly. I decided to follow Janet. She had perhaps twenty yards start of me by now, and then, just as I started off, she staggered, collapsed without a sound, and lay quite still. . . .

I stopped dead. That was involuntary. If she had gone down with a twisted ankle, or had simply tripped I should have run on, to her. But this was so sudden and so complete that for a moment I thought, idiotically, that she had been shot.

The stop was only momentary. Then I went on again.

Dimly I was aware of the man away on the left still shouting, but I did not bother about him. I hurried towards her....

But I did not reach her.

I went out so completely that I never even saw the ground come up to hit me....

CHAPTER 2

All Quiet in Midwich

As I said, all was normal in Midwich on the 26th. I have looked into the matter extensively, and can tell you where practically everyone was, and what they were doing that evening.

The Scythe and Stone, for instance, was entertaining its regulars in their usual numbers. Some of the younger villagers had gone to the pictures in Trayne – mostly the same ones who had gone there the previous Monday. In the post office Miss Ogle was knitting beside her switchboard, and finding, as usual, that real life conversation was more interesting than the wireless. Mr Tapper, who used to be a jobbing gardener before he won something fabulous in a football pool, was in a bad temper with his prized colour-television set which had gone on the blink again in its red circuit, and was abusing it in language that had already driven his wife to bed. Lights still burnt in one or two of the new laboratories shouldered on to The Grange, but there was nothing unusual in that; it was common for one or two Researchers to conduct their mysterious pursuits late into the night.

But although all was so normal, even the most ordinary-seeming day is special for someone. For instance, it was, as I have said, my birthday, so it happened that our cottage was closed and dark. And up at Kyle Manor it happened, also, to be the day when Miss Ferrelyn Zellaby put it to Mr Alan (temporarily Second-Lieutenant) Hughes that, in practice, it takes more than two to make an engagement; that it would be a friendly gesture to tell her father about it.

Alan, after some hesitation and demur, allowed himself to be persuaded into Gordon Zellaby's study to make him acquainted with the situation.

He found the master of Kyle Manor spread comfortably

about a large armchair, his eyes closed, and his elegantly white head leaning against the chair's right wing, so that at first sight he appeared to have been lulled to sleep by the excellently reproduced music that pervaded the room. Without speaking, or opening his eyes, however, he dispelled this impression by waving his left hand at another easy chair and then putting his finger to his lips for silence.

Alan tiptoed to the indicated chair, and sat down. There then followed an interlude during which all the phrases that he had summoned to the tip of his tongue drained back somewhere beyond its root, and for the next ten minutes or so he occupied himself by a survey of the room.

One wall was covered from floor to ceiling by books which broke off only to allow the door by which he had entered. More books, in lower bookcases, ran round most of the room, halting in places to accommodate the french-windows, the chimney-piece, where flickered a pleasant though not quite necessary fire, and the record player. One of the several glass-fronted cases was devoted to the Zellaby Works in various editions and languages, with room on the bottom shelf for a few more.

Above this case hung a sketch in red chalk of a handsome young man who could, after some forty years, still be seen in Gordon Zellaby. On another case a vigorous bronze recorded the impression he had made on Epstein some twenty-five years later. A few signed portraits of other notable persons hung here and there on the walls. The space above and about the fireplace was reserved for more domestic mementoes. Along with portraits of Gordon Zellaby's father, mother, brother, and two sisters, hung likenesses of Ferrelyn, and her mother (Mrs Zellaby Number 1).

A portrait of Angela, the present Mrs Gordon Zellaby, stood upon the centre piece and focus of the room, the large, leather-topped desk where the Works were written.

Reminder of the Works caused Alan to wonder whether his timing might not have been more propitious, for a new Work was in process of gestation. This was made manifest by a certain distraitness in Mr Zellaby at present.

'It always happens when he's brewing,' Ferrelyn had explained. 'Part of him seems to get lost. He goes off on long walks and can't make out where he is and rings up to be brought home, and so on. It's a bit trying while it lasts, but it gets all right again once he eventually starts to write the book. While it's on, we just have to be firm with him, and see he has his meals, and all that.'

The room in general, with its comfortable chairs, convenient lights, and thick carpet, struck Alan as a practical result of its owner's views on the balanced life. He recalled that in *While We Last*, the only one of the Works he had read as yet, Zellaby had treated ascetism and over-indulgence as similar evidences of maladjustment. It had been an interesting, but, he thought, gloomy book; the author had not seemed to him to give proper weight to the fact that the new generation was more dynamic, and rather more clear-sighted than those that had preceded it. . . .

At last the music tied itself up with a neat bow, and ceased. Zellaby stopped the machine by a switch on the arm of his chair, opened his eyes, and regarded Alan.

'I hope you don't mind,' he apologized. 'One feels that once Bach has started his pattern he should be allowed to finish it. Besides,' he added, glancing at the playing-cabinet, 'we still lack a code for dealing with these innovations. Is the art of the musician less worthy of respect simply because he is not present in person? What is the gracious thing? – For me to defer to you, for you to defer to me, or for both of us to defer to genius – even genius at second-hand? Nobody can tell us. We shall never know.

'We don't seem to be good at integrating novelties with our social lives, do we? The world of the etiquette book fell to pieces at the end of the last century, and there has been no code of manners to tell us how to deal with anything invented since. Not even rules for an individualist to break, which is itself another blow at freedom. Rather a pity, don't you think?'

'Er, yes,' said Alan. 'I – er – '

'Though, mind you,' Mr Zellaby continued, 'it is a trifle *démodé* even to perceive the existence of the problem. The true fruit of this century has little interest in coming to living-terms with innovations; it just greedily grabs them all as they come along. Only when it encounters something really big does it become aware of a social problem at all, and then, rather than make concessions, it yammers for the impossibly easy way out, uninvention, suppression – as in the matter of The Bomb.'

'Er – yes, I suppose so. What I – '

Mr Zellaby perceived a lack of fervour in the response.

'When one is young,' he said understandingly, 'the unconventional, the unregulated, hand-to-mouth way of life has a romantic aspect. But such, you must agree, are not the lines on which to run a complex world. Luckily, we in the West still retain the skeleton of our ethics, but there are signs that the old bones are finding the weight of new knowledge difficult to carry with confidence, don't you think?'

Alan drew breath. Recollections of previous entanglements in the web of Zellaby discourse forced him to the direct solution.

'Actually, sir, it was on quite another matter I wanted to see you,' he said.

When Zellaby noticed the interruptions of his audible reflections he was accustomed to take them in mild good part. He now postponed further contemplation of the ethical skeleton to inquire:

'But of course, my dear fellow. By all means. What is it?'

'It's that – well, it's about Ferrelyn, sir.'

'Ferrelyn? Oh yes. I'm afraid she's gone up to London for a couple of days to see her mother. She'll be back tomorrow.'

'Er – it was today she came back, Mr Zellaby.'

'Really?' exclaimed Zellaby. He thought it over. 'Yes, you're quite right. She was here for dinner. You both were,' he said triumphantly.

'Yes,' said Alan, and holding his chance with determination, he ploughed ahead with his news, unhappily conscious that not one stone of his prepared phrases remained upon another, but getting through it somehow.

Zellaby listened patiently until Alan finally stumbled to a conclusion with:

'So I do hope, sir, that you will have no objection to our becoming officially engaged,' and at that his eyes widened slightly.

'My dear fellow, you overestimate my position. Ferrelyn is a sensible girl, and I have no doubt whatever that by this time she and her mother know *all* about you, and have, together, reached a well-considered decision.'

'But I've never even met Mrs Holder,' Alan objected.

'If you had, you would have a better grasp of the situation. Jane is a great organizer,' Mr Zellaby told him, regarding one of the pictures on the mantel with benevolence. He got up.

'Well, now, you have performed your part very creditably; so I, too, must behave as Ferrelyn considers proper. Would you care to assemble the company while I fetch the bottle?'

A few minutes, with his wife, his daughter, and his prospective son-in-law grouped about him, he lifted his glass.

'Let us now drink,' announced Zellaby, 'to the adjunction of fond spirits. It is true that the institution of marriage as it is proclaimed by Church and state displays a depressingly mechanistic attitude of mind towards partnership – one not unlike, in fact, that of Noah. The human spirit, however, is tough, and it quite often happens that love is able to survive this coarse, institutional thumbing. Let us hope, therefore – '

'Daddy,' Ferrelyn broke in, 'it's after ten, and Alan has to get back to camp in time, or he'll be cashiered, or something. All you really have to say is "long life and happiness to you both".'

'Oh,' said Mr Zellaby. 'Are you sure that's enough? It seems very brief. However, if you think it suitable, then I say it, my dear. Most wholeheartedly I say it.'

He did.

Alan set down his empty glass.

'I'm afraid what Ferrelyn said was right, sir. I shall have to leave now,' he said.

Zellaby nodded sympathetically.

'It must be a trying time for you. How much longer will they keep you?'

Alan said he hoped to be free of the army in about three months. Zellaby nodded again.

'I expect the experience will turn out to have value. Sometimes I regret the lack of it myself. Too young for one war, tethered to a desk in the Ministry of Information in the next. Something more active would have been preferable. Well, good night, my dear fellow. It's – ' He broke off, struck by a sudden thought. 'Dear me, I know we all call you Alan, but I don't believe I know your other name. Perhaps we ought to have that in order.'

Alan told him, and they shook hands again.

As he emerged into the hall with Ferrelyn he noticed the clock.

'I say, I'll have to step on it. See you tomorrow, darling. Six o'clock. Good night, my sweet.'

They kissed fervently but briefly in the doorway, and he broke away down the steps, bounding towards the small red car parked on the drive. The engine started and roared. He gave a final wave, and, with a spurt of gravel from the rear wheels, dashed away.

Ferrelyn watched the rear lights dwindle and vanish She stood listening until the erstwhile roar became a distant hum, and then closed the front door. On her way back to the study she noticed that the hall clock now showed ten-fifteen.

Still, then, at ten-fifteen nothing in Midwich was abnormal.

With the departure of Alan's car peace was able to settle down again over a community which was, by and large, engaged in winding up an uneventful day in expectation of a no less uneventful morrow.

Many cottage windows still threw yellow beams into the mild evening where they glistered in the dampness of an earlier shower. The occasional surges of voices and laughter which swept the place were not local; they originated with a well-handled studio-audience miles away and several days ago, and formed merely a background against which most of the village was preparing for bed. Many of the very old and very young had gone there already, and wives were now filling their own hot-water bottles.

The last customers to be persuaded out of The Scythe and Stone had lingered for a few minutes to get their night-eyes and gone their ways, and by ten-fifteen all but one Alfred Wait and a certain Harry Crankhart, who were still engaged in argument about fertilizers, had reached their homes.

Only one event of the day still impended – the passage of the bus that would be bringing the more dashing spirits back from their evening in Trayne. With that over, Midwich could finally settle down for the night.

In the Vicarage, at ten-fifteen, Miss Polly Rushton was thinking that if only she had gone to bed half an hour ago she could be enjoying the book that now lay neglected on her knees, and how much pleasanter that would be than listening to the present contest between her uncle and aunt. For, on one side of the room Uncle Hubert, the Reverend Hubert Leebody, was attempting to listen to a Third Programme disquisition on the Pre-Sophoclean Conception of the Oedipus Complex, while, on the other, Aunt Dora was telephoning. Mr Leebody, determined that scholarship should not be submerged by piffle, had already made two advances in volume, and still had forty-five degrees of knob turning in reserve. He could not be blamed for failing to guess that what was striking him as a particularly nugatory exchange of feminine concerns could turn out to be of importance. No one else would have guessed it, either.

The call was from South Kensington, London, where a Mrs Cluey was seeking the support of her lifelong friend Mrs

Leebody. By ten-sixteen she had reached the kernel of the matter.

'Now, tell me, Dora – and, mind, I do want your *honest* opinion on this: do you think that in Kathy's case it should be white satin, or white brocade?'

Mrs Leebody stalled. Clearly this was a matter where the word 'honest' was relative, and it was inconsiderate of Mrs Cluey, to say the least, to phrase her question with no perceptible bias. Probably satin, thought Mrs Leebody, but she hesitated to risk the friendship of years on a guess. She tried for a lead.

'Of course, for a very young bride . . . but then one wouldn't call Kathy such a *very* young bride, perhaps . . .'

'Not *very* young,' agreed Mrs Cluey, and waited.

Mrs Leebody dratted her friends' importunity, and also her husband's wireless programme which made thinking and finesse difficult.

'Well,' she said at last, 'both can look charming, of course, but for Kathy I really think – '

At which point her voice abruptly stopped. . . .

Far away in South Kensington Mrs Cluey joggled the rest impatiently, and looked at her watch. Presently she pressed the bar down for a moment, and then dialled O.

'I wish to make a complaint,' she said. 'I have just been cut off in the middle of a most important conversation.'

The exchange told her it would try to reconnect her. A few minutes later it confessed failure.

'Most inefficient,' said Mrs Cluey. 'I shall put in a written complaint. I refuse to pay for a minute more than we had – indeed, I really don't see why I should pay for that, in the circumstances. We were cut off at ten-seventeen exactly.'

The man at the exchange responded with formal tact, and made a note of the time, for reference – 22.17 hrs 26th Sept. . . .

CHAPTER 3

Midwich Rests

FROM ten-seventeen that night, information about Midwich becomes episodic. Its telephones remained dead. The bus that should have passed through it failed to reach Stouch, and a truck that went to look for the bus did not return. A notification from the R.A.F. was received in Trayne of some unidentified flying object, not, repeat not, a service machine, detected by radar in the Midwich area, possibly making a forced landing. Someone in Oppley reported a house on fire in Midwich, with, apparently, nothing being done about it. The Trayne fire appliance turned out – and thereafter failed to make any reports. The Trayne police despatched a car to find out what had happened to the fire-engine, and that, too, vanished into silence. Oppley reported a second fire, and still, seemingly, nothing being done, Constable Gobby, in Stouch, was rung up, and sent off on his bicycle to Midwich; and no more was heard of him, either. . . .

*

The dawn of the 27th was an affair of slatternly rags soaking in a dishwater sky, with a grey light weakly filtering through. Nevertheless, in Oppley and in Stouch cocks crowed, and other birds welcomed it more melodiously. In Midwich, however, no birds sang.

In Oppley and Stouch, too, as in other places, hands were soon reaching out to silence alarm clocks, but in Midwich the clocks rattled on till they ran down.

In other villages sleepy-eyed men left their cottages and encountered their work-mates with sleepy good mornings; in Midwich no one encountered anyone.

For Midwich lay entranced. . . .

While the rest of the world began to fill the day with

clamour, Midwich slept on. . . . Its men and women, its horses, cows, and sheep; its pigs, its poultry, its larks, moles, and mice all lay still. There was a pocket of silence in Midwich, broken only by the frouing of the leaves, the chiming of the church clock, and the gurgle of the Opple as it slid over the weir beside the mill. . . .

And while the dawn was still a poor, weak thing an olive-green van, with the words 'Post Office Telephones' just discernible upon it, set out from Trayne with the object of putting the rest of the world into touch with Midwich again.

In Stouch it paused at the village call box to inquire whether Midwich had yet shown any signs of life. Midwich had not; it was still as deeply incommunicado as it had been since 22.17 hrs. The van restarted and rattled on through the uncertainly gathering daylight.

'Cor!' said the lineman to his driver companion. 'Cor! That there Miss Ogle ain't 'alf goin' to cop 'erself a basinful of 'Er Majesty's displeasure over this little lot.'

'I don't get it,' complained the driver. ' 'F you'd asked me I'd of said the old girl was *always* listenin' when there was anyone on the blower, day or night. Jest goes to show,' he added, vaguely.

A little out of Stouch, the van swung sharply to the right, and bounced along the by-road to Midwich for half a mile or so. Then it rounded a corner to encounter a situation which called for all the driver's presence of mind.

He had a sudden view of a fire-engine, half heeled over, with its near-side wheels in the ditch, and a black saloon car which had climbed half-way up the bank on the other side a few yards further on, with a man and a bicycle lying half in the ditch behind it. He pulled hard over, attempting an S turn which would avoid both vehicles, but before he could complete it his own van ran on to the narrow verge, bumped along for a few more yards, then ploughed to a stop, with its side in the hedge.

Half an hour later the first bus of the day, proceeding at a light-hearted speed, since it never had a passenger before it picked up the Midwich children for school in Oppley, rattled round the same corner to jamb itself neatly into the gap between the fire-engine and the van, and block the road completely.

On Midwich's other road – that connecting it with Oppley – a similar tangle of vehicles gave at first sight the impression that the highway had, overnight become a dump. And on that side the mail-van was the first vehicle to stop without becoming involved.

One of its occupants got out, and walked forward to investigate the disorder. He was just approaching the rear of the stationary bus when, without any warning, he quietly folded up, and dropped to the ground. The driver's jaw fell open, and he stared. Then, looking beyond his fallen companion, he saw the heads of some of the bus passengers, all quite motionless. He reversed hastily, turned, and made for Oppley and the nearest telephone.

Meanwhile the similar state of affairs on the Stouch side had been discovered by the driver of a baker's van, and twenty minutes later almost identical action was taking place on both the approaches to Midwich. Ambulances swept up with something of the air of mechanized Galahads. Their rear doors opened. Uniformed men emerged, fastening their tunic buttons, and providently pinching the embers from half-smoked cigarettes. They surveyed the pile-ups in a knowledgeable, confidence-inspiring way, unrolled stretchers, and prepared to advance.

On the Oppley road the two leading bearers approached the prone postman competently, but then, as the one in the lead drew level with the body, he wilted, sagged, and subsided across the last casualty's legs. The hind bearer goggled. Out of a babble behind him his ears picked up the word 'Gas!' he dropped the stretcher-handles as if they had turned hot, and stepped hastily back.

There was a pause for consultation. Presently the ambulance driver delivered a verdict, shaking his head.

'Not our kind of job,' he said, with the air of one recalling a useful Union decision. 'More like the fire chaps' pigeon, I'd say.'

'The army's, I reckon,' said the bearer. 'Gas masks, not just smoke masks, is what's wanted here.'

CHAPTER 4

Operation Midwich

ABOUT the time that Janet and I were approaching Trayne, Lieutenant Alan Hughes was standing side by side with Leading-Fireman Norris on the Oppley road. They were watching while a fireman grappled at the fallen ambulance-man with a long ceiling-hook. Presently the hook lodged, and began to haul him in. The body was dragged across a yard and a half of tarmac – and then sat up abruptly, and swore.

It seemed to Alan that he had never heard more beautiful language. Already, the acute anxiety with which he had arrived on the scene had been allayed by the discovery that the victims of whatever-it-was were quietly, but quite definitely, breathing as they lay there. Now it was established that one, at least, of them showed no visible ill effects of quite ninety minutes' experience of it.

'Good,' Alan said. 'If he's all right, it looks as if the rest may be – though it doesn't get us much nearer to knowing *what* it is.'

The next to be hooked and pulled out was the postman. He had been there somewhat longer than the ambulance-man, but his recovery was every bit as spontaneous and satisfactory.

'The line seems to be quite sharp – and stationary,' Alan added. 'Whoever heard of a perfectly stationary gas – and with a light wind blowing, too? It doesn't make sense.'

'Can't be droplet stuff evaporating off the ground, either,' said the Leading-Fireman. 'Kind of hits 'em like a hammer. I never heard of a droplet one like that, did you?'

Alan shook his head. 'Besides,' he agreed, 'anything really volatile would have cleared by now. What's more, it wouldn't have vaporized last night and caught the bus and the rest.

The bus was due in Midwich at ten-twenty-five – and I came over this bit of road myself only a few minutes before that. There wasn't anything wrong with it then. In fact, that must be the bus I met just running into Oppley.'

'I wonder how far it stretches?' mused the Leading-Fireman. 'Must be fairly wide, or we'd see things what were trying to come this way.'

They continued to gaze in perplexity towards Midwich. Beyond the vehicles the road continued with a clear, innocent-looking, slightly shining, surface to the next turn. Just like any other road almost dry after a shower. Now that the morning mist had lifted it was possible to see the tower of Midwich church jutting above the hedges. When one disregarded the immediate foreground, the prospect was the very negation of mystery.

The firemen, assisted by Alan's squad, continued to drag out the forms within easy reach. Their experience seemed to leave no impression on the victims. Each one, on coming clear, sat up alertly, and maintained with obvious truth that he needed no help from the ambulance men.

The next job was to clear an inverted tractor out of the way so that the further vehicles and their occupants could be pulled clear.

Alan left his Sergeant and the Leading-Fireman directing the work, and climbed over a stile. The field-path beyond climbed a small rise, and gave him a better view of the Midwich terrain. He was able to see several roofs, including those of Kyle Manor, and The Grange, also the topmost stones of the Abbey ruins, and two drifts of grey smoke. A placid scene. But a few further yards brought him to a point where he could see four sheep lying motionless in a field. The sight troubled him, not because he now thought it likely that any real harm had come to the sheep, but because it indicated that the barrier-zone was wider than he had hoped. He contemplated the creatures and the landscape beyond, and noticed two cows on their sides still further away. He watched them for a minute or two to make sure there was no movement, and then turned and walked thoughtfully back to the road.

'Sergeant Decker,' he called.

The sergeant came over, and saluted.

'Sergeant,' said Alan, 'I want you to get hold of a canary – in a cage, of course.'

The sergeant blinked.

'Er – a canary, sir?' he asked, uneasily.

'Well, I suppose a budgerigar would do as well. There ought to be some in Oppley. You'd better take the jeep. Tell the owner there'll be compensation if necessary.'

'I – er – '

'Cut along now, Sergeant. I want that bird here as soon as you can manage it.'

'Very good, sir. Er – a canary,' the sergeant added, to make sure.

'Yes,' said Alan.

*

I became aware that I was slithering along the ground, face down. Very odd. One moment I was hurrying towards Janet, then, with no interval at all, this . . .

The motion stopped. I sat up to find myself surrounded by a collection of people. There was a fireman, engaged in disentangling a murderous-looking hook from my clothing. A St John Ambulance man regarding me with a professionally hopeful eye. A very young private carrying a pail of whitewash, another holding a map, and an equally young corporal armed with a bird-cage on the end of a long pole. Also an unencumbered officer. In addition to this somewhat surrealistic collection there was Janet, still lying where she had fallen. I got to my feet just as the fireman, having freed his hook, reached it towards her, and caught the belt of her mackintosh. He began to pull, and of course the belt broke, so he reached it across her, and began to roll her towards us. At the second time over, she sat up, looking disarranged, and indignant.

'Feeling all right, Mr Gayford?' asked a voice beside me.

I looked round and recognized the officer as Alan Hughes whom we had met at the Zellabys' a couple of times.

'Yes,' I said. 'But what's going on here?'

He disregarded that for the moment, and helped Janet to her feet. Then he turned to the corporal.

'I'd better get back to the road. Just carry on with this, Corporal.'

'Yes, sir,' said the corporal. He lowered his pole from the vertical, and with the cage still dangling at its end, thrust it forward tentatively. The bird fell off its perch, and lay on the sanded floor of the cage. The corporal withdrew the cage. The bird gave a slightly indignant tweet, and hopped back on its perch. One watching private stepped forward with his bucket and daubed a little whitewash on the grass, the other made a mark on his map. The party then moved along a dozen yards or so, and repeated the performance.

This time it was Janet who inquired what on earth was happening. Alan explained as much as he knew, and added:

'There's obviously no chance of getting into the place while this lasts. Much your best course would be to make for Trayne, and wait there for the all-clear.'

We looked after the corporal's party, just in time to see the bird fall off its perch once more, and then across the innocent fields to Midwich. After our experience there did not appear to be any useful alternative. Janet nodded. So we thanked young Hughes, and presently parted from him to make our way back to the car.

At the The Eagle Janet insisted that we should book a room for the night, just in case . . . and then went up to it. I gravitated to the bar.

The place was quite unusually full for noon, and almost entirely of strangers. The majority of them were talking somewhat histrionically in small groups or pairs; though a few individuals were drinking privately and thoughtfully. I wormed my way to the counter with some difficulty, and as I was worming it back again, drink in hand, a voice at my shoulder said:

'Now, what on earth would you be doing in this lot, Richard?'

The voice was familiar, and so, when I looked round, was the face, though it took me a second or two to place it – there was not only the veil of years to be drawn aside, but a military cap had to be juggled into the place of the present tweed. But when this had been done, I was delighted.

'My dear Bernard!' I exclaimed. 'This is wonderful! Come along out of this mob.' And I seized his arm, and towed him into the lounge.

The sight of him made me feel young again: took me back to the beaches, the Ardennes, the Reichswald, and the Rhine. It was a good meeting. I sent the waiter for more drinks. It took about half an hour for the first ebullition to level out, but when it did:

'You never answered my first question,' he reminded me, looking at me carefully. 'I'd no idea you'd gone in for that sort of thing.'

'What sort of thing?' I inquired.

He lifted his head slightly, towards the bar.

'The Press,' he explained.

'Oh, is that it! I was wondering why the invasion.'

One eyebrow descended a little.

'Well, if you're not part of it, what are you?' he said.

'I just live in these parts,' I told him.

At that moment Janet came into the lounge, and I introduced him.

'Janet dear, this is Bernard Westcott. He used to be Captain Westcott when we were together, but I know he became a Major, and now – ?'

'Colonel,' admitted Bernard, and greeted her charmingly.

'I am so glad,' Janet told him. 'I've heard a lot about you. I know one says that, but this time it happens to be true.'

She invited him to lunch with us, but he said that he had

business to attend to, and was already overdue. His tone of regret was genuine enough for her to say:

'Dinner, then? At home, if we can get there, but here if we are still exiled?'

'At home?' queried Bernard.

'In Midwich,' she explained. 'It's about eight miles away.'

Bernard's manner changed slightly.

'You *live* in Midwich?' he inquired, looking from her to me. 'Have you been there long?'

'About a year now,' I told him. 'We'd normally be there now, but – ' I explained how we came to be stranded at The Eagle.

He thought for some moments after I finished, and then seemed to come to a decision. He turned to Janet.

'Mrs Gayford, I wonder if you would excuse me if I were to take your husband along with me? It's this Midwich business that has brought me here. I think he might be able to help us, if he's willing.'

'To find out what's happened, you mean?' Janet asked.

'Well – let's say in connexion with it. What do you think?' he added to me.

'If I can, of course. Though I don't see. . . . Who is *us*?' I inquired

'I'll explain as we go,' he told me 'I really ought to have been there an hour ago. I'd not drag him off like this, if it weren't important, Mrs Gayford. You'll be all right on your own here?'

Janet assured him that The Eagle was a safe place, and we rose.

'Just one thing,' he added before we left, 'don't let any of those fellows in the bar pester you. Get them slung out if they try. They're all a bit peevish since they've learnt that their editors won't be touching this Midwich business. Not a word to any of 'em. Tell you more about it later.'

'Very well. Agog, but silent. That's me,' Janet agreed as we left.

*

H.Q. had been established a little back from the affected area, on the Oppley road. At the police-block Bernard produced a pass which earned him a salute from the constable on duty, and we passed through without further trouble. A very young three-pipper sitting forlornly in a tent brightened up at our arrival, and decided that as Colonel Latcher was out inspecting the lines it was his duty to put us in the picture.

The caged-birds had now, it seemed, finished their job, and been returned to their doting and reluctantly public-spirited owners.

'We'll probably have protests from the R.S.P.C.A., as well as claims for damages when they contract croup or something,' said the Captain, 'but here's the result.' And he produced a large-scale map showing a perfect circle almost two miles in diameter, with Midwich Church lying somewhat south and a little east of its centre.

'That's *it*,' he explained, 'and as far as we can tell it *is* a circle, not just a belt. We've got an o.p. on Oppley church tower, and no movement in the area has been observed – and there are a couple of chaps lying in the road outside the pub who haven't moved, either. As to *what* it is, we're not much further.

'We've established that it is static, invisible, odourless, non-registering on radar, non-echoing on sound, immediate in effect on at least mammals, birds, reptiles, and insects; and apparently has no after-effects – at least, no direct effects, though naturally the people in the bus and the others who were in it for some time are feeling roughish from exposure. But that's about as far as we go. Frankly, as to what it really is, we haven't a clue yet.'

Bernard asked him a few questions which elicited little more, and then we made our way in search of Colonel Latcher. We found him after a while, in company with an older man who turned out to be the Chief Constable of Winshire. Both of them, with some lesser lights in attendance, were standing on a slight rise regarding the terrain. Their grouping suggested an eighteenth-century engraving of generals watching a battle that was not going too well, only there was no visible battle. Bernard introduced himself and me. The Colonel regarded him intently.

'Ah!' he said. 'Ah yes. You're the chap on the phone who told me this had to be kept quiet.'

Before Bernard could reply, the Chief Constable came in:

'*Kept quiet!* Kept quiet, indeed. A two-mile circle of country completely blanketed by this thing, and you'd like it kept quiet.'

'That was the instruction,' said Bernard. 'The Security – '

'But how the devil do they think – ?'

Colonel Latcher cut in, heading him off.

'We've done our best to put it around as a surprise tactical exercise. Bit thin, but it makes something to say. Had to say something. Trouble is, for all we know it may be some little trick of our own gone wrong. So much damned secrecy nowadays that nobody knows anything. Don't know what the other chap has; don't even know what you may have to use yourself. All these scientist fellers in back rooms ruining the profession. Can't keep up with what you don't know. Soldiering'll soon be nothing but wizards and wires.'

'The news agencies are on to it already,' grumbled the Chief Constable. 'We've headed some of 'em off. But you know what they are. They'll be sneaking round some way, pushing their noses into it, and having to be pulled out. And how are we going to keep *them* quiet?'

'That, at least, needn't worry you much,' Bernard told him. 'There's been a Home Office advice on this already. Very sore they are. But I think it will hold. It really depends on whether it turns out to have enough sensation in it to make trouble worth while.'

'H'm,' said the Colonel, looking out across the somnolent scene again. 'And I suppose *that* depends on whether, from a newspaper view, the sleeping beauty would be a sensation, or a bore.'

*

Quite an assortment of people kept on turning up in the course of the next hour or two, all apparently representing the interests of various departments, civil and military. A larger tent was erected beside the Oppley road, and in it a conference was called for 16.30. Colonel Latcher led off with a review of the situation. It did not take long. Just as he was concluding it a Group Captain arrived. He marched in with a malevolent air, and slapped a large photograph down on to the table in front of the Colonel.

'There you are, gentlemen,' he said grimly. 'That cost two good men in one good aircraft, and we were lucky not to lose another. I hope it was worth it.'

We crowded round to study the photograph, and compare it with the map.

'What's *that*?' asked a Major of Intelligence, pointing.

The object he indicated showed as a pale oval outline, with a shape, judging by the shadows, not unlike the inverted bowl of a spoon. The Chief Constable bent down, peering more closely.

'I can't imagine,' he admitted. 'Looks as if it *might* be some unusual kind of building – only it can't be. I was round by the Abbey ruins myself less than a week ago, and there was no sign of anything there then; besides, that's British Heritage Association property. They don't build, they just prop things up.'

One of the others looked from the photograph to the map, and back again.

'Whatever it is, it's in just about the mathematical centre of the trouble,' he pointed out. 'If it wasn't there a few days ago, it must be something that's landed there.'

'Unless it could be a rick, with a very bleached cover,' someone suggested.

The Chief Constable snorted. 'Look at the scale, man – and the shape. It'd have to be the size of a dozen ricks, at least.'

'Then what the devil is it?' inquired the Major.

One after another we studied it through the magnifier.

'You couldn't get a lower altitude picture?' suggested the Major.

'Trying that was how we lost the aircraft,' the Group Captain told him curtly.

'How far up does the whatsit – this affected area – extend?' someone asked.

The Group Captain shrugged. 'You could find that out by flying into it,' he said. 'This,' he added, tapping the photograph, 'was taken at ten thousand. The crew noticed no effect there.'

Colonel Latcher cleared his throat.

'Two of my officers suggest that the area may be hemispherical in form,' he remarked.

'So it may,' agreed the Group Captain, 'or it may be rhomboidal, or dodecahedral.'

'I gather,' said the Colonel mildly, 'that they observed birds flying into it; getting a fix on them at the moment they became affected. They claim to have established that the edge of the zone does not extend vertically like a wall – that it definitely is not a cylinder, in fact. The sides contract slightly. From that they argue that it must be either domed, or conical. They say their evidence favours a hemisphere, but they have had to work on too small a segment of too large an arc to be certain.'

'Well, that's the first contribution we've had for some time,' acknowledged the Group Captain. He pondered, 'If they're right about a hemisphere, that should give it a ceiling of about five thousand over the centre. I suppose they didn't have any helpful ideas on how we establish that without losing another aircraft?'

'As a matter of fact,' Colonel Latcher said, diffidently, 'one of them did. He suggested that perhaps a helicopter dangling a canary in a cage on a few hundred feet of line and slowly reducing height – Well, I know it sounds a bit – '

'No,' said the Group Captain. 'It's an idea. Sounds like the same fellow who got the perimeter taped.'

'It is.' Colonel Latcher nodded.

'Quite a line of his own in ornithological warfare,' commented the Group Captain. 'I think perhaps we can improve on the canary, but we're grateful for the idea. A bit too late for it today. I'll lay it on for early tomorrow, with pictures from the lowest safe altitude while there's a good cross-light.'

The Intelligence Major emerged from silence.

'Bombs, I think,' he said reflectively. 'Fragmentation, perhaps.'

'Bombs?' asked the Group Captain, with raised brows.

'Wouldn't do any harm to have some handy. Never know what these Ivans are up to. Might be a good idea to have a wham at it, anyway. Stop it getting away. Knock it out so that we can have a proper look at it.'

'Bit drastic at this stage,' suggested the Chief Constable. 'I mean, wouldn't it be better to take it intact, if possible.'

'Probably,' agreed the Major, 'but meanwhile we are just allowing it to go on doing whatever it came to do, while it holds us off with this whatever-it-is.'

'I don't see what it *could* have come to do in Midwich,' another officer put in, 'therefore I imagine that it force-landed, and is using this screen to prevent interference while it makes repairs.'

'There's The Grange. . . . ' someone said tentatively.

'In either case, the sooner we get authority to disable it further, the better,' said the Major. 'It had no business over our territory, anyway. Real point is, of course, that it mustn't get away. Much too interesting. Apart from the thing itself, that screen effect could be very useful indeed. I shall recommend taking any action necessary to secure it; intact if possible; but damaged if necessary.'

There was considerable discussion, but it came to little since almost everyone present seemed to hold no more than a watching and reporting brief. The only decisions I can recall were that parachute flares would be dropped every hour for observation purposes, and that the helicopter would attempt to get more informative photographs in the morning; beyond that nothing definite had been achieved when the conference broke up.

I did not see why I had been taken along there at all – or, for the matter of that, why Bernard had been there, for he had made not a single contribution to the conference. As we drove back I asked:

'Is it out of order for me to inquire where you come into this?'

'Not altogether. I have a professional interest.'

'The Grange?' I suggested.

'Yes. The Grange comes within my scope, and naturally anything untoward in its neighbourhood interests us. This, one might call very untoward, don't you think?'

'Us' I had already gathered from his self-introduction before the conference, could be either Military Intelligence in general, or his particular department of it.

'I thought,' I said, 'that the Special Branch looked after that kind of thing.'

'There are various angles,' he said, vaguely, and changed the subject.

We managed to get him a room at The Eagle, and the three of us dined together. I had hoped that after dinner he might make good his promise to 'explain later', but though we talked of a number of things, including Midwich, he was clearly avoiding any more mention of his professional interest in it. But for all that it was a good evening that left me wondering how one can be so careless as to let some people drift out of one's life.

Twice in the course of the evening I rang up the Trayne police to inquire whether there had been any change in the Midwich situation, and both times they reported that it was quite unaltered. After the second, we decided it was no good waiting up, and after a final round we retired.

'A nice man,' said Janet, as our door closed. 'I was afraid it might be old-warriors-together which is so boring for wives, but he didn't let it be a bit like that. Why did he take you along this afternoon?'

'That's what's puzzling me,' I confessed. 'He seemed to have second thoughts and become more reserved altogether once we actually got close to it.'

'It really is very queer,' Janet said, as if the whole thing had just struck her afresh. 'Didn't he have anything at all to say about what it is?'

'Neither he, nor any of the rest of them,' I assured her. 'About the one thing they've learnt is what we could tell them – that you don't know when it hits you, and there's no sign afterwards that it did.'

'And that at least is encouraging. Let's hope that no one in the village comes to any more harm than we did,' she said.

*

While we were still sleeping, on the morning of the 28th, a met. officer gave it as his opinion that ground mist in Midwich would clear early, and a crew of two boarded a helicopter. A wire cage containing a pair of lively but perplexed ferrets was handed in after them. Presently the machine took off, and whimmered noisily upwards.

'They reckon,' remarked the pilot, 'that six thousand will be dead safe, so we'll try at seven thou. for luck. If that's okay, we'll bring her down slowly.'

The observer settled his gear, and occupied himself with teasing the ferrets until the pilot told him:

'Right. You can lower away now, and we'll make the trial crossing at seven.'

The cage went through the door. The observer let three hundred feet of line unreel. The machine came round, and the pilot informed ground that he was about to make a preliminary run over Midwich. The observer lay on the floor, observing the ferrets, through glasses.

They were doing fine at present, clambering with non-stop sinuousness all round and over one another. He took the glasses off them for a moment, and turned towards the village ahead, then:

'Oy, Skipper,' he said.

'Uh?'

'That thing we're supposed to photograph, by the Abbey.'

'What about it?'

'Well, either it was a mirage, or it's flipped off,' said the observer.

CHAPTER 5

Midwich Reviviscit

AT almost the same moment that the observer made his discovery, the picket at the Stouch-Midwich road was carrying out its routine test. The sergeant in charge threw a lump of sugar across the white line that had been drawn across the road, and watched while the dog, on its long lead, dashed after it. The dog snapped up the sugar, and crunched it.

The sergeant regarded the dog carefully for a moment, and walked close to the line himself. He hesitated there, and then stepped across it. Nothing happened. With increasing confidence, he took a few more paces. Half a dozen rooks cawed as they passed over his head. He watched them flap steadily away over Midwich.

'Hey, you there, Signals,' he called. 'Inform H.Q. Oppley. Affected area reduced, and believed clear. Will confirm after further tests.'

*

A few minutes earlier, in Kyle Manor, Gordon Zellaby had stirred with difficulty, and given out a sound like a half-groan. Presently he realized that he was lying on the floor; also, that the room which had been brightly lit and warm, perhaps a trifle over-warm, a moment ago, was now dark, and clammily cold.

He shivered. He did not think he had ever felt quite so cold. It went right through so that every fibre ached with it. There was a sound in the darkness of someone else stirring. Ferrelyn's voice said, shakily:

'What's happened . . . ? Daddy . . . ? Angela . . . ? Where are you?'

Zellaby moved an aching and reluctant jaw to say:

'I'm here, nearly f-frozen. Angela, my dear . . . ?'

'Just here, Gordon,' said her voice unsteadily, close behind him.

He put out a hand which encountered something, but his fingers were too numbed to tell him what it was.

There was a sound of movement across the room.

'Gosh, I'm stiff! Oo-oo-ooh! Oh, dear!' complained Ferrelyn's voice. 'Oo-ow-oo! I don't believe these are my legs at all.' She stopped moving for a moment. 'What's that rattling noise?'

'My t-teeth, I th-think,' said Zellaby, with an effort.

There was more movement, followed by a stumbling sound. Then a clatter of curtain-rings, and the room was revealed in a grey light.

Zellaby's eyes went to the grate. He stared at it in disbelief. A moment ago he had put a new log on the fire, now there was nothing there by a few ashes. Angela, sitting up on the carpet a yard away from him, and Ferrelyn by the window, were both staring at the grate, too.

'What on earth – ?' began Ferrelyn.

'The ch-champagne?' suggested Zellaby.

'Oh, really, Daddy . . . !'

Against the protest of every joint Zellaby tried to get up. He found it too painful, and decided to stay where he was for a bit. Ferrelyn crossed unsteadily to the fireplace. She reached a hand towards it, and stood there, shivering.

'I think it's dead,' she said.

She tried to pick up *The Times* from the chair, but her fingers were too numb to hold it. She looked at it miserably, and then managed to scrumble it between her stiff hands, and stuff it into the grate. Still using both hands she succeeded in lifting some of the smaller bits of wood from the basket and dropping them on the paper.

Frustration with the matches almost made her weep.

'My fingers *won't*,' she wailed miserably.

In her efforts she spilt the matches on the hearth. Somehow she managed to light one by rubbing the box on them. It caught another. She pushed them all closer to the paper bulging out of the grate. Presently it caught, too, and the flame blossomed up like a wonderful flower.

Angela got up, and staggered stiffly closer. Zellaby made his approach on all fours. The wood began to crackle. They crouched towards it, greedy for warmth. The numbness in their outstretched fingers began to give way to a tingling. After a while the Zellaby spirit began to show signs of revival.

'Odd,' he remarked through teeth that still showed a tendency to chatter, 'odd that I should have to live to my present age before appreciating the underlying soundness of fire-worship.'

On both the Oppley and Stouch roads there was a great starting up and warming of engines. Presently two streams of ambulances, fire appliances, police cars, jeeps, and military trucks started to converge on Midwich. They met at the Green. The civilian transport pulled up, and its occupants piled out. The military trucks for the most part headed for Hickham Lane, bound for the Abbey. An exception to both categories was a small red car that turned off by itself and went bouncing up the drive of Kyle Manor to stop in grooves of gravel by the front door.

Alan Hughes burst into the Zellaby study, pulled Ferrelyn out of the huddle by the fire, and clutched her firmly.

'Darling!' he exclaimed, still breathing hard. 'Darling! Are you all right?'

'Darling!' responded Ferrelyn, rather as if it were an answer.

After a considerate interval Gordon Zellaby remarked:

'We, also, are all right, we believe, though bewildered. We are also somewhat chilled. Do you think – ?'

Alan seemed to become aware of them for the first time.

'The – ' he began, and then broke off as the lights came on. 'Good-oh,' he said. 'Hot drinks in a jiffy.' And departed, towing Ferrelyn after him.

' "Hot drinks in a jiffy," ' murmured Zellaby. 'Such music in a simple phrase!'

*

And so, when we came down to breakfast, eight miles away, it was to be greeted with the news that Colonel Westcott had gone out a couple of hours before; and that Midwich was as near awake again as was natural to it.

CHAPTER 6

Midwich Settles Down

THERE was still a police picket on the Stouch road, but as residents of Midwich we passed through promptly, to drive on through a scene which looked much as usual, and reach our cottage without further hindrance.

We had wondered more than once what state of affairs we might find there, but there proved to have been no need for alarm. The cottage was intact, and exactly as we had left it. We went in and resettled ourselves just as we had intended to on the previous day, with no inconvenience except that the milk in the refrigerator had gone off, on account of the cut in the electricity supply. Indeed, within half an hour of returning the happenings of the previous day were beginning to seem unreal; and when we went out and talked to our neighbours we found that for those who had actually been involved the feeling of unreality was even more pronounced.

Nor was that surprising, for, as Mr Zellaby pointed out, their knowledge of the affair was limited to an awareness that they had failed to go to bed one night and had awakened, feeling extremely cold, one morning: the rest was a matter of hearsay. One had to believe that they had during the interval missed a day, for it was improbable that the rest of the world could be collectively mistaken; but, speaking for himself, it had not even been an interesting experience, since the prime requisite of interest was, after all, consciousness. He therefore proposed to disregard the whole matter, and do his best to forget that he had been cheated out of one of the days which he found to be passing, in proper sequence, far too quickly.

Such a dismissal turned out for a time to be surprisingly easy, for it is doubtful whether the affair – even had it not lain beneath the intimidating muzzles of the Official Secrets Act – could at this stage have made a really useful newspaper sensation. As a dish, it had a number of promising aromas, but it proved short on substance. There were, in all, eleven casualties, and something might have been made of them, but even they lacked the details to excite a blasé readership, and the stories of the survivors were woefully undramatic, for they had nothing to tell but their recollections of a cold awakening.

We were able, therefore, to assess our losses, dress our wounds, and generally readjust ourselves from the experience which afterwards became known as the Dayout, with a quite unexpected degree of privacy.

Of our eleven fatalities: Mr William Trunk, a farm-hand, his wife, and their small son, had perished when their cottage burnt down. An elderly couple called Stagfield had been lost in the other house that caught fire. Another farm-hand, Herbert Flagg, had been discovered dead from exposure in close, and not easily explained, proximity to the cottage occupied by Mrs Harriman, whose husband was at work in his bakery at the time. Harry Crankhart, one of the two men whom the Oppley church-tower observers had been able to see lying in front of the Scythe and Stone had also been found dead from exposure. The other four were all elderly persons in whom neither the sulfas nor the mycetes had been able to check the progress of pneumonia.

Mr Leebody preached a thanksgiving sermon on behalf of the rest of us at an unusually well-attended service the following Sunday, and with that, and his conduct of the last of the funerals, the dream-like quality of the whole affair became established.

It is true that for a week or so there were a few soldiers about, and there was quite a deal of coming and going in official cars, but the centre of this interest did not lie within the village itself, and so disturbed it little. The visible focus of attention was close to the Abbey ruins where a guard was posted to protect a large dent in the ground which certainly looked as if something massive had rested there for a while. Engineers had measured this phenomenon, made sketches, and taken photographs of it. Technicians of various kinds had then tramped back and forth across it, carrying mine-detectors, geiger-counters, and other subtle gear. Then, abruptly, the military lost all interest in it, and withdrew.

Investigations at The Grange went on a little longer, and among those occupied with them was Bernard Westcott. He dropped in to see us several times, but he told us nothing of what was going on, and we asked no details. We knew no more than the rest of the village did – that there was a security check in progress. Not until the evening of the day it was finished, and after he had announced his departure for London the following day, did he speak much of the Dayout and its consequences. Then, following a lull in conversation, he said:

'I've got a proposition to make to you two. If you'd care to hear it.'

'Let's hear it and see,' I told him.

'Essentially it is this: we feel that it is rather important for us to keep an eye on this village for a time, and know what goes on here. We could introduce one of our own men to help keep us posted, but there are points against that. For one thing, he would have to start from scratch; and it takes time for any stranger to work into the life of any village, and, for another, it is doubtful whether we could justify the detachment of a good man to full-time work here at present – and if he were not full-time it is equally doubtful whether he could be of much use. If, on the other hand, we could get someone reliable who already knows the place and the people to keep us posted on possible developments it would be more satisfactory all round. What do you think?'

I considered for a moment.

'Not, at first hearing, very much,' I told him. 'It rather depends, I suppose, what is involved.' I glanced across at Janet. She said, somewhat coldly:

'It rather sounds as if we are being invited to spy on our friends, and neighbours. I think perhaps a professional spy might suit you better.'

'This,' I backed her up, 'is our home.'

He nodded, rather as if that were what he had expected.

'You consider yourselves a part of this community?' he said.

'We are trying to be, and, I think, beginning to be,' I told him.

He nodded again. 'Good – At least, good if you feel that you have begun to have an obligation towards it. That's what's needed. It can well do with someone who has its welfare at heart to keep an eye on it.'

'I don't see quite why. It seems to have got along very well without for a number of centuries . . . or, at least, should I say that the attentions of its own inhabitants have served it well enough.'

'Yes,' he admitted. 'True enough – until now. Now, however, it needs, and is getting, some outside protection. It seems to me that the best chance of giving it that protection depends quite largely on our having adequate information on what goes on inside it.'

'What sort of protection? – and from what?'

'Chiefly, at present, from busybodies,' he said. 'My dear fellow, surely you don't think it was an *accident* that the Midwich Dayout wasn't splashed across the papers *on* the Dayout? Or that there wasn't a rush of journalists of all kinds pestering the life out of everyone here th moment it lifted?'

'Of course not,' I said. 'Naturally I knew there was the security angle – you told me as much yourself – and I was not surprised at that. I don't know what goes on at The Grange, but I do know it is very hush.'

'It wasn't simply The Grange that was put to sleep,' he pointed out. 'It was everything for a mile around.'

'But it included The Grange. That must have been the focal point. Quite possibly the influence, whatever it is, doesn't have less than that range – or perhaps the people, whoever they were, thought it safer to have that much elbow room for safety.'

'That's what the village thinks?' he asked.

'Most of it – with a few variations.'

'That's the sort of thing I want to know. They all pin it on The Grange, do they?'

'Naturally. What other reason could there be – in Midwich?'

'Well then, suppose I tell you I have reason to believe that The Grange had nothing whatever to do with it. And that our very careful investigations do no more than confirm that?'

'But that would make nonsense of the whole thing,' I protested.

'Surely not – not, that is, any more than any accident can be regarded as a form of nonsense.'

'Accident? You mean a forced landing?'

Bernard shrugged. 'That I can't tell you. It's possible that the accident lay more in the fact that The Grange happened to be located where the landing was made. But my point is this: almost everyone in this village has been exposed to a curious and quite unfamiliar phenomenon. And now you, and all the rest of the place, are assuming it is over and finished with. Why?'

Both Janet and I stared at him.

'Well,' she said, 'it's come, and it's gone, so why not?'

'And it simply came, and did nothing, and went away again, and had no effect on anything?'

'I don't know. No visible effect – beyond the casualties, of course, and they mercifully can't have known anything about it,' Janet replied.

'No *visible* effect,' he repeated. 'That means rather little nowadays, doesn't it? You can, for instance, have quite a serious dose of X-rays, gamma-rays, and others, without immediate visible effect. You needn't be alarmed, it *is* just an instance. If any of them had been present we should have detected them. They were not. But something that we were unable to detect was present. Something quite unknown to us that is capable of inducing – let's call it artificial sleep. Now, that is a very remarkable phenomenon – quite inexplicable to us, and not a little alarming. Do you really think one is justified in airily assuming that such a peculiar incident can just happen and then cease to happen, and have no effect? It may be so, of course, it may have no more effect than an aspirin tablet; but surely one should keep an eye on things to see whether that is so or not?'

Janet weakened a little.

'You mean, you want us, or someone, to do that for you. To watch for, and note, any effects?'

'What I'm after is a reliable source of information on Midwich as a whole. I want to be kept posted and up to date on how things are here so that if it should become necessary to take any steps I shall be aware of the circumstances, and be better able to take them in good time.'

'Now you're making it sound like a kind of welfare work,' Janet said.

'In a way, that's what it is. I want a regular report on Midwich's state of health, mind, and morale so that I can keep a fatherly eye on it. There's no question of spying. I want it so that I can act for Midwich's benefit, should it be necessary.'

Janet looked at him steadily for a moment.

'Just what are you expecting to happen here, Bernard?' she asked.

'Would I have to make this suggestion to you if I knew?' he countered. 'I'm taking precautions. We don't know what this thing is, or does. We can't slap on a quarantine order without evidence. But we can watch for evidence. At least, you can. So what do you say?'

'I'm not sure,' I told him. 'Give us a day or two to think it over, and I'll let you know.'

'Good,' he said. And we went on to talk of other things.

Janet and I discussed the matter several times in the next few days. Her attitude had modified considerably.

'He's got something up his sleeve, I'm sure,' she said. 'But what?'

I did not know. And:

'It isn't as if we were being asked to watch a particular person, is it?'

I agree that it was not. And:

'It wouldn't be really different in principle from what a Medical Officer of Health does, would it?'

Not very different, I thought. And:

'If we don't do it for him, he'd have to find someone else to do it. I don't really see who he'd get, in the village. It wouldn't be very nice, or efficient, if he did have to introduce a stranger, would it?'

I supposed not.

So, mindful of Miss Ogle's strategic situation in the post office, I wrote, instead of telephoning, to Bernard telling him that we thought we saw our way clear to cooperation provided we could be satisfied over one or two details, and received a reply suggesting that we should arrange a meeting when we next came to London. The letter showed no feeling of urgency, and merely asked us to keep our eyes open in the meantime.

We did. But there was little for them to perceive. A fortnight after the Dayout, only very small rumples remained in Midwich's placidity.

The small minority who felt that Security had cheated them of national fame and pictures in the newspapers had become resigned: the rest were glad that the interruption of their ways had been no greater. Another division of local opinion concerned The Grange and its occupants. One school held that the place must have some connexion with the event, and but for its mysterious activities the phenomenon would never have visited Midwich. The other considered its influence as something of a blessing.

Mr Arthur Crimm, O.B.E., the Director of the Station, was the tenant of one of Zellaby's cottages, and Zellaby, encountering him one day, expressed the majority view that the village was indebted to the researchers.

'But for your presence, and the consequent Security interest,' he said, 'we should without doubt have suffered a visitation far worse than that of the Dayout. Our privacy would have been ravaged, our susceptibilities outraged by the three modern Furies, the awful sisterhood of the printed word, the recorded word, and the picture. So, against your inconveniences, which I am sure have been considerable, you can at least set our gratitude that the Midwich way of life has been preserved, largely intact.'

Miss Polly Rushton, almost the only visitor to the district to be involved, concluded her holiday with her uncle and aunt, and returned home to London. Alan Hughes found himself, to his disgust, not only inexplicably posted to the north of Scotland, but also listed for release several weeks later than he had expected, and was spending much of his time up there in documentary argument with his regimental record office, and most of the rest of it, seemingly, in correspondence with Miss Zellaby. Mrs Harriman, the baker's wife, after thinking up a series of not very convincing circumstances which could have led to the discovery of Herbert Flagg's body in her front garden, had taken refuge in attack and was belabouring her husband with the whole of his known and suspected past. Almost everyone else went on as usual.

Thus, in three weeks the affair was nearly an historical incident. Even the new tombstones that marked it might – or, at any rate, quite half of them might – have been expected so to stand in a short time, from natural causes. The only newly created widow, Mrs Crankhart, rallied well, and showed no intention of letting her state depress her, nor indeed harden.

Midwich had, in fact, simply twitched – curiously, perhaps, but only very slightly – for the third or fourth time in its thousand-year doze.

*

And now I come to a technical difficulty, for this, as I have explained, is not my story; it is Midwich's story. If I were to set down my information in the order it came to me I should be flitting back and forth in the account, producing an almost incomprehensible hotchpotch of incidents out of order, and effects preceding causes. Therefore it is necessary that I rearrange my information, disregarding entirely the dates and times when I acquired it, and put it into chronological order. If this method of approach should result in the suggestion of uncanny perception, or disquieting multiscience, in the writer, the reader must bear with it the assurance that it is entirely the product of hindsight.

It was, for instance, not current observation, but later inquiry which revealed that a little while after the village had seemingly returned to normal there began to be small swirls of localized uneasiness in its corporative peace; certain disquiets that were, as yet, isolated and unacknowledged. This would be somewhere about late November, even early December – though perhaps in some quarters slightly earlier. Approximately, that is, about the time that Miss Ferrelyn Zellaby mentioned in the course of her almost daily correspondence with Mr Hughes that a tenuous suspicion had perturbingly solidified.

In what appears to have been a not very coherent letter, she explained – or, perhaps one should say, intimated – that she did not see how it could be, and, in fact, according to all she had learnt, it couldn't be, so she did not understand it at all, but the fact was that, in some mysterious way, she seemed to have started a baby – well, actually 'seemed' wasn't quite the right word because she was pretty sure about it, really. So did he think he could manage a weekend leave, because one did rather feel that it was the sort of thing that needed some talking over . . . ?

CHAPTER 7

Coming Events

IN point of fact, investigations have shown that Alan was not the first to hear Ferrelyn's news. She had been worried and puzzled for some little time, and two or three days before she wrote to him had made up her mind that the time had come for the matter to be known in the family circle: for one thing, she badly needed advice and explanation that none of the books she consulted seemed able to give her; and, for another, it struck her as more dignified than just going on until somebody should guess. Angela, she decided, would be the best person to tell first – Mother, too, of course, but a little later on, when the organizing was already done; it looked like one of those occasions when Mother might get terribly executive about everything.

Decision, however, had been rather easier to take than action. On the Wednesday morning Ferrelyn's mind was fully made up. At some time in that day, some relaxed hour, she would draw Angela quietly aside and explain how things were....

Unfortunately, there hadn't seemed to be any part of Wednesday when people were really relaxed. Thursday morning did not feel suitable somehow, either, and in the afternoon Angela had had a Women's Institute meeting which made her look tired in the evening. There was a moment on Friday afternoon that might have done – and yet it did not seem quite the kind of thing one could raise while Daddy showed his lunch visitor the garden, preparatory to bringing him back for tea. So, what with one thing and another, Ferrelyn arose on Saturday morning with her secret still unshared.

'I'll really *have* to tell her today – even if everything doesn't seem absolutely right for it. A person could go on this way for weeks,' she told herself firmly, as she finished dressing.

Gordon Zellaby was at the last stage of his breakfast when she reached the table. He accepted her good-morning kiss absent-mindedly, and presently took himself off to his routine – once briskly round the garden, then to the study, and the Work in progress.

Ferrelyn ate some cornflakes, drank some coffee, and accepted a fried egg and bacon. After two nibbles she pushed the plate away decisively enough to arouse Angela from her reflections.

'What's the matter?' Angela inquired from her end of the table. 'Isn't it fresh?'

'Oh, there's nothing *wrong* with it,' Ferrelyn told her. 'I just don't happen to feel eggy this morning, that's all.'

Angela seemed uninterested, when one had half-hoped she would ask why. An inside voice seemed to prompt Ferrelyn: 'Why not now? After all, it can't really make much difference *when*, can it?' So she took a breath. By way of introducing the matter gently she said:

'As a matter of fact, Angela, I was sick this morning.'

'Oh, indeed,' said her stepmother, and paused while she helped herself to butter. In the act of raising her marmaladed toast, she added: 'So was I. Horrid, isn't it?'

Now she had taxied on to the runway, Ferrelyn was going through with it. She squashed the opportunity of diverting, forthwith:

'I think,' she said, steadily, 'that mine was rather special kind of being sick. The sort,' she added, in order that it should be perfectly clear, 'that happens when a person might be going to have a baby, if you see what I mean.'

Angela regarded her for a moment with thoughtful interest, and nodded slowly.

'I do,' she agreed. With careful attention she buttered a further area of toast, and added marmalade. Then she looked up again.

'So was mine,' she said.

Ferrelyn's mouth fell a little open as she stared. To her astonishment, and to her confusion, she found herself feeling slightly shocked. . . . But. . . . Well, after all, why not? Angela was only sixteen years older than herself, so it was all very natural really, only . . . well, somehow one just hadn't expected it. . . . It didn't seem quite. . . . After all, Daddy was a triple grandfather by his first marriage. . . .

Besides, it was all so unexpected. . . . It somehow hadn't seemed likely. . . . Not that Angela wasn't a wonderful person, and one was very fond of her . . . but, sort, of as a capable elder sister. . . . It needed a bit of readjusting to. . . .

She went on staring at Angela, unable to find the right-sounding thing to say, because everything had somehow turned the wrong way round. . . .

Angela was not seeing Ferrelyn. She was looking straight down the table, out of the window at something much further away than the bare, swaying branches of the chestnut. Her dark eyes were bright and shiny.

The shininess increased and sparkled into two drops sparkling on her lower lashes. They welled, overflowed, and ran down Angela's cheeks.

A kind of paralysis still held Ferrelyn. She had never seen Angela cry. Angela wasn't that kind of person. . . .

Angela bent forward, and put her face in her hands. Ferrelyn jumped up as if she had been suddenly released. She ran to Angela, put her arms round her, and felt her trembling. She held her close, and stroked her hair, and made small, comforting sounds.

In the pause that followed Ferrelyn could not help feeling that a curious element of miscasting had intruded. It was not an exact reversal of roles, for she had had no intention of weeping on Angela's shoulder; but it was near enough to it to make one wonder if one were fully awake.

Quite soon, however, Angela ceased to shake. She drew longer, calmer breaths, and presently sought for a handkerchief.

'Phew!' she said. 'Sorry to be such a fool, but I'm so happy.'

'Oh' Ferrelyn responded, uncertainly.

Angela blew, blinked, and dabbed.

'You see,' she explained, 'I've not really dared to believe it myself. Telling it to somebody else suddenly made it real. And I've always wanted to, so much, you see. But then nothing happened, and went on not happening, so I began to think – well, I'd just about decided I'd have to try to forget about it, and make the best of things. And now it's really happening after all, I – I – ' She began to weep again, quietly and comfortably.

A few minutes later she pulled herself together, gave a final pat with the bunched handkerchief, and decisively put it away.

'There,' she said, 'that's over. I never thought I was one to enjoy a good cry, but it does seem to help.' She looked at Ferrelyn. 'Makes one thoroughly selfish, too – I'm sorry, my dear.'

'Oh, that's all right. I'm glad for you,' Ferrelyn said, generously she thought because, after all, one had been a bit anti-climaxed. After a pause, she went on:

'Actually, I don't feel weepy about it myself. But I do feel a bit frightened. . . . '

The word caught Angela's attention, and dragged her thoughts from self-contemplation. It was not a response she expected from Ferrelyn. She looked at her step-daughter for a thoughtful moment, as if the full import of the situation were only just reaching her.

'Frightened, my dear?' she repeated. 'I don't think you need feel that. It isn't very proper, of course, but – well, we shan't get anywhere by being puritanical about it. The first thing to do is to make sure you're right.'

'I *am* right,' Ferrelyn said, gloomily. 'But I don't understand it. It's different for you, being married, and so on.'

Angela disregarded that. She went on:

'Well, then, the next thing must be to let Alan know.'

'Yes, I suppose so,' agreed Ferrelyn, without eagerness.

'Of course it is. And you don't need to be frightened of that. Alan won't let you down. He adores you.'

'Are you sure of that, Angela?' doubtfully.

'Why, yes, you silly. One only has to look at him. Of course, it's all quite reprehensible, but I shouldn't be surprised if you find he's delighted. Naturally, it will – Why, Ferrelyn, what's the matter?' She broke off, startled by Ferrelyn's expression.

'But – but you don't understand, Angela. It wasn't Alan.'

The look of sympathy died from Angela's face. Her expression went cold. She started to get up.

'No!' exclaimed Ferrelyn, desperately, 'you *don't* understand, Angela. It isn't that. *It wasn't anybody! That's* why I'm frightened....'

*

In the course of the next fortnight, three of the Midwich young women sought confidential interviews with Mr Leebody. He had baptized them when they were babies; he knew them, and their parents, well. All of them were good, intelligent, and certainly not ignorant, girls. Yet each of them told him, in effect: 'It *wasn't anybody*, Vicar. *That's* why I'm frightened....'

When Harriman, the baker, chanced to hear that his wife had been to see the doctor, he remembered that Herbert Flagg's body had been found in his front garden, and he beat her up, while she tearfully protested that Herbert hadn't come in, and that she'd not had anything to do with him, or with any other man.

Young Tom Dorry returned home on leave from the navy after eighteen months' foreign service. When he learned of his wife's condition, he picked up his traps and went over to his mother's cottage. But she told him to go back and stand by the girl because she was frightened. And when that didn't move him, she told him that she herself, respectable widow for years was – well, not exactly frightened, but she couldn't for the life of her say how it had happened. In a bemused state Tom Dorry did go back. He found his wife lying on the kitchen floor, with an empty aspirin bottle beside her, and he pelted for the doctor.

One not-so-young woman suddenly bought a bicycle, and pedalled it madly for astonishing distances, with fierce determination.

Two young women collapsed in over-hot baths.

Three inexplicably tripped, and fell downstairs.

A number suffered from unusual gastric upsets.

Even Miss Ogle, at the post office, was observed eating a curious meal which involved bloater-paste spread half an inch thick, and about half a pound of pickled gherkins.

A point was reached when Dr Willers' mounting anxiety drove him into urgent conference with Mr Leebody at the Vicarage, and, as if to underline the need for action, their talk was terminated by a caller in agitated need of the doctor.

It turned out less badly than it might have done. Luckily the word 'poison' appeared on the disinfectant bottle in conformity with regulations, and was not to be taken as literally as Rosie Platch had thought. But that did not alter the tragic intention. When he had finished, Dr Willers was trembling with an impotent, targetless anger. Poor little Rosie Platch was only seventeen. . . .

CHAPTER 8

Heads Together

THE tranquillity that Gordon Zellaby had been pleasantly regaining after the wedding of Alan and Ferrelyn two days before, was dissipated by the irruption of Dr Willers. The doctor, still upset by the near-tragedy of Rosie Platch, was in an agitated state which gave Zellaby some difficulty in grasping his purpose.

By stages, however, he discovered that the doctor and the vicar had agreed to ask for his help – or, more importantly, it seemed, Angela's help – over something that was far from clear, and that the misadventure to the Platch child had brought Willers on his mission earlier than he had intended.

'So far we've been lucky,' Willers said, 'but this is the second attempted suicide, in a week. At any moment there may be another; perhaps a successful one. We *must* get this thing out in the open, and relieve the tension. We cannot afford any more delay.'

'As far as I am concerned, it is certainly not in the open. What thing is this?' inquired Zellaby.

Willers stared at him for a moment, and then rubbed his forehead.

'Sorry,' he said. 'I've been so wound up with it lately; I forgot you mightn't know. It's all these inexplicable pregnancies.'

'Inexplicable?' Zellaby raised his eyebrows.

Willers did his best to explain why they were inexplicable.

'The whole thing is so incomprehensible,' he concluded, 'that the vicar and I have been driven back on to the theory that it must in some way be connected with the other incomprehensible thing we have had here – the Dayout.'

Zellaby regarded him thoughtfully for several moments. One thing about which there could be no doubt at all was the genuineness of the doctor's anxiety.

'It seems a curious theory,' he suggested, cautiously.

'It's a more than curious situation,' replied Willers. 'However, that can wait. What can't wait is a lot of women who are on the verge of hysteria. Some of them are my patients, more of them are going to be, and unless this state of tension is resolved quickly – ' He left the sentence unfinished, with a shake of his head.

' "A lot of women"?' Zellaby repeated. 'Somewhat vague. How many?'

'I can't say for certain,' Willers admitted.

'Well, in round figures? We need some idea of what we have to deal with.'

'I should say – oh, about sixty-five to seventy.'

'*What!*' Zellaby stared at him, incredulously.

'I told you it is the devil of a problem.'

'But, if you're not sure, why pitch on sixty-five?'

'Because that's my estimate – it's a pretty rough estimate, I admit – but I *think* you'll find it's about the number of women of childbearing age in the village,' Willers told him.

*

Later that evening, after Angela Zellaby, looking tired and shocked, had gone to bed, Willers said:

'I'm very sorry to have had to inflict this, Zellaby – but she would have had to know soon, in any case. My hope is that the others can take it only half as staunchly as your wife has.'

Zellaby gave a sombre nod.

'She *is* grand, isn't she? I wonder how you or I would have stood up to a shock like that?'

'It's a hell of a thing,' Willers agreed. 'So far, most of the married women will have been easy in their minds, but now, in order to stop the unmarried going neurotic, we've got to upset them, too. But there's no way round that, that I can see.'

'One thing that has been worrying me all the evening is *how much* we ought to tell them,' Zellaby said. 'Should we leave the thing a mystery, and let them draw conclusions eventually for themselves – or is there a better way?'

'Well, damn it, it *is* a mystery, isn't it?' the doctor pointed out.

'The *how* is a very mysterious mystery,' Zellaby admitted. 'But I don't think there can be much doubt as to *what* has happened. Nor, I imagine, do you – unless you're deliberately trying to avoid it.'

'You tell me,' suggested Willers. 'Your line of reasoning may be different. I hope it is.'

Zellaby shook his head.

'The conclusion – ' he began, and then suddenly broke off, staring at the picture of his daughter.

'My God!' he exclaimed. 'Ferrelyn, too . . . ?'

He turned his head slowly towards the doctor. 'I suppose the answer is that you just don't know?'

Willers hesitated.

'I can't be sure,' he said.

Zellaby pushed back his white hair, and lapsed back in his chair. He remained staring at the pattern of the carpet for a full minute, in silence. Then he roused himself. With a studied detachment of manner, he observed:

'There are three – no, perhaps four – possibilities that suggest themselves. You would, I think, have mentioned it had there been any evidence of the explanation that will at once occur to the more obvious-minded? Besides, there are other points against that which I shall come to shortly.'

'Quite so,' agreed the doctor.

Zellaby nodded. 'Then, it is possible, is it not, in some of the lower forms at any rate, to induce parthenogenesis?'

'But not, as far as is known, among any of the higher forms – certainly not among mammals.'

'Quite. Well then, there is artificial insemination.'

'There is,' admitted the doctor.

'But you don't think so.'

'I don't.'

'Nor do I. And that,' Zellaby went on, a little grimly,

'leaves the possibility of implantation, which *could* result in what someone – Huxley, I fancy – has called "xenogenesis". That is, the production of a form that could be unlike that of the parent – or, should one perhaps say, "host"? – It would not be the true parent.'

Dr Willers frowned.

'I've been hoping that that might not occur to them,' he said.

Zellaby shook his head.

'A hope, my dear fellow, that you would do better to abandon. It may not occur to them straight away, but it is the explanation – if that is not too definite a word – that the intelligent ones are bound to arrive at before long. For, look here. We can agree, can we not, to dismiss parthenogenesis? – there has never been a reliably documented case?'

The doctor nodded.

'Well then, it will soon become as clear to them as it is to me, and must be to you, that both crude assault and a.i. are put right out of court by sheer mathematics. And this, incidentally, would seem to apply to parthenogenesis, too, if that were possible. By the law of averages it simply is not possible in any sizeable group of women taken at random, for more than twenty-five per cent of them to be in the same stage of pregnancy at the same time.'

'Well – ' began the doctor, doubtfully.

'All right, let us make a concession to, say, thirty-three and a third per cent – which is high. But then, if your estimate of the incidence is right, or anywhere near right, the present situation is still statistically quite impossible. Ergo, whether we like it or not, we are thrown back upon the fourth, and last possibility – that implantation of fertilized ova must have taken place during the Dayout.'

Willers was looking very unhappy, and still not altogether convinced.

'I'd question your "and last" – there *could* be other possibilities that have not occurred to us.'

With a touch of impatience, Zellaby said:

'Can you suggest any form of conception that does not come up against that mathematical barrier? – No? Very well. Then it follows that this *cannot* be conception: therefore it *must* be incubation.'

The doctor sighed.

'All right. I'll grant you that,' he said. 'For myself, I am only incidentally concerned about *how* it happened: my anxiety is for the welfare of those who are, and are going to be, my patients. . . .'

'You will be concerned, later on,' Zellaby put in, 'because, since they are all at the same stage now, it follows that the births are going to occur – barring accidents – over a quite limited period later on. All round about the end of June, or the first week in July – everything else being normal, of course.'

'At present,' Willers continued firmly, 'my chief worry is to decrease their anxiety, not to increase it. And for that reason we must do our best to stop this implantation idea getting about, for as long as we can. It's panicky stuff. For their good I ask you to pooh-pooh, convincingly, any suggestion of the kind that may come your way.'

'Yes,' agreed Zellaby, after consideration. 'Yes. I agree. Here, we really do have a case for benign censorship, I think.' He frowned. 'It is difficult to appreciate how a woman sees these matters: all that I can say is that if I were to be called upon, even in the most propitious circumstances, to bring forth life, the prospect would awe me considerably: had I any reason to suspect that it might be some unexpected form of life, I should probably go quite mad. Most women wouldn't, of course; they are mentally tougher, but some might, so a convincing dismissal of the possibility will be best.'

He paused, considering.

'Now we ought to get down to giving my wife a line to work on. There are various angles to be covered. One of the most tricky is going to be publicity – or, rather, no publicity.'

'Lord, yes,' said Willers. 'Once the Press get hold of it –'

'I know. God help us if they do. Day-by-day commentary, with six months of gloriously mounting speculation to go. *They* certainly wouldn't miss the xenogenesis angle. More likely to run a forecasting competition. All right, then; M.I. managed to keep the Dayout out of the papers; we'll have to see what they can do about this.

'Now, let's rough out the approach for her....'

CHAPTER 9

Keep it Dark

THE canvassing for attendance at what was not very informatively described as a 'Special Emergency Meeting of Great Importance to every Woman in Midwich' was intensive. We ourselves were visited by Gordon Zellaby who managed to convey a quite dramatic sense of urgency through a considerable wordage which gave practically nothing away. His parrying of attempts to pump him only added to the interest.

Once people had been convinced that it was not simply a matter of another Civil Defence drive, or any other of the hardy regulars, they developed a strong curiosity as to what it could possibly be that could put the doctor, the vicar, their wives, the district-nurse, and both the Zellabys, too, to the trouble of seeing that everyone was called on and given a personal invitation. The very evasiveness of the callers, backed by their reassurances that there would be nothing to pay, no collection, and a free tea for all, had caused inquisitiveness to triumph even in the naturally suspicious, and there were few empty seats.

The two chief convenors sat on the platform with Angela Zellaby, looking a little pale, between them. The doctor smoked, with a nervous intensity. The vicar seemed lost in an abstraction from which he would rouse himself now and then to make a remark to Mrs Zellaby who responded to it with an absent-minded air. They allowed ten minutes for laggards, then the doctor asked for the doors to be closed, and opened the proceedings with a brief, but still uninformative, insistence on their importance. The vicar then added his support. He concluded:

'I earnestly ask every one of you here to listen very carefully indeed to what Mrs Zellaby has to say. We are greatly indebted to her for her willingness to put the matter before you. And I want you to know in advance that she has the endorsement of Dr Willers and myself for everything she is going to tell you. It is, I assure you, only because we feel that this matter may come more acceptably and, I am sure, more ably, from a woman to women that we have burdened her with the task.

'Dr Willers and I will now leave the hall, but we shall remain on the premises. When Mrs Zellaby has finished we shall, if you wish, return to the platform, and do our best to answer questions. And now I ask you to give Mrs Zellaby your closest attention.'

He waved the doctor ahead of him, and they both went out by a door at the side of the platform. It swung-to behind them, but did not close entirely.

Angela Zellaby drank from a glass of water on the table before her. She looked down for a moment at her hands resting on her notes. Then she raised her head, waiting for the murmurs to die down. When they had, she looked her audience over carefully as if noticing every face there.

'First,' she said, 'I must warn you. What I have to tell you is going to be difficult for me to say, difficult for you to believe, too difficult for any of us to understand at present.' She paused, dropped her eyes, and then looked up once more.

'I,' she said, 'am going to have a baby. I am very, very glad, and happy about it. It is natural for women to want babies, and to be happy when they know they are coming. It is *not* natural, and it is *not* good to be afraid of them. Babies should be joy and fun. Unhappily, there are a number of women in Midwich who are not able to feel like that. Some of them are miserable, ashamed, and afraid. It is for their benefit we have called this meeting. To help the unhappy ones, and to assure them that they need be none of these things.'

She looked steadily round her audience again. There was a sound of caught breath here and there.

'Something very, very strange has happened here. And it has not happened just to one or two of us, but to almost all of us – to almost all the women in Midwich who are capable of bearing children.'

The audience sat motionless and silent, every eye fixed upon her as she put the situation before them. Before she had finished, however, she became aware of some disturbance and shushing going on on the right-hand side of the hall. Glancing over there, she saw Miss Latterly and her inseparable companion, Miss Lamb, in the middle of it.

Angela stopped speaking, in mid-sentence, and waited. She could hear the indignant tone of Miss Latterly's voice, but not its words.

'Miss Latterly,' she said clearly. 'Am I right in thinking that you do not find yourself personally concerned with the subject of this meeting?'

Miss Latterly stood up, she spoke in a voice trembling with indignation.

'You most certainly are, Mrs Zellaby. I have never in all my life – '

'Then, since this is a matter of the gravest importance to many people here, I hope you will refrain from further interruptions – Or perhaps you would prefer to leave us?'

Miss Latterly stood firm, looking back at Mrs Zellaby.

'This is – ' she began, and then changed her mind. 'Very well, Mrs Zellaby,' she said. 'I shall make my protest against the extraordinary aspersions you have made on our community, at another time.'

She turned with dignity, and paused, clearly to allow Miss Lamb to accompany her exit.

But Miss Lamb did not move. Miss Latterly looked down at her, with an impatient frown. Miss Lamb continued to sit fast.

Miss Latterly opened her lips to speak, but something in Miss Lamb's expression checked her. Miss Lamb ceased to meet her eyes. She looked straight before her, while a tide of colour rose until her whole face was a burning flush.

An odd, small sound escaped from Miss Latterly. She put out a hand, and grasped a chair to steady herself. She stared down at her friend without speaking. In a few seconds she grew haggard, and looked ten years older. Her hand dropped from the chair back. With a great effort she pulled herself together. She lifted her head decisively, looking round with eyes that seemed to see nothing. Then, straight-backed, but a little uncertain in her steps, she made her way up the aisle to the back of the hall, alone.

Angela waited. She expected a buzz of comment, but there was none. The audience looked shocked and bewildered. Every face turned back to her, in expectation. In the silence she picked up where she had stopped, trying to reduce by matter-of-factness the emotional tension which Miss Latterly had increased. With an effort she continued factually to the end of her preliminary statement, and then broke off.

The expected buzz of comment rose quickly enough this time. Angela took a drink from her glass of water, and rolled her bunched handkerchief between her damp palms while she watched the audience carefully.

She could see Miss Lamb leaning forward with a handkerchief pressed to her eyes while kindly Mrs Brant beside her tried to comfort her. Nor was Miss Lamb by any means the only one finding relief in tears. Over those bent heads the sound of voices, incredulous, high-pitched with consternation and indignation, grew. Here and there, one or two were behaving a little hysterically, but there was nothing like the outburst she had feared. She wondered to what extent an inkling awareness had blunted the shock.

With a feeling of relief and rising confidence she went on observing them for several minutes. When she decided that the first impact had had long enough to register, she rapped the table. The murmurs died away, there were a few sniffs, and then rows of expectant faces turned towards her once more. Angela took a deep breath, and started in again.

'Nobody,' she said, 'nobody but a child, or a child-minded person, expects life to be fair. It is not, and this is going to be harder on some of us than on others. Nevertheless, fair or unfair, whether we like it or not, we are all of us, married and single alike, in the same boat. There is no ground for, and consequently no place for, disparagement of some of us by others. All of us have been placed outside the conventions, and if any married woman here is tempted to consider herself more virtuous than her unmarried neighbour, she might do well to consider how, if she were challenged, she could *prove* that the child she now carries is her husband's child.

'This is a thing that has happened to all of us. We must make it bind us together for the good of all. There is no blame upon any of us, so there must be no differentiation between us, *except* – ' She paused, and then repeated: '*Except* that those who have not the love of a husband to help them will have more need of our sympathy and care.'

She continued to elaborate that for a while until she hoped it had made its mark. Then she turned to another aspect.

'This,' she told them forcefully, 'is *our* affair – there could not well be any matter more personal to each of us. I am sure, and I think you will agree with me, that it should remain so. It is for us to handle, ourselves; without outside interference.

'You must all know how the cheap papers seize upon anything to do with birth, particularly anything unusual. They make a peepshow of it, as if the people concerned were freaks in a fairground. The parents' lives, their homes, their children, are no longer their own.

'We have all read of one instance of a multiple birth where the papers took it up, then the medical profession backed by the government, with the result that the parents were virtually deprived of their own children quite soon after they were born.

'Well I, for one, do not intend to lose my child that way, and I expect and hope that all of you will feel the same. Therefore, unless we want to have, first, a great deal of unpleasantness – for I warn you that if this should become generally known it will be argued in every club and pub, with a great many nasty insinuations – unless then, we want to be exposed to that, and then to the very real probability that our babies will be taken away from us on one excuse or another by doctors and scientists, we must, every one of us, resolve not to mention, or even hint outside the village, at the present state of affairs. It is in our power to see that it remains Midwich's affair, to be managed, not as some newspaper, or Ministry, decides, but as the people of Midwich themselves wish it decided.

'If people in Trayne, or elsewhere, are inquisitive, or strangers come here asking questions, we must, for our babies' sakes, and our own, tell them nothing. But we must not simply be silent and secretive, as if we were concealing something. We must make it seem that there *is* nothing unusual in Midwich at all. If we all cooperate, and our men are made to understand that they must cooperate too, no interest will be aroused, and people will leave us alone – as they should do. It is not their business, it is *ours*. There is no one, no one at all who has a better right, or a higher duty, to protect our children from exploitation than we who are to be their mothers.'

She surveyed them steadily, almost individually once more, as she had at the start. Then she concluded:

'I shall now ask the Vicar and Dr Willers to come back. If you will excuse me for a few minutes I will join them here later. I know there must be a great many questions you are wanting to ask.'

She slipped off into the little room at the side.

'Excellent, Mrs Zellaby. Really excellent,' said Mr Leebody.

Dr Willers took her hand, and pressed it.

'I think you've done it, my dear,' he told her, as he followed the vicar on to the platform.

Zellaby guided her to a chair. She sat down, and leant back with her eyes closed. Her face was pale, and she looked exhausted.

'I think you'd better come home,' he told her.

She shook her head.

'No, I'll be all right in a few minutes. I must go back.'

'They can manage. You've done your part, and very well, too.'

She shook her head again.

'I know what those women must be feeling. This is absolutely crucial, Gordon. We've got to let them ask questions and talk – talk as long as they like. Then they'll have got over the first shock by the time they go. They've got to get used to the idea. A feeling of mutual support is what they need. I *know* – I want it, too.'

She put a hand to her head, and pushed back her hair.

'You know, it isn't true, Gordon, what I said just now.'

'Which part, my dear? You said a lot, you know.'

'About my being glad and happy. Two days ago it was quite, quite true. I wanted the baby, yours and mine, so very much. Now I'm frightened about it – I'm frightened, Gordon.'

He tightened his arm round her shoulders. She rested her head against his, with a sigh.

'My dear, my dear,' he said, stroking her hair gently. 'It's going to be all right. We'll look after you.'

'Not to *know*,' she exclaimed. 'To know there's something growing there – and not to be sure how, or what. . . . It's so – so abasing, Gordon. It makes me feel like an animal.'

He kissed her cheek softly, and went on stroking her hair.

'You're not to worry,' he told her. 'I'm prepared to bet that when he or she comes you'll take one look and say: "Oh dear, there's that Zellaby nose." But, if not, we face it together. You're not alone, my dear, you must never feel that you are alone. I'm here, and Willers is here. We're here to help you, always, all the time.'

She turned her head, and kissed him.

'Gordon, darling,' she said. Then she pulled away and sat up. 'I must get back,' she announced.

Zellaby gazed after her a moment. Then he moved a chair closer to the unclosed door, lit a cigarette, and settled himself to listen critically to the mood of the village as it showed in its questions.

CHAPTER 10

Midwich Comes to Terms

THE task for January was to cushion the shock and steer the reactions, and thus to establish an attitude. The initiation meeting could be considered a success. It let the air in, and a lot of anxiety out; and the audience, tackled while it was still in a semi-stunned condition, had for the most part accepted the suggestion of communal solidarity and responsibility.

It was only to be expected that a few individuals should hold aloof, but they were no more anxious than the rest to have their private lives invaded and exposed, and their roads jammed with motor-coaches while goggling loads of sightseers peered in at their windows. Moreover, it was not difficult for the two or three who hankered for limelight to perceive that the village was in a mood to subdue any active non-cooperator by boycott. And if Mr Wilfred Williams thought a little wistfully at times of the trade that might have come to The Scythe and Stone, he proved a staunch supporter – and sensitive to the requirements of longer-term goodwill.

Once the bewilderment of the first impact had been succeeded by the feeling that there were capable hands at the helm; when the pendulum-swing among the young unmarried women from frightened wretchedness to smug bumptiousness had settled down; and when an air of readiness to turn-to, not vastly dissimilar from that which preceded the annual fête and flower-show, began to be apparent, the self-appointed committee could feel that at least it had succeeded in getting things on to the right lines.

The original Committee of the Willers, the Leebodys, the Zellabys, and Nurse Daniels, had been augmented by ourselves, and also by Mr Arthur Crimm who had been co-opted to represent the interests of several indignant researchers at

The Grange who now found themselves embroiled, willy-nilly, in the domestic life of Midwich.

But though the feeling at the committee meeting held some five days after the Village Hall meeting could be fairly summarized as 'so far, so good', members were well aware that the achievement could not be left to take care of itself. The attitude that had been successfully induced might, it was felt, slip back all too easily into normal conventional prejudices if it were not carefully tended. For some time, at least, it would have to be sustained and fortified.

'What we need to produce,' Angela summed up, 'is something like the companionship of adversity, but without suggesting that it is an adversity – which, indeed, as far as we know, it is not.'

The sentiment gained the approval of everyone but Mrs Leebody, who looked doubtful.

'But,' she said hesitantly, 'I think we ought to be *honest*, you know.'

The rest of us looked at her inquiringly. She went on:

'Well, I mean, it *is* an adversity, isn't it? After all, a thing like this wouldn't happen to us for no reason, would it? There must be a reason; so isn't it our duty to search for it?'

Angela regarded her with a small, puzzled frown.

'I don't think I quite understand. . . . ' she said.

'Well,' explained Mrs Leebody, 'when things – unusual things like this – suddenly happen to a community there *is* a reason. I mean, look at the plagues of Egypt, and Sodom and Gomorrah, and that kind of thing.'

There was a pause. Zellaby felt impelled to relieve the awkwardness.

'For my part,' he observed, 'I regard the plagues of Egypt as an unedifying example of celestial bullying; a technique now known as power-politics. As for Sodom – ' He broke off and subsided as he caught his wife's eye.

'Er – ' said the vicar, since something seemed to be expected of him. 'Er – '

Angela came to his rescue.

'I really don't think you need worry about that, Mrs Leebody. Barrenness is, of course, a classical form of curse; but I really can't remember any instance where retribution took the form of fruitfulness. After all, it scarcely seems reasonable, does it?'

'That would depend on the fruit,' Mrs Leebody said, darkly.

Another uneasy silence followed. Everybody, except Mr Leebody, regarded Mrs Leebody. Dr Willers' eyes swivelled to catch those of Nurse Daniels, and then went back to Dora Leebody who showed no discomfort at being the centre of attention. She glanced round at all of us in an apologetic manner.

'I am sorry, but I am afraid I am the cause of it all,' she confided.

'Mrs Leebody – ' the doctor began.

She raised her hand reprovingly.

'You are kind,' she said. 'I know you want to spare me. But there is a time for confession. I am a sinner, you see. If I had had my child twelve years ago, none of this would have happened. Now I must pay for my sin by bearing a child that is not my husband's. It is all quite clear. I am very sorry to have brought this down on the rest of you. But it is a judgement, you see. Just like the plagues. . . . '

The vicar, flushed and troubled, broke in before she could continue: 'I think – er – perhaps if you will excuse us – '

There was a general pushing back of chairs. Nurse Daniels crossed quietly to Mrs Leebody's side, and began a conversation with her. Dr Willers watched them for a moment until he became aware of Mr Leebody beside him, mutely inquiring. He laid a hand reassuringly on the vicar's shoulder.

'It has been a shock to her. Not surprising at all. I fully expected a number of cases before this. I'll get Nurse Daniels to see her home and give her a sedative. Very likely a good sleep will make all the difference. I'll look in tomorrow morning.'

A few minutes later we dispersed, in a subdued and thoughtful mood.

*

The policy advocated by Angela Zellaby was carried out with considerable success. The latter part of January saw the introduction of such a programme of social activities and helpful neighbourliness as we felt would leave only the most determined non-cooperators with the isolation, or the time, to brood.

In late February I was able to report to Bernard that things were going, on the whole, smoothly – more smoothly, at any rate than we had dared to hope at first. There had been a few sags in the graph of local confidence, and would doubtless be others, but, so far, recoveries had been speedy. I gave him details of the happenings in the village since my last report, but information regarding the attitude and views prevailing at The Grange which he had asked for I could not supply. Either the researchers were of the opinion that the affair somehow came within the compass of their oaths of secrecy, or else they were of the opinion that it was safer to act as if it did.

Mr Crimm continued to be their only link with the village, and it seemed to me that to get any more information I must either have authority to reveal to him the official nature of my interest, or Bernard would have to tackle him himself. Bernard preferred the latter course, and a meeting was arranged for Mr Crimm's next visit to London.

He called in on us on the way back, feeling at liberty to spill some of his troubles, which seemed to be largely concerned with his Establishments Section.

'They do so worship tidiness,' he complained. 'I just don't know what we are going to do when my six problems start to raise matters of allowances and absences, and make an undisguisable mess of their nice tidy leave-rosters. And then, too, there'll be the effect on our work schedule. I put it to Colonel Westcott that if his Department really is seriously concerned to keep the matter quiet, they'll only be able to do it by stepping in officially, at a high level. Otherwise, we shall have to give explanations before long. I think he sees my point there. But, for the life of me, I can't see why that particular aspect should be of such interest to M.I., can you?'

'Now that is a pity,' Janet told him. 'One of our hopes when we heard that you were going to see him was that *you* might learn enough to enlighten *us*.'

*

Life appeared to be going on smoothly enough in Midwich for the present, but it was only a little later that one of the undercurrents broke surface, and gave us a flutter of anxiety.

After the committee meeting which she had brought to a premature close, Mrs Leebody ceased, not altogether surprisingly, to play any further active part in the promotion of village harmony. When she did reappear after a few days' rest, she seemed to have recovered her balance by a decision to regard the whole unfortunate situation as a distasteful subject.

On one of the early days in March, however, the Vicar of St Mary's, in Trayne, accompanied by his wife, brought her home in their car. They had found her, he reported to Mr Leebody, with some embarrassment, preaching in Trayne market, from an upturned box.

'Er – preaching?' said Mr Leebody, a new uneasiness mingling with his concern. 'I – er – can you tell me what about?'

'Oh, well – well quite fantastical, I'm afraid,' the Vicar of St Mary's told him, evasively.

'But I think I ought to know. The doctor will be sure to ask about it when he arrives.'

'Well – er – it was in the nature of a call to repentance; on a note of – er – revivalist doom. The people of Trayne must repent and pray forgiveness for fear of wrath, retribution, and hellfire. Rather nonconformist, I'm afraid. Lurid, you know. And, it seems, they must particularly avoid having anything to do with the people of Midwich who are already suffering under divine disapproval. If the Trayne people do not take heed, and mend their ways, punishment will inevitably descend on them, too.'

'Oh,' said Mr Leebody, keeping his tone level. 'She did not say what form our suffering here is taking?'

'A visitation,' the Vicar of St Mary's told him. 'Specifically, the infliction of a plague of – er – babies. That, of course, was causing some degree of ribaldry. A lamentable business altogether. Of course, once my wife had drawn my attention to Mrs Leebody's – er – condition, the matter became more intelligible, though still more distressing. I – oh, here *is* Dr Willers, now.' He broke off with relief.

*

A week later, in the middle of the afternoon, Mrs Leebody took up a position on the lowest step of the War Memorial, and began to speak. She was dressed for the occasion in a garment of hessian, her feet were bare, and there was a smudge of ash on her forehead. Fortunately there were not many people about at the time, and she was persuaded home again by Mrs Brant before she had well begun. Word was all round the village in an hour, but her message, whatever it may have been, remained undelivered.

Midwich heard the quickly following news of Dr Willers' recommendation to rest in a nursing-home with sympathy rather than surprise.

*

About mid-March Alan and Ferrelyn made their first visit since their marriage. With Ferrelyn putting in the time until Alan's release in a small Scottish town entirely among strangers, Angela had been against causing her worry by attempting to explain the Midwich state of affairs in a letter; so, now, it had to be laid before them.

Alan's expression of concern deepened as the predicament was explained. Ferrelyn listened without interruption, but with a swift glance now and then at Alan's face. It was she who broke the silence that followed.

'You know,' she said, 'I had a sort of feeling all along that there was something funny. I mean, it oughtn't – ' she broke off, struck apparently by an ancillary thought. 'Oh, how dreadful! I kind of shot-gunned poor Alan. This probably makes it coercion, or undue influence, or something heinous. Could it be grounds for divorce? Oh, dear. Do you want a divorce, darling?'

Zellaby's eyes crinkled a little at the corners as he watched his daughter.

Alan put his hand over hers.

'I think we ought to wait a bit, don't you?' he told her.

'Darling,' said Ferrelyn, twining her fingers in his. Turning her head after a long look at him, she caught her father's expression. Treating him to a determinedly unresponsive look, she turned to Angela, and asked for more details of the village's reactions. Half an hour later they went out, leaving the two men alone together. Alan barely waited for the door to latch before he broke out.

'I say, sir, this *is* a bit of a facer, isn't it?'

'I'm afraid it is,' Zellaby agreed. 'The best consolation I can offer is that we find the shock wears off. The most painful part is the opening assault on one's prejudices – I speak for our sex, of course. For the women that is, unfortunately, only the first hurdle.'

Alan shook his head.

'This is going to be a terrible blow for Ferrelyn, I'm afraid – as it must have been to Angela,' he added, a little hurriedly. 'Of course, one can't expect her, Ferrelyn, I mean, to take in all the implications at once. A thing like this needs a bit of absorbing. . . . '

'My dear fellow,' said Zellaby, 'as Ferrelyn's husband you have the right to think all sorts of things about her, but one of the things you must not do, for your own peace of mind, is to underestimate her. Ferrelyn, I assure you, was away ahead of you. I doubt whether she's missed a trick. She was certainly far enough ahead to move in with a lightweight remark because she knew that if she seemed worried, you would worry about her.'

'Oh, do you think so?' said Alan, a little flatly.

'I do,' said Zellaby. 'Furthermore, it was sensible of her. A fruitlessly worrying male is a nuisance. The best thing he can do is to disguise his worry, and stand staunchly by, impersonating a pillar of strength while performing certain practical and organizational services. I offer you the fruit of somewhat intensive experience.

'Another thing he can do is represent Modern Knowledge and Commonsense – but tactfully. You can have no idea of the number of venerable saws, significant signs, old wives' sooths, gipsies' warnings, and general fiddle-faddle that has been thrown up by this in the village, lately. We have become a folklorist's treasure-chest. Did you know that in our circumstances it is dangerous to pass under a lych-gate on a Friday? Practically suicide to wear green? Very unwise indeed to eat seed-cake? Are you aware that if a dropped knife, or needle, sticks point down in the floor it will be a boy? No? I thought you might not be. But never mind. I am assembling a bouquet of these cauliflowers of human wisdom in the hope that they may keep my publishers quiet.'

Alan inquired with belated politeness after the progress of the Current Work. Zellaby sighed sadly.

'I am supposed to deliver the final draft of *The British Twilight* by the end of next month. So far I have written three chapters of this supposedly contemporary study. If I could remember what they deal with, I've no doubt I should find them obsolete by now. It ruins a man's concentration to have a crêche hanging over his head.'

'What is amazing me as much as anything is that you've managed to keep it quiet. I'd have said you hadn't a chance,' Alan told him.

'I *did* say it,' Zellaby admitted. 'And I'm still astonished. I think it must be a kind of variant on The Emperor's Clothes theme – either that, or an inversion of the Hitler Big Lie – a truth too big to be believed. But, mind you, both Oppley and Stouch are saying unneighbourly things about some of us that they've noticed, though they appear to have no idea of the real scale. I'm told that there is a theory current in both of them that we have all been indulging in one of those fine old uninhibited rustic frenzies on Hallowe'en. Anyway, several of the inhabitants almost gather their skirts aside as we pass. I must say that our people have restrained themselves commendably, under some provocation.'

'But do you mean that only a mile or two away they've no idea what's really happened?' Alan asked incredulously.

'I'd not say that, so much as that they don't want to believe it. They must have heard fairly fully I imagine, but they choose to believe that that is all a tale to cover up something more normal, but disgraceful. Willers was right when he said that a kind of self-protective reflex would defend the ordinary man and woman from disquieting beliefs – That is unless it should get into print. On the word of a newspaper, of course, eighty or ninety per cent would swing to the opposite extreme, and believe anything. The cynical attitude in the other villages really helps. It means that a newspaper is unlikely to get anything to go on unless it is directly informed by someone inside the village.

'Internal stresses were worst for the first week or two after our announcement. Several of the husbands were awkward to handle, but once we got it out of their heads that it was some elaborate system of whitewashing or spoofing, and when they discovered that none of the others was in a position to make a butt of them, they became more reasonable, and less conventional.

'The Lamb-Latterly breach was mended after a few days, when Miss Latterly got over the shock, and Miss Lamb is now being cosseted with a devotion scarcely to be distinguished from tyranny.

'Our leading rebel for some time was Tilly. . . . Oh, you must have seen Tilly Foresham – jodhpurs, roll-neck, hacking-jacket, dragged hither and thither by the whim of fate in the form of three golden retrievers. . . . She protested indignantly for some time that she would not mind much if she happened to *like* babies; but, as she much preferred puppies, the whole thing was particularly hard on her. However, she seems now to have given in, though grudgingly.'

Zellaby rambled on for a time with anecdotes of the emergency, concluding with the one in which Miss Ogle had been narrowly headed off from making the first payment, in her own name, for the most resplendent perambulator that Trayne could offer.

After a pause, Alan prompted:

'You did say that about ten who might be expected to be involved actually are not?'

'Yes. And five of those were in the bus on the Oppley road, and therefore under observation during the Dayout – that has at least done something to dispel the idea of a fertilizing gas which some seemed to be inclined to adopt as one of the new scientific horrors of our age,' Zellaby told him.

CHAPTER 11

Well Played, Midwich

'I AM really sorry,' Bernard Westcott wrote to me early in May, 'that circumstances preclude well-deserved official congratulations to your village on the success of the operation to date. It has been conducted with a discretion and communal loyalty which, frankly, has astonished us; most of us here were of the opinion that it would prove necessary to take official action well before this. Now, with only some seven weeks to go before D-day, we are hopeful that we may get through without it.

'The matter which has given us the greatest concern so far was in connexion with Miss Frazer, on Mr Crimm's staff, and so, one might say, not the fault of the village proper – nor even of the lady herself.

'Her father, a naval commander, retired, and a fire-eater of some truculence, was bent on trouble – all set to get questions asked in the House about loose-living and orgiastic goings-on in government establishments. Anxious, apparently, to make a Fleet Street holiday of his daughter. Luckily we were able to arrange for suitably influential people to have a few effective words with him in time.

'What is your own opinion? Do you think Midwich will last it out?'

That was far from easy to answer. If there were no major upset, I thought it might stand a good chance: on the other hand, one could not fail to be anxiously aware of the unexpected, lurking round any corner – the small detonator that might set things off.

We had had our ups and downs, though, and managed to get through them. Sometimes, they seemed to come from nowhere and spread like an infection. The worst, which looked at one time like becoming a panic, was allayed by Dr Willers who hurriedly arranged X-ray facilities and was able to show that all appeared to be quite normal.

The general attitude in May one could describe as a bracing-up, with here and there an impatient desire to let battle commence. Dr Willers, normally an ardent advocate of having one's baby in Trayne hospital, had reversed his usual advice. For one thing, it would, particularly if there should be anything untoward about the babies, render all attempts to keep the matter quiet utterly useless. For another, Trayne did not have the beds to cope with such a phenomenon as a simultaneous application by the whole female population of Midwich – and that alone would certainly have been fuel for publicity – so he went on wearing and flogging himself to make the best local arrangements he could. Nurse Daniels, too, was tireless, and it was a matter for thanksgiving by the whole village that she had happened to be away from home at the critical time of the Dayout. Willers, it was understood, had a temporary assistant booked for the first week in June, and a sort of commando of midwives signed-up for later on. The small committee-room in the Village Hall had been requisitioned as a supply-base, and several large cartons from firms of manufacturing chemists had already arrived.

Mr Leebody was working himself dead tired, too. There was much sympathy for him on account of Mrs Leebody, and he was more regarded in the village than he ever had been before. Mrs Zellaby was holding resolutely to her solidarity line, and, aided by Janet, continued to proclaim that Midwich would meet whatever was to come with a united front, and unafraid. It was, I think, chiefly on account of their work that we had come so far with – except in the matter of Mrs Leebody and one or two others – so little psychosomatic trouble.

Zellaby had operated, as might be expected, in less definable capacities, one of which he described as chief liquidator of the all-my-eye-and-crystal-balls division, and he had shown a pretty knack of causing nonsense to wilt, without putting backs up. One suspected that he was also supplying quite a little help where there was need and hardship.

Mr Crimm's worries with his Establishments Branch continued. He had been making increasingly urgent appeals to Bernard Westcott, and reached the point of saying that the only thing that would save a scandal throughout the Civil Service soon would be for his research project to be switched, and quickly, from ministerial to War Office control. Bernard, it seemed, was trying to achieve that, insisting the while that the whole affair *must* be kept quiet for just as long as it was possible to hold it.

'Which, from the Midwich point of view,' said Mr Crimm, with a shrug, 'is all to the good. But what the devil it can matter to M.I. I still don't begin to see....'

*

By mid-May there was a perceptible change. Hitherto, the spirit of Midwich had been not ill-attuned with that of the burgeoning season all around. It would be too much to say that it now went out of tune, but there was a certain muting of its strings. It acquired an air of abstraction; a more pensive mien.

'This,' remarked Willers to Zellaby, one day, 'is where we begin to stiffen the sinews.'

'Some quotations,' said Zellaby, 'are greatly improved by lack of context, but I take your meaning. One of the things that isn't helping is the nattering of stupid old women. What with one thing and another, it is such an exceptionally good wicket for beldames. I wish they could be stopped.'

'They're only one of the hazards. There are plenty more.'

Zellaby pondered glumly for a little, then he said:

'Well, we can only keep on trying. I suppose we have done pretty well not to have more trouble with it some time ago.'

'A lot better than one thought possible – and nearly all of it due to Mrs Zellaby,' the doctor told him.

Zellaby hesitated, and then made up his mind.

'I'm rather concerned about her, Willers. I wonder if you could – well, have a talk with her.'

'A talk?'

'She's more worried than she has let us see. It came out a bit a couple of nights ago. Nothing particular to start it. I happened to look up and found her staring at me, as though she were hating me. She doesn't you know. . . . Then, as if I had said something, she broke out: "It's all very well for a man. He doesn't have to go through this sort of thing, and he knows he never will have to. How *can* he understand? He may *mean* as well as a saint, but he's always on the outside. He can never *know* what it's like, even in a normal way – so what sort of an idea can he have of *this*? – Of how it feels to lie awake at night with the humiliating knowledge that one is simply being used? – As if one were not a person at all, but just a kind of mechanism, a sort of incubator. . . . And then go on wondering, hour after hour, night after night, *what* – just *what* it may be that one is being forced to incubate. *Of course* you can't understand how that feels – how could you! It's degrading, it's intolerable. I shall crack soon. I know I shall. I can't go on like this much longer." '

Zellaby paused, and shook his head.

'There's so damned little one can do. I didn't try to stop her. I thought it would be better for her to let it out. But I'd be glad if you would talk to her, convince her. She knows that all the tests and X-rays show normal development – but she's got it into her head that it would be professionally necessary for you to say that, in any case. And I suppose it would.'

'It's true – thank heaven,' the doctor told him. 'I don't know what the devil I'd have done if it weren't – but I know we couldn't have just gone on as we have. I assure you the patients can't be more relieved that it is so than I am. So don't you worry, I'll set her mind at rest on that point, at any rate. She's not the first to think it, and she'll certainly not be the last. But, as soon as we get one thing nailed, they'll find others to worry themselves with.

'This is going to be a very, very dodgy time all round....'

*

In a week, it began to look as if Willers' prophecy would prove a pale understatement. The feeling of tension was contagious, and almost palpably increasing day by day. At the end of another week Midwich's united front had weakened sadly. With self-help beginning to show inadequacy, Mr Leebody had to bear more and more of the weight of communal anxiety. He did not spare any pains. He arranged special daily services, and for the rest of the day drove himself on from one parishioner to another, giving what encouragement he could.

Zellaby found himself quite superfluous. Rationalism was in disfavour. He maintained an unusual silence, and would have accepted invisibility, too, had it been offered.

'Have you noticed,' he inquired, dropping in one evening at Mr Crimm's cottage, 'have you noticed the way they glare at one? Rather as if one had been currying favour with the Creator in order to be given the other sex. Quite unnerving at times. Is it the same at The Grange?'

'It began to be,' Mr Crimm admitted, 'but we got them away on leave a day or two ago. Those who wanted to go home have gone there. The rest are in billets arranged by the doctor. We are getting more work done, as a result. It was becoming a little difficult.'

'Understatement,' said Zellaby. 'As it happens, I have never worked in a fireworks factory, but I know just what it must be like. I feel that at any moment something ungoverned, and rather horrible, may break out. And there's nothing one can do but wait, and hope it doesn't happen. Frankly, how we are going to get through another month or so of it, I don't know.' He shrugged and shook his head.

*

At the very moment of that despondent shake, however, the situation was in the process of being unexpectedly improved.

For Miss Lamb, who had adopted the custom of a quiet evening stroll, carefully supervised by Miss Latterly, that evening underwent a misadventure. One of the milk-bottles neatly arranged outside the back door of their cottage had somehow been overturned, and, as they left, Miss Lamb stepped on it. It rolled beneath her foot, and she fell. . . .

Miss Latterly carried her back indoors, and rushed to the telephone. . . .

*

Mrs Willers was still waiting up for her husband when he came back, five hours later. She heard the car drive up, and when she opened the door he was standing on the threshold, dishevelled, and blinking at the light. She had seen him like that only once or twice in their married life, and caught his arm anxiously.

'Charley. Charley, my dear, what is it? Not – ?'

'Rather drunk, Milly. Sorry. Take no notice,' he said.

'Oh, Charley! Was the baby – ?'

'Reaction, m'dear. Jus' reaction. Baby's perfect, you see. Nothing wrong with the baby. Nothing 't all. Perfect.'

'Oh, thank God for that,' exclaimed Mrs Willers, meaning it as fervently as she had ever meant any prayer.

'Got golden eyes,' said her husband. 'Funny – but nothing against having golden eyes, is there?'

'No, dear, of course not.'

'Perfect, 'cept for golden eyes. Not wrong at all.'

Mrs Willers helped him out of his coat, and steered him into the sitting-room. He dropped into a chair and sat there slackly, staring before him.

'S-so s-silly, isn't it?' he said. 'All that worrying. And now it's perfect. I – I – I – ' He burst suddenly into tears, and covered his face with his hands.

Mrs Willers sat down on the arm of his chair, and laid her arm round his shoulders.

'There, there, my darling. It's all right, dear. It's over now.' She turned his face towards her own, and kissed him.

'Might've been black, or yellow, or green, or like a monkey. X-rays no good to tell that,' he said. ' 'F the women of Midwich do the right thing by Miss Lamb, should be window to her, in the church.'

'I know, my dear, I know. But you don't need to worry about that any more. You said it's perfect.'

Dr Willers nodded emphatically several times.

'That's right. Perfect,' he repeated, with another nod. ' 'Cept for golden eyes. Golden eyes are all right. Perfect.... Lambs, my dear, lambs may safely graze . . . safely graze. ... Oh, God, I'm tired, Milly....'

*

A month later Gordon Zellaby found himself pacing the floor of the waiting-room in Trayne's best nursing-home, and forced himself to stop it and sit down. It was a ridiculous way to behave at his age, he told himself. Very proper in a young man, no doubt, but the last few weeks had brought the fact that he was no longer a young man rather forcibly to his notice. He felt about twice the age he had a year ago. Nevertheless, when, ten minutes later, a nurse rustled starchily in, she found him pacing the room again.

'It is a boy, Mr Zellaby,' she said. 'And I have Mrs Zellaby's special instructions to tell you he *has* the Zellaby nose.'

CHAPTER 12

Harvest Home

ON a fine afternoon in the last week of July, Gordon Zellaby, emerging from the post office, encountered a small family-party coming from the church. It centred about a girl who carried a baby wrapped in a white woollen shawl. She looked very young to be the baby's mother; scarcely more than a schoolgirl. Zellaby beamed benevolently upon the group and received their smiles in return, but when they had passed his eyes followed the child carrying her child, a little sadly.

As he approached the lych-gate, the Reverend Hubert Leebody came down the path.

'Hullo, Vicar. Still signing up the recruits, I see,' he said.

Mr Leebody greeted him, nodded, and fell into step beside him.

'It's easing off now, though,' he said. 'Only two or three more to come.'

'Making it one hundred per cent?'

'Very nearly. I must confess I had scarcely expected that, but I fancy they feel that though it can't exactly regularize matters, it does go some way towards it. I'm glad they do.' He paused reflectively. 'This one,' he went on, 'young Mary Histon, she's chosen the name Theodore. Chose it all on her own, I gather. And I must say I rather like that.'

Zellaby considered for a moment, and nodded.

'So do I, Vicar. I like it very much. And, you know, that embodies no mean tribute to you.'

Mr Leebody looked pleased, but shook his head.

'Not to me,' he said. 'That a child like Mary should want to call her baby "the gift of God" instead of being ashamed of it is a tribute to the whole village.'

'But the village had to be shown how, in the name of humanity, it ought to behave.'

'Teamwork,' said the Vicar. 'Teamwork, with a fine captain in Mrs Zellaby.'

They continued for a few paces in silence, then Zellaby said:

'Nevertheless, the fact remains that, however the girl takes it, she has been robbed. She has been swept suddenly from childhood into womanhood. I find that saddening. No chance to stretch her wings. She has to miss the age of true poetry.'

'One would like to agree – but, in point of fact, I doubt it,' said Mr Leebody. 'Not only are poets, active or passive, rather rare, but it suits more temperaments than our times like to pretend to go straight from dolls to babies.'

Zellaby shook his head regretfully.

'I expect you're right. All my life I have deplored the Teutonic view of women, and all my life ninety per cent of them have been showing me that they don't mind it a bit.'

'There are some who certainly have not been robbed of anything,' Mr Leebody pointed out.

'You're right. I've just been looking in on Miss Ogle. She hasn't. Still a bit bewildered, perhaps, but delighted too. You'd think it was all some kind of conjuring trick she had invented for herself, without knowing how.'

He paused, and then went on: 'My wife tells me that Mrs Leebody will be home in a few days. We were most happy to hear that.'

'Yes. The doctors are very pleased. She's made a wonderful recovery.'

'And the baby is doing well?'

'Yes,' said Mr Leebody, a shade unhappily. 'She adores the baby.'

He paused at a gate which gave entrance to the garden of a large cottage set well back from the road.

'Ah, yes,' Zellaby nodded. 'And how *is* Miss Foresham?'

'Very busy at the moment. A new litter. She still maintains that a baby is less interesting than puppies, but I think I notice a weakening of conviction.'

'There are signs of that even in the most indignant,' Zellaby agreed. 'For my part, however, that is as a male, I must admit to finding things a bit flat and after-the-battle.'

'It has been a battle,' agreed Mr Leebody, 'but battles, after all, are just the highlights of a campaign. There are more to come.'

Zellaby looked at him more attentively. Mr Leebody went on:

'Who *are* these children? There's something about the way they look at one with those curious eyes. They are – strangers, you know.' He hesitated, and added: 'I realize it is not a way of thinking that will commend itself to you, but I find myself continually returning to the idea that this must be some kind of test.'

'But by whom, of whom?' said Zellaby.

Mr Leebody shook his head.

'Possibly we shall never know. Though it has already shown itself something of a test of us here. We *could* have rejected the situation that was thrust upon us, but we accepted it as our own concern.'

'One hopes,' said Zellaby, 'one hopes that we did right.'

Mr Leebody looked startled.

'But what else – ?'

'I don't know. How is one to know with – strangers?'

Presently they parted; Mr Leebody to make his call, Zellaby to continue his stroll, with a thoughtful air. Not until he was approaching the Green did his attention turn outward, and then it was caught by Mrs Brinkman, still at some distance. One moment she was hurrying along towards him behind a new and shiny perambulator; the next, she had stopped dead, and was looking down into it in a helpless, troubled fashion. Then she picked the baby up and carried it the few yards to the War Memorial. There she sat down on the second step, unbuttoned her blouse, and held the baby to her.

Zellaby continued his stroll. As he drew near he raised his somewhat ramshackle hat. An expression of annoyance came over Mrs Brinkman's face, and a suffusion of pink, but she did not move. Then, as if he had spoken, she said defensively:

'Well, it's natural enough, isn't it?'

'My dear lady, it's classical. One of the great symbols.' Zellaby assured her.

'Then go away,' she told him, and abruptly began to weep.

Zellaby hesitated. 'Is there anything I can – ?'

'Yes. Go *away*,' she repeated. 'You don't think I *want* to make an exhibition of myself, do you?' she added, tearfully.

Zellaby was still irresolute.

'She's hungry,' Mrs Brinkman said. 'You'd understand if yours was one of the Dayout babies. Now, will you please *go away*!'

It did not seem the moment to pursue the matter further. Zellaby lifted his hat once more, and did as he was required. He went on, with a puzzled frown on his brow as he realized that somewhere he had missed a trick; something had been kept from him.

Half-way up the drive to Kyle Manor the sound of a car behind made him draw in to the side for it to pass. It did not pass, however. It drew up beside him. Turning, he saw not the tradesman's van he had assumed it to be, but a small black car with Ferrelyn at the wheel.

'My dear,' he said, 'how nice to see you. I had no idea you were coming. I wish they wouldn't forget to tell me things.'

But Ferrelyn did not give him smile for smile. Her face, a little pale, remained tired-looking.

'Nobody had any idea I was coming – not even me. I didn't intend to come.' She looked down at the baby in the carry-cot on the passenger seat beside her. 'He *made* me come,' she said.

CHAPTER 13

Midwich Centrocline

ON the following day there returned to Midwich, first, Dr Margaret Haxby from Norwich, with baby. Miss Haxby was no longer on the staff of The Grange, having resigned two months before, nevertheless it was to The Grange she went, demanding accommodation. Two hours later came Miss Diana Dawson, from the neighbourhood of Gloucester, also with baby, also demanding accommodation. She presented slightly less of a problem than Miss Haxby since she was still a member of the staff, though not due to return from leave for some weeks yet. Third, came Miss Polly Rushton from London, with baby, in a state of distress and confused emotions, asking help and shelter of her uncle, the Reverend Hubert Leebody.

The day after that, two more ex-staff from The Grange arrived, with their babies, admitting their resignations from the Service, but at the same time making it perfectly clear that it was The Grange's duty to find them a room of some kind in Midwich. In the afternoon, young Mrs Dorry, who had been staying in Devonport to be near her husband in his latest posting, arrived unexpectedly, with her baby, and opened up her cottage.

And on the next day there showed up from Durham, with baby, the remaining member of The Grange staff involved. She, too, was technically on leave, but insisted that a place must be found for her. Finally appeared Miss Latterly, with Miss Lamb's baby, urgently returning from Eastbourne whither she had taken Miss Lamb for recuperation.

This influx was observed with varying emotions. Mr Leebody welcomed his niece warmly, as though she were putting it within his power to make some amends. Dr Willers was perplexed and disconcerted – as was Mrs Willers, who feared it might cause him to postpone the much-needed holiday she had arranged for him. Gordon Zellaby had the air of one regarding an interesting phenomenon with judicial reserve. The person upon whom the development pressed most immediately was, without doubt, Mr Crimm. He was beginning to wear a distraught look.

A number of urgent reports went in to Bernard. Janet's and mine was to the effect that the first, and probably the worst, hurdle had been crossed, and the babies had arrived without nationwide obstetrical interest, BUT *if* he still wished to avoid publicity the new situation *must* be dealt with promptly. Plans for the care and support of the children would have to be established on a sound, official footing.

Mr Crimm urged that the irregularities appearing in his personnel records were now on a scale that had taken them beyond his control, and that unless there was swift intervention at a higher level, there was soon going to be an almighty rumpus.

Dr Willers felt it necessary to turn in three reports. The first was in medical language, for the record. The second expressed his opinions in more colloquial terms, for the lay. Among the points he made were these:

'The survival rate of one hundred per cent – resulting in 31 males and 30 females of this special type – means that only superficial study has been possible, but of the characteristics observed, the following are common to them all:

'Most striking are the eyes. These appear to be quite normal in structure; the iris, however, is, to the best of my knowledge, unique in its colouring, being of a bright, almost fluorescent-looking gold, and is the same shade of gold in all.

'The hair, noticeably soft and fine, is, as well as I can describe it, of a slightly darkened blond shade. In section, under the microscope, it is almost flat on one side, while the other is an arc; the shape being close to that of a narrow D. Specimens taken from eight of the babies are precisely similar. I can find no record of such a hair-type being observed hitherto. The finger and toe nails are a trifle narrower than is usual, but there is no suggestion of claw formation – indeed, one would judge them to be slightly flatter than the average. The shape of the occiput may be a little unusual, but it is too early to be definite about that.

'In a former report it was surmised that the origin might be attributable to some process of xenogenesis. The very remarkable similarity of the children; the fact that they are certainly not hybrids of any known species, as well as all the circumstances attending gestation, tend, in my view to support this opinion. Additional evidence may accrue when the blood-groups can be determined – that is to say, when the blood circulating ceases to be that of the mother's group, and becomes that of the individual.

'I have been unable to find any record of a case of human xenogenesis, but I know of no reason why it should not be possible. This explanation has naturally occurred to those involved. The more educated women entirely accept the thesis that they are host-mothers, rather than true mothers; the less educated find in it an element of humiliation, and so tend to ignore it.

'In general: the babies all appear to be perfectly healthy although they do not show the degree of "chubbiness" one expects at their age: the size of the head in relation to the body is that normally found in a somewhat older child: a curious, but slight, silvery sheen on the skin has given concern to some of the mothers, but is common to all, and would appear to be normal to the type.'

After reading through the rest of his report, Janet took him up on it severely.

'Look here,' she said. 'What about the return of all the mothers and babies – all this compulsion business? You can't just skip that altogether.'

'A form of hysteria giving rise to collective hallucination – probably quite temporary,' said Willers.

'But *all* the mothers, educated or not, agree that the babies can, and *do*, exert a form of compulsion. Those who were away didn't want to come back here; they came because they *had* to. I've talked to all of them, and what they *all* say is that they suddenly became aware of a feeling of distress – a sense of need which they somehow knew could only be relieved by coming back here. Their attempts to describe it vary because it seems to have affected them in different ways – one felt stifled, another said it was like hunger or thirst, and another, that it was like having a great noise battering at one. Ferrelyn says she simply suffered from intolerable jitters. But, whichever way it took them, they felt it was associated with the babies, and that the only way to relieve it was to bring them back here.

'And that even goes for Miss Lamb, too. She felt just the same, but she was ill in bed at the time, and couldn't possibly come. So what happened? The compulsion switched on to Miss Latterly, and she was unable to rest until she had acted as Miss Lamb's proxy and brought the baby back here. Once she had parked it here with Mrs Brant she felt free of the compulsion, and was able to return to Miss Lamb, in Eastbourne.'

'If,' said Doctor Willers, heavily, '*if* we take all old wives' – or young wives' – tales at face value; *if* we remember that the majority of feminine tasks are deadly dull, and leave the mind so empty that the most trifling seed that falls there can grow into a riotous tangle, we shall not be surprised by an outlook on life which has the disproportion and the illogical inconsequence of a nightmare, where values are symbolic rather than literal.

'Now, what do we have here? A number of women who are the victims of an improbable, and as yet unexplained, phenomenon: and a number of resultant babies which are not quite like other babies. By a dichotomy familiar to us all, a woman requires her own baby to be perfectly normal, and at the same time superior to all other babies. Well, when any of these women concerned is isolated from the rest with her own baby, it is bound to become more strongly borne in upon her that her golden-eyed baby is not, in relation to the other babies she sees, quite normal. Her sub-conscious becomes defensive, and keeps it up until a point is reached where the facts must either be admitted, or somehow sublimated. The easiest way to sublimate the situation is to transfer the irregularity into an environment where it no longer appears irregular – if there is such a place. In this case there *is* one, and one only – Midwich. So they pick up their babies, and back they come, and everything is comfortably rationalized for the time being.'

'It seems to me that there is certainly *some* rationalizing going on,' Janet said. 'What about Mrs Welt?'

On the occasion she was referring to, Mrs Brant had gone into Mrs Welt's shop one morning to find her engaged in jabbing a pin into herself again and again, and weeping as she did it. This had not seemed good to Mrs Brant, so she had dragged her off to see Willers. He gave Mrs Welt some kind of sedative, and when she felt better she had explained that in changing the baby's napkin she had pricked him with a pin. Whereupon, by her account, the baby had just looked steadily at her with its golden eyes, and *made* her start jabbing the pin into herself.

'Well, really!' objected Willers. 'If you can cite me a plainer case of hysterical remorse – hair-shirts, and all that – I shall be interested to hear it.'

'And Harriman, too?' Janet persisted.

For Harriman had one day made his appearance in Willers' surgery in a shocking mess. Nose broken, couple of teeth knocked out, both eyes blacked. He had been set on, so he said, by three unknown men – but no one else had seen these men. On the other hand, two of the village boys claimed that through his window they had seen Harriman furiously bashing himself with his own fists. – And the next day someone noticed a bruise on the side of the Harriman baby's face.

Dr Willers shrugged.

'If Harriman were to complain of being set upon by a troupe of pink elephants, it would not greatly surprise me,' he said.

'Well, if you aren't going to put it in, I shall write an additional report,' said Janet.

And she did. She concluded it:

'This is *not*, in my opinion, or in anyone's opinion but Dr Willers', a matter of hysteria, but of simple fact.

'The situation should, in my view, be recognized, not explained away. It needs to be examined and understood. There is a tendency among the weaker-willed to become superstitious about it, and to credit the babies with magical powers. This sort of nonsense does no one any good, and invites exploitation by what Zellaby calls "the beldame underground". There ought to be an unbiased investigation.'

An investigation, though on more general lines, was also the theme of Dr Willers third report which was in the form of a protest that wound up:

'In the first place, I do not see why M.I. is concerned in this at all: in the second, that it should be, apparently, an exclusive concern of theirs is outrageous.

'It is disgracefully *wrong*. Somebody should be making a thorough study of these children – I am keeping notes, of course, but they are only an ordinary G.P.'s observations. There ought to be a team of experts on the job. I kept quiet before the births because I thought, and still think, that it was better for everyone, and for the mothers in particular, but now that need is over.

'One has got used to the idea of military interference with science in a number of fields – a lot of it totally unnecessary – but this is really preposterous! It is nothing less than a scandal that such a phenomenon as this should continue to be hushed up so that it is going practically unobserved.

'If it is not simply a piece of obstructionism, it is still a scandal. It must be possible for something to be done, within the provisions of the Official Secrets Act, if necessary. A wonderful opportunity for the study of comparative development is simply being thrown away.

'Think of all the trouble that has been taken to observe mere quins and quads, and then look at the material for study that we have here. Sixty-one similars – so similar that most of their ostensible mothers cannot tell them apart.

(They will deny that, but it is true.) Think of the work that should be taking place on the comparative effects of environment, conditioning, association, diet, and all the rest of it. What is going on here is a burning of books before they have been written. Something *must* be done about it before more chances are lost.'

All these representations resulted in a prompt visit from Bernard, and an afternoon of rather acrimonious discussion. The discussion broke up only partly mollified by his promises to stir the Ministry of Health into swift, practical action.

*

After the others had left, he said:

'Now that official interest in Midwich is bound to become more overt, it might be very useful – and, indeed, might help to avoid awkwardness later on – if we could enlist Zellaby's sympathy. Do you think you could arrange for me to meet him?'

I rang up Zellaby who agreed at once, so after dinner I took Bernard up to Kyle Manor, and left him there to talk. He returned to our cottage about a couple of hours later, looking thoughtful.

'Well,' asked Janet, 'and what do you make of the sage of Midwich?'

Bernard shook his head, and looked at me.

'He's got me wondering,' he said. 'Most of your reports have been excellent, Richard, but I doubt whether you got him quite right. Oh, there *is* a lot of chatter which sounds like hot air, I know, but what you gave me was too much of the manner, and too little of the matter.'

'I'm sorry if I misled you,' I admitted. 'The trouble about Zellaby is that his matter is frequently elusive, and often allusive. Not much that he says is reportable fact; he is given to mentioning things *en passant*, and by the time you've thought it over you don't know whether he followed them up with serious deductions, or was simply playing with hypotheses – nor, for that matter, are you at all sure how much he implied, and how much you inferred. It makes things difficult.'

Bernard nodded, understandingly.

'I appreciate that now. I've just had some of it. He spent quite ten minutes towards the end telling me that it is only recently that he has come to wonder whether civilization is not, biologically speaking, a form of decadence. From that he went on to wonder whether the gap between *homo sapiens* and the rest was not too wide; with the suggestion that it might have been better for our development had we had to contend with the conditions of some other sapient, or at least semi-sapient, species. I'm sure he wasn't being altogether irrelevant – but I'm hanged if I can really pin down the relevance. One thing seems pretty clear though; erratic as he seems, he doesn't miss a lot. . . . Incidentally, he is strong on the same line as the doctor concerning expert observation – particularly on this "compulsion", but in his case for the opposite reason: he doesn't consider it hysterical, and is anxious to know what it is.

'By the way, you seem to have missed one trick – did you know his daughter tried to take her baby for a drive in her car the other day?'

'No,' I said, 'what do you mean, "tried"?'

'Just that after about six miles she had to give up, and come back again. He doesn't like it. As he put it: for a child to be tied to its mother's apron strings is bad, but for a mother to be tied to a baby's apron strings is serious. He feels it is time he took some steps about it.'

CHAPTER 14

Matters Arising

FOR various reasons almost three weeks went by before Alan Hughes was free to come for a week-end visit, so that Zellaby's expressed intention of taking steps had to be postponed until then.

By this time the disinclination of the Children (now beginning to acquire an implied capital C, to distinguish them from other children) to be removed from the immediate neighbourhood had become a phenomenon generally recognized in the village. It was a nuisance, since it involved finding someone to look after the baby when its mother went to Trayne, or elsewhere, but not regarded with any great seriousness – more, indeed, as a foible; just another inconvenience added to the inconveniences inevitable with babies, anyway.

Zellaby took a less casual view of it, but waited until the Sunday afternoon before putting the matter to his son-in-law. Reasonably certain, then, of a spell without interruption he led Alan to deck-chairs under the cedar tree on the lawn where they would not be overheard. Once they were seated he came to the point with quite unusual directness.

'What I want to say, my boy, is this: I'd feel happier if you can get Ferrelyn away from here. And the sooner, I think, the better.'

Alan looked at him with an expression of surprise which became changed into a slight frown.

'I should have thought it fairly clear that there is nothing I want more than to have her with me.'

'Of course it is, my dear fellow. One could not fail to realize that. But at the moment I am concerned with something more important than interfering in your private affairs; I am not thinking of what either of you wants, or would like, so much as what needs to be done – for Ferrelyn's sake, not for yours.'

'She wants to come away. She set out to come once,' Alan reminded him.

'I know. But she tried to take the baby with her: it brought her back, just as it brought her here before, and just, it appears, as it will if she tries again. Therefore you must take her away without the baby. If you can persuade her to that, we can arrange to have it excellently looked after here. The indications are that if it is not actually with her it will not – probably cannot – exert any influence stronger than that of natural affection.'

'But according to Willers –'

'Willers is making a loud blustering noise to prevent himself from being frightened. He's refusing to see what he doesn't want to see. I don't suppose it matters very much what casuistries he uses to comfort himself, as long as they don't take in the rest of us.'

'You mean that this hysteria he talks about isn't the real reason for Ferrelyn and the rest coming back here?'

'Well, what is hysteria? A functional disorder of the nervous system. Naturally there has been considerable strain upon the nervous systems of many of them, but the trouble with Willers is that he stops before he ought to begin. Instead of facing it, and honestly inquiring why the reaction should take this particular form, he hides in a smoke-screen of generalities about a long period of sustained anxiety, and so on. I don't blame the man. He's had enough for the time being; he's tired out, and he deserves a rest. But that doesn't mean we must let him obscure the facts, which is what he is trying to do. For instance, even if he has observed it, he has not admitted that none of this "hysteria" has ever been known to manifest itself without one of the babies being present.'

'Is that so?' Alan asked, surprised.

'Without exception. This sense of compulsion occurs only in the vicinity of one of the babies. Separate the baby from the mother – or perhaps one should say remove the mother from the neighbourhood of *any* of the babies – and the compulsion at once begins to lessen, and gradually dies away. It takes longer to fade in some than in others, but that is what happens.'

'But I don't see – I mean, how is it done?'

'I've no idea. There could, one supposes, be an element akin to hypnotism, perhaps, but, whatever the mechanism, I am perfectly satisfied that it is exerted wilfully and with purpose by the child. One would instance the case of Miss Lamb: when it was physically impossible for her to comply, the compulsion was promptly switched to Miss Latterly, who had previously felt none of it, with the result that the baby had its way, and got back here, as did the rest.

'And since they got back, no one has managed to take one of them more than six miles from Midwich.

'Hysteria, says Willers. One woman starts it, the rest subconsciously accept it, and so exhibit the same symptoms. But if the baby is parked with a neighbour here the mother is able to go to Trayne, or anywhere else she wants to, without any hindrance. That, according to Willers, is simply because her subconscious hasn't been led to expect anything to happen when she is on her own, so it doesn't.

'But my point is this: Ferrelyn cannot take the baby; but if she makes up her mind to go, and leave it here, there's nothing to stop her. Your job is to help to make up her mind for her.'

Alan considered.

'Sort of put out an ultimatum – make her choose between baby and me? That's a bit tough and – er – fundamental, isn't it?' he suggested.

'My dear fellow, the baby's put the ultimatum already. What you have to do is to clarify the situation. The only possible compromise would be for you to surrender to the baby's challenge, and come to live here, too.'

'Which I couldn't, anyway.'

'Very well, then. Ferrelyn has been dodging the issue for

some weeks now, but sooner or later she must face it. Your job is first to make her recognize the hurdle, and then help her over it.'

Alan said slowly:

'It's quite a thing to ask, though, isn't it?'

'Isn't the other quite a thing to ask of a man – when it isn't his baby?'

'H'm,' Alan remarked. Zellaby went on:

'And it isn't really her baby, either, or I'd not be talking quite like this. Ferrelyn and the rest are the victims of an imposition: they have been cheated into an utterly false position. Some kind of elaborate confidence trick has made them into what the veterinary fellows call host-mothers; a relationship more intimate than that of the foster-mother, but similar in kind. This baby has absolutely nothing to do with either of you – except that, by some process not yet explained, she was placed in a situation which forced her to nourish it. So far is it from belonging to either of you that it doesn't correspond to any known racial classification. Even Willers has to admit that.

'But if the type is unknown, the phenomenon is not – our ancestors, who did not have Willers' blind faith in the articles of science – had a word for it: they called such beings changelings. None of this business would have seemed as strange to them as it does to us because they had only to suffer religious dogmatism, which was not so dogmatic as scientific dogmatism.

'The idea of the changeling, therefore, far from being novel, is both old and so widely distributed that it is unlikely to have arisen, or to have persisted, without cause, and occasional support. True, one has not encountered the idea of it taking place on such a scale as this, but quantity does not, in this case, affect the quality of the event; it simply confirms it. All these sixty-one golden-eyed children we have here are intruders, changelings: they are cuckoo-children.

'Now, the important thing about the cuckoo is not how the egg got into the nest, nor why that nest was chosen; the real matter for concern comes after it has been hatched – what, in fact, it will attempt to do next. And that, whatever it may be, will be motivated by its instinct for survival, an instinct characterized chiefly by utter ruthlessness.'

Alan pondered a little.

'You really think you've got a sound analogy there?' he asked, uneasily.

'I'm perfectly certain of it,' Zellaby asserted.

The two of them fell silent for some little time, Zellaby lying back in his chair with his hands behind his head, Alan staring unseeingly across the lawn. At length:

'All right,' he said. 'I suppose most of us have been hoping that once the babies arrived things would straighten out. I admit that it doesn't look like it now. But what are you expecting to happen?'

'I'm just being expectant, not specific – except that I don't think it will be anything pleasant,' Zellaby replied. 'The cuckoo survives because it is tough and single-purposed. That is why I hope you will take Ferrelyn away – and keep her away.

'Nothing satisfactory can come of this, at best. Do your utmost to make her forget this changeling in order that she may have a normal life. It will be difficult at first, no doubt, but not so hard if she has a child that is really her own.'

Alan rubbed the furrows on his forehead.

'It *is* difficult,' he said. 'In spite of the way it happened, she does have a maternal feeling for it – a well, a sort of physical affection, and a sense of obligation, you know.'

'But of course. That's how it works. That's why the poor hen works herself to death feeding the greedy cuckoo-chick. It's a form of confidence-trick, as I told you – the callous exploitation of a natural proclivity. The existence of such a proclivity is important to the continuation of a species, but, after all, in a civilized society we cannot afford to give way to *all* the natural urges, can we? In this case, Ferrelyn must simply refuse to be blackmailed through her better instincts.'

'If,' said Alan slowly, 'if Angela's child had turned out to be one of them, what would you have done?'

'I should have done what I am advising you to do for Ferrelyn. Taken her away. I should also have cut off our connexion with Midwich by selling this house, fond as we both are of it. I may have to do that yet, even though she is not directly involved. It depends how the situation develops. One waits to see. The potentialities are unknown, but I don't care for the logical implications. Therefore the sooner Ferrelyn is out of it, the happier I shall be. I don't propose to say anything about it to her myself. For one thing it is a matter for you to settle between you; for another, there is the risk that by crystallizing a not very clear misgiving I might do the wrong thing – make it appear as a challenge to be met, for instance. You have a positive alternative to offer. However, if it is difficult, and you need something to tip the balance, Angela and I will back you up quite fully.'

Alan nodded slowly.

'I hope that won't be necessary – I don't think it will be. We both know really that we can't just go on like this. Now you've given me a push, we'll get it settled.'

They continued to sit, in silent contemplation. Alan was aware of some relief that his fragmentary feelings and suspicions had been collected for him into a form which warranted action. He was also considerably impressed, for he could recall no previous conversation with his father-in-law in which Zellaby, spurning one tempting diversion after another, had held so stoutly to his course. Moreover, the speculations which could arise were interesting and numerous. He was on the point of raising one or two of them himself when he was checked by the sight of Angela crossing the lawn towards them.

She sat down in the chair on the other side of her husband, and demanded a cigarette. Zellaby gave her one and held out the match. He watched her take the first few puffs.

'Trouble?' he inquired.

'I'm not quite sure. I've just had Margaret Haxby on the telephone. She's gone.'

Zellaby lifted his eyebrows.

'You mean, cleared out?'

'Yes. She was speaking from London.'

'Oh,' said Zellaby, and lapsed into thought. Alan asked who Margaret Haxby was.

'Oh, I'm sorry. You probably don't know her. She's one of Mr Crimm's young ladies – or was. One of the brightest of them, I understand. Academically Dr Margaret Haxby – Ph.D., London.'

'One of the – er – afflicted?' Alan inquired.

'Yes. And one of the most resentful,' Angela said. 'Now she's made up her mind to beat it, and gone – leaving Midwich holding the baby. Literally.'

'But where do you come in, my dear?' Zellaby inquired.

'Oh, she just decided I was a reliable subject for official notification. She said she'd have rung Mr Crimm, but he's away today. She wanted to arrange about the baby.'

'Where is it now?'

'Where she was staying. In the older Mrs Dorry's cottage.'

'And she's just walked out on it?'

'That's it. Mrs Dorry doesn't know yet. I'll have to go and tell her.'

'This could be awkward,' Zellaby said. 'I can see a pretty panic starting up among the other women who've taken these girls in. They'll all be throwing them out overnight before they get left in the cart, too. Can't we stall? Give Crimm time to get back and do something? After all, his girls aren't a village responsibility – not primarily, anyway. Besides, she might change her mind.'

Angela shook her head.

'Not this one, I think. She's not done it on the spur of the moment. She's been over it pretty carefully, in fact. Her line is: She never asked to come to Midwich, she was simply posted here. If they'd posted her to a yellow-fever area they'd be responsible for the consequences; well, they posted her here, and through no fault of her own she caught this instead; now it's up to them to deal with it.'

'H'm,' said Zellaby. 'One has a feeling that *that* parallelism is not going to be accepted in government circles nem. con. However . . . ?'

'Anyway, that's her contention. She repudiates the child entirely. She says she is no more responsible for it than if it had been left on her doorstep, and there is, therefore, no reason why she should put up with, or be expected to put up with, the wrecking of her life, or her work, on account of it.'

'With the upshot that it is now thrown on the parish – unless she intends to pay for it, of course.'

'Naturally, I asked about that. She said that the village and The Grange could fight out the responsibility between them; it certainly was not hers. She will refuse to pay anything, since payment might be legally construed as admission of liability. Nevertheless, Mrs Dorry, or any other person of good character who cares to take the baby on, will receive a rate of two pounds a week, sent anonymously and irregularly.'

'You're right, my dear. She *has* been thinking it out; this is going to need looking into. What is the effect if this repudiation is allowed to go unchallenged? I imagine legal responsibility for the child has to be established somewhere. How is that done? Get the Relieving Officer in, and slap a court order on her, do you suppose?'

'I don't know, but she's thought of something of the kind happening. If it does, she intends to fight it in court. She claims that medical evidence will establish that the child cannot possibly be hers; from this it will be argued that as she was placed *in loco parentis* without her knowledge or consent, she cannot be held responsible. Failing this, it is still open to her to bring an action against the Ministry for negligence resulting in her being placed in a position of jeopardy; or it might be for conniving at assault; or, possibly, procuring. She isn't sure.'

'I should think not,' said Zellaby. 'It ought to be an interesting indictment to frame.'

'Well, she didn't seem to think it was likely to come to that,' Angela admitted.

'I imagine she's perfectly right there,' agreed Zellaby. 'We have made our own efforts, but the unperceived official machinations to keep all this quiet must have been quite considerable. Even the evidence brought to dispute a court order would be manna to journalists of all nations. In fact, the issue of such an order would probably bring Dr Haxby a considerable fortune, one way and another. Poor Mr Crimm – and poor Colonel Westcott. They are going to be worried, I'm afraid. I wonder just what their powers in the matter are . . . ?' He lapsed into thought for some moments before he went on:

'My dear, I've just been talking to Alan about getting Ferrelyn away. This seems to make it a little more urgent. Once it becomes generally known, others may decide to follow Margaret Haxby's example, don't you think?'

'It may make up their minds for some of them,' Angela agreed.

'In which case, and supposing an inconvenient number should take the same course, don't you think there is a possibility of some counter-move to stop more desertions.'

'But if, as you say, they don't want publicity – ?'

'Not by the authorities, my dear. No, I was wondering what would happen if it were to turn out that the children are as opposed to being deserted as they are to being removed.'

'But you don't really think – ?'

'I don't know. I'm simply doing my best to place myself in the situation of a young cuckoo. As such, I fancy I should resent anything that appeared likely to lessen attention to my comfort and well-being. Indeed, one does not even have to be a cuckoo to feel so. I just air the suggestion, you understand, but I do feel that it is worth making sure that Ferrelyn is not trapped here if something of the sort should happen.'

'Whether it does or not, she'll be better away,' Angela agreed. 'You could start by suggesting two or three weeks away while we see what happens,' she told Alan.

'Very well,' Alan said. 'It does give me a handle to start with. Where is she?'

'I left her on the veranda.'

The Zellabys watched him cross the lawn and disappear round a corner of the house. Gordon Zellaby lifted an eyebrow at his wife.

'Not very difficult, I think,' Angela said. 'Naturally she's longing to be with him. The obstacle is her sense of obligation. The conflict is doing her harm, wearing her out.'

'How much affection does she really have for the baby?'

'It's hard to say. There is so much social and traditional pressure on a woman in these things. One's self-defensive instinct is to conform to the approved pattern. Personal honesty takes time to assert itself – if it is ever allowed to.'

'Not with Ferrelyn, surely?' Zellaby looked hurt.

'Oh, it will with her, I'm sure. But she hasn't got there yet. It's a bit much to face, you know. She's had all the inconvenience and discomfort of bearing the baby, as much as if it were her own – and now, after all that, she has to readjust to the biological fact that it is not, that she is only what you call a "host-mother" to it. That must take a lot of doing.'

She paused, looking thoughtfully across the lawn. 'I now say a little prayer of thanksgiving every night,' she added. 'I don't know where it goes to, but I just want it to be known somewhere how grateful I am.'

Zellaby reached out, and took her hand. After some minutes, he observed:

'I wonder if a sillier and more ignorant catachresis than "Mother Nature" was ever perpetrated? It is because Nature is ruthless, hideous, and cruel beyond belief that it was necessary to invent civilization. One thinks of wild animals as savage, but the fiercest of them begins to look almost domesticated when one considers the viciousness required of a survivor in the sea; as for the insects, their lives are sustained only by intricate processes of fantastic horror. There is no conception more fallacious than the sense of cosiness implied by "Mother Nature". Each species must strive to survive, and that it will do, by every means in its power, however foul – unless the instinct to survive is weakened by conflict with another instinct.'

Angela seized the pause to put in, with a touch of impatience:

'I've no doubt you are gradually working round to something, Gordon.'

'Yes,' Zellaby owned. 'I am working round again to cuckoos. Cuckoos are very determined survivors. So determined that there is really only one thing to be done with them once one's nest is infested. I am, as you know, a humane man; I think I may even say a kindly man, by disposition.'

'You may, Gordon.'

'As a further disadvantage, I am a civilized man. For these reasons I shall not be able to bring myself to approve of what ought to be done. Nor, even when we perceive its advisability, will the rest of us. So, like the poor hen-thrush we shall feed and nurture the monster, and betray our own species. . . .

'Odd, don't you think? We could drown a litter of kittens that is no sort of threat to us – but these creatures we shall carefully rear.'

Angela sat motionless for some moments. Then she turned her head and looked at him, long and steadily.

'You *mean* that – about what *ought* to be done, don't you, Gordon?'

'I do, my dear.'

'It isn't like you.'

'As I pointed out. But then, it is a situation I have never been in before. It has occurred to me that "live and let live" is a piece of patronage which can only be afforded by the consciously secure. I now find, when I feel – as I never expected to feel – my situation at the summit of creation to be threatened, that I don't like it a bit.'

'But, Gordon, dear, surely this is all a little exaggerated. After all, a few unusual babies. . . .'

'Who can at will produce a neurotic condition in mature

women – and don't forget Harriman, too – in order to enforce their wishes.'

'It may wear off as they get older. One has heard sometimes of odd understanding, a kind of psychic sympathy. . . .'

'In isolated cases, perhaps. But in sixty-one inter-connected cases! No, there's no tender sympathy with these, and they trail no clouds of glory, either. They are the most practical, sensible, self-contained babies anyone ever saw – they are also quite the smuggest, and no wonder – they can get anything they want. Just at present they are still at a stage where they do not want very much, but later on – well, we shall see. . . .'

'Dr Willers says –' his wife began, but Zellaby cut her short impatiently.

'Willers rose to the occasion magnificently – so well that it's not surprising that he's addled himself into behaving like a damned ostrich now. His faith in hysteria has become practically pathological. I hope his holiday will do him good.'

'But, Gordon, he does at least *try* to explain it.'

'My dear, I am a patient man, but don't try me too far. Willers has never tried to *explain* any of it. He has accepted certain facts when they became inescapable; the rest he has attempted to explain away – which is quite different.'

'But there must *be* an explanation.'

'Of course.'

'Then what do you think it is?'

'We shall have to wait until the children are old enough to give us some evidence.'

'But you do have some ideas?'

'Nothing very cheering, I'm afraid.'

'But what?'

Zellaby shook his head. 'I'm not ready,' he said again. 'But as you are a discreet woman I will put a question to you. It is this: If you were wishful to challenge the supremacy of a society that was fairly stable, and quite well weaponed, what would you do? Would you meet it on its own terms by launching a probably costly, and certainly destructive, assault? Or, if time were of no great importance, would you prefer to employ a version of a more subtle tactic? Would you, in fact, try somehow to introduce a fifth column, to attack it from within?'

CHAPTER 15

Matters to Arise

THE next few months saw a number of changes in Midwich.

Dr Willers handed over his practice to the care of a locum, the young man who had helped him during the crisis, and, accompanied by Mrs Willers, went off, in a state of mingled exhaustion and disgust with authority, on a holiday that was said to be taking him round the world.

In November we had an epidemic of influenza which carried off three elderly villagers, and also three of the Children. One of them was Ferrelyn's boy. She was sent for, and came hurrying home at once, but arrived too late to see him alive. The others were two of the girls.

Well before that, however, there had been the sensational evacuation of The Grange. A fine bit of service organization: the researchers first heard about it on the Monday, the vans arrived on Wednesday, and by the week-end the house and the expensive new laboratories stood blank-windowed and empty, leaving the villagers with the feeling that they had seen a piece of pantomime magic, for Mr Crimm and his staff had gone, too, and all that was left were four of the golden-eyed babies for whom foster-parents had to be found.

A week later a desiccated-looking couple called Freeman moved into the cottage vacated by Mr Crimm. Freeman introduced himself as a medical man specializing in social psychology, and his wife, too, it appeared, was a doctor of medicine. We were led to understand, in a cautious way, that their purpose was to study the development of the Children on behalf of an unspecified official body. This, after their own fashion, they presumably did, for they were continually lurking and peering about the village, often insinuating themselves into the cottages, and not infrequently to be found on one of the seats on the Green, pondering weightily and watchfully. They had an aggressive discretion which verged upon the conspiratorial, and tactics which, within a week of their arrival, caused them to be generally resented and referred to as the Noseys. Doggedness, however, was another of their characteristics, and they persisted in the face of discouragement until they gained the kind of acceptance accorded to the inevitable.

I checked on them with Bernard. He said they were nothing to do with his department, but their appointment was authentic. We felt that if they were to be the only outcome of Willers' anxiety for study of the Children, it was as well that he was away.

Zellaby offered, as indeed did all of us, a few cooperative overtures to them, but made no headway. Whatever department was employing them had picked winners for discretion, but we felt that, importantly as discretion might be regarded in the larger sphere, a little more sociability within the community could have brought them fuller information with less effort. Still, there it was: they *might*, for all we knew, be turning in useful reports somewhere. All we could do was let them prowl in their chosen fashion.

However interesting, scientifically, the Children may have been during the first year of their lives there was little about them during that time to cause further misgiving. Apart from their continued resistance to any attempt to remove any of them from Midwich, the reminders of their compulsive powers were mostly mild and infrequent. They were, as Zellaby had said, remarkably sensible and self-sufficient babies – as long as nobody neglected them, or crossed their wishes.

There was very little about them at this stage to support the ominous ruminations of the beldame group, or, for that matter, the differently cast, but scarcely less gloomy, prognostications of Zellaby himself, and, as the time passed with unexpected placidity, Janet and I were not the only ones who began to wonder whether we had not all been misled, and if the unusual qualities in the children were not fading, perhaps to dwindle into insignificance as they should grow older.

And then, early in the following summer, Zellaby made a discovery which appeared to have escaped the Freemans, for all their conscientious watching.

He turned up at our cottage one sunny afternoon, and ruthlessly routed us out. I protested at having my work interrupted, but he was not to be put off.

'I know, my dear fellow, I know. I have a picture of my own publisher, with tears in his eyes. But this is important. I need reliable witnesses.'

'Of what?' inquired Janet, with little enthusiasm. But Zellaby shook his head.

'I am making no leading statements, incubating no germs. I am simply asking you to watch an experiment, and draw your own conclusions. Now here,' he fumbled in his pockets, 'is our apparatus.'

He laid on the table a small ornamental wooden box about half as big again as a matchbox, and one of those puzzles consisting of two large nails so bent that they are linked together, but will, when held in the right positions, slide easily apart. He picked up the wooden box, and shook it. Something rattled inside.

'Barley-sugar,' he explained. 'This is one of the products of feckless Nipponese ingenuity. It has no visible means of opening, but slide aside this bit of the marquetry here, and it opens without difficulty, and here's your barley-sugar. Why anybody should trouble himself to construct such a thing is known only to the Japanese, but, for us it will, I think, turn out to have a useful purpose, after all. Now, which of the Children, male, shall we try it on first?'

'None of these babies is quite one year old yet,' Janet pointed out, a little chillingly.

'In every respect, except that of actual duration, they are, as you very well know, quite well-developed two-year-olds,' Zellaby countered. 'And in any case, what I am proposing is not exactly an intelligence test . . . or, is it . . . ?' He broke off uncertainly. 'I must admit that I'm not sure about that. However, it doesn't greatly matter. Just name the child.'

'All right. Mrs Brant's,' said Janet. So to Mrs Brant's we went.

Mrs Brant showed us through into her small back-garden where the child was in a play-pen on the lawn. He looked, as Zellaby had pointed out, every bit of two years old, and brightly intelligent at that. Zellaby gave him the little box. The boy took it, looked at it, found that it rattled, and shook it delightedly. We watched him decide that it must be a box, and try unsuccessfully to open it. Zellaby let him go on playing with it for a bit, and then produced a piece of barley-sugar, and traded it for the return of his box, still unopened.

'I don't see what that's supposed to show,' Janet said, as we left.

'Patience, my dear,' Zellaby said, reprovingly. 'Which shall we try next, male again?'

Janet suggested the Vicarage as convenient. Zellaby shook his head.

'No that won't do. Polly Rushton's baby girl would very likely be on hand, too.'

'Does that matter? It all seems very mysterious,' said Janet.

'I want my witnesses satisfied,' said Zellaby. 'Try another.'

We settled for the elder Mrs Dorry's. There, he went through the same performance, but, after playing with the box a little, the child offered it back to him, looking up expectantly. Zellaby, however, did not take it from him. Instead, he showed the child how to open the box, and then let him do it for himself, and take out the sweet. Zellaby thereupon put another piece of barley-sugar in the box, closed it, and presently handed it to him again.

'Try once more,' he suggested, and we watched the little boy open it easily, and achieve a second sweet.

'Now,' said Zellaby as we left, 'we go back to Exhibit One, the Brant child.'

In Mrs Brant's garden again, he presented the child in the

play-pen with the box, just as he had before. The child took it eagerly. Without the least hesitation he found and slid back the movable bit of marquetry, and extracted the sweet, as if he had done it a dozen times before. Zellaby looked at our dumbfounded expressions with an amused twinkle. Once more he retrieved and reloaded the box.

'Well,' he said, 'name another boy.'

We visited three, up and down the village. None of them showed the least puzzlement over the box. They opened it as if it were perfectly familiar to them, and made sure of the contents without delay.

'Interesting, isn't it?' remarked Zellaby. 'Now let's start on the girls.'

We went through the same procedure again, except that this time it was to the third, instead of to the second, Child that he showed the secret of opening the box. After that, matters went just as before.

'Fascinating, don't you think?' beamed Zellaby. 'Like to try them with the nail-puzzle?'

'Later, perhaps,' Janet told him. 'Just at present I should like some tea.' So we took him back with us to the cottage.

'That box idea was a good one,' Zellaby congratulated himself modestly, while wolfing a cucumber sandwich. 'Simple, incontestable, and went off without a hitch, too.'

'Does that mean you've been trying other ideas on them?' Janet inquired.

'Oh, q ite a number. Some of them were a bit too complicated, though, and others not fully conclusive – besides, I hadn't got hold of the right end of the stick to begin with.'

'Are you quite sure you have now – because I'm not at all sure that I have?' Janet told him. He looked at her.

'I rather think you must have – and that Richard has, too. You don't need to be shy of admitting it.'

He helped himself to another sandwich, and looked inquiringly at me.

'I suppose,' I told him, 'that you are wanting me to say

that your experiment has shown that what one of the boys knows, all the boys know, though the girls do not; and *vice versa*. All right then, that *is* what it appears to show – unless there is a catch somewhere.'

'My dear fellow – !'

'Well, you must admit that what it *appears* to show is a little more than anyone is likely to be able to swallow at one gulp.'

'I see. Yes. Of course, I myself arrived at it by stages,' he nodded.

'But,' I said, 'it *is* what we were intended to infer?'

'Of course, my dear fellow. Could it be clearer?' He took the linked nails from his pocket and dropped them on the table. 'Take these, and try for yourselves – or, better still, devise your own little test, and apply it. You'll find the inference – at least the preliminary inference – inescapable.'

'To appreciate takes longer than to grasp,' I said, 'but let's regard it as a hypothesis which I accept for the moment –'

'Wait a minute,' put in Janet. 'Mr Zellaby, are you claiming that if I were to tell anything to any one of the boys, all the rest would know it?'

'Certainly – provided, of course, that it was something simple enough for them to understand at this stage.'

Janet looked highly sceptical.

Zellaby sighed.

'The old trouble,' he said. 'Lynch Darwin, and you show the impossibility of evolution. But, as I said, you've only to apply your own tests.' He turned back to me. 'You were allowing the hypothesis . . . ?' he suggested.

'Yes,' I agreed, 'and you said that was the *preliminary* inference. What is the next one?'

'I should have thought that just that one contained implications enough to capsize our social system.'

'Couldn't this be something like – I mean, a more developed form of the sort of sympathetic understanding that's sometimes found between twins?' Janet asked.

Zellaby shook his head.

'I think not – or else it has developed far enough to have acquired new features. Besides, we don't have here one single group *en rapport*; we have two separate groups of rapport, apparently without cross-connexions. Now, if that is so, and we have seen that it is, a question that immediately presents itself is this: to what extent is any of these Children an individual? Each is physically an individual, as we can see – but is he so in other ways? If he is sharing consciousness with the rest of the group, instead of having to communicate with others with difficulty, as we do, can he be said to have a mind of his own, a separate personality as we understand it? I don't see that he can. It seems perfectly clear that if A, B, and C share a common consciousness, then what A expresses is also what B and C are thinking, and that way action taken by B in particular circumstances is exactly that which would be taken by A and C in those circumstances – subject only to modifications arising from physical differences between them, which may, in fact, be considerable in so far as conduct is very susceptible to conditions of the glands, and other factors in the physical individual.

'In other words if I ask a question to any of these boys I shall get exactly the same answer from whichever I choose to ask: if I ask him to perform an action, I shall get more or less the same result, but it is likely to be more successful with some who happen to have better physical coordination than others – though, in point of fact, with such close similarity as there is among the Children the variation will be small.

'But my point is this: it will not be an individual who answers me, or performs what I ask, it will be an item of the group. And in that alone lie plenty of further questions, and implications.'

Janet was frowning. 'I still don't quite – '

'Let me put it differently,' said Zellaby. 'What we have *seemed* to have here is fifty-eight little individual entities. But appearances have been deceptive, and we find that what we actually have are *two* entities only – *a* boy, and *a* girl: though the boy has thirty component parts each with the physical structure and appearance of individual boys; and the girl has twenty-eight component parts.'

There was a pause. Presently:

'I find that rather hard to take,' said Janet, with careful understatement.

'Yes, of course,' agreed Zellaby. 'So did I.'

'Look here,' I said, after a further pause. 'You are putting this forward as a serious proposition? I mean, it isn't just a dramatic manner of speaking?'

'I am stating a fact – having shown you the evidence first.'

I shook my head. 'All you showed us was that they are able to communicate in some way that I don't understand. To proceed from that to your theory of non-individualism is too much of a jump.'

'On that piece of evidence alone, perhaps so. But you must remember that, though this is the first you have seen, I have already conducted a number of tests, and not one of them has contradicted the idea of what I prefer to call collective-individualism. Moreover, it is not as strange, *per se*, as it appears at first sight. It is quite a well established evolutionary dodge for getting round a shortcoming. A number of forms that appear at first sight to be individuals turn out to be colonies – and many forms cannot survive at all unless they create colonies which operate as individuals. Admittedly the best examples are among the lower forms, but there's no reason why it should be confined to them. Many of the insects come pretty near it. The laws of physics prevent them increasing in size, so they contrive greater efficiency by acting as a group. We ourselves combine in groups consciously, instead of by instinct, for the same purposes. Very well, why shouldn't nature produce a more efficient version of the method by which we clumsily contrive to overcome our own weakness? Another case of nature copying art, perhaps?

'After all, we are up against the barriers to further development, and we have been for some time – unless we are to stagnate we must find some way of getting round them.

G. B. S. proposed, you will remember, that the first step should be to extend the term of human life to three hundred years. That might be one way – and no doubt the extension of individual life would have a strong appeal to so determined an individualist – but there are others, and, though this is not perhaps a line of evolution one would expect to find among the higher animals, it is obviously not impracticable – though, of course, that is by no means to say that it is bound to be successful.'

A quick glance at Janet's expression showed me that she had dropped out. When she has decided that someone is talking nonsense she makes a quick decision to waste no more effort upon it, and pulls down an impervious mental curtain. I went on pondering, looking out of the window.

'I feel, I think,' I said presently, 'rather like a chameleon placed on a colour it can't quite manage. If I have followed you, you are saying that in each of these two groups the minds are in some way – well – pooled. Would that imply that the boys have, collectively, a normal brain-power multiplied by thirty, and the girls have it multiplied by twenty-eight?'

'I think not,' said Zellaby, quite seriously, 'and it certainly does not mean normal abilities to the power of thirty, thank heaven – that would be beyond any comprehension. It does appear to mean multiplication of intelligence in some degree, but at their present stage I don't see how that can be estimated – if it ever could be. That may portend tremendous things. But what seems to me of more immediate importance is the degree of will-power that has been produced – the potentialities of that strike me as very serious indeed. One has no idea how these compulsions are exerted, but I fancy that if it can be explored we might find that when a certain degree of will is, so as to speak, concentrated in one vessel a Hegelian change takes place – that is, that in more than a critical quantity it begins to display a new quality. In this case, a power of direct imposition.

'That, however, I frankly admit is speculative – and I can

now foresee a devil of a lot to speculate about and investigate.'

'The whole thing sounds incredibly complicated to me – if you are right.'

'In detail, in the mechanics, yes,' Zellaby admitted, 'but in principle, I think, not nearly so much as would appear at first sight. After all, you would agree that the essential quality of man is the embodiment of a spirit?'

'Certainly,' I nodded.

'Well, a spirit is a living force, therefore it is not static, therefore it is something which must either evolve, or atrophy. Evolution of a spirit assumes the eventual development of a greater spirit. Suppose, then, that this greater spirit, this super spirit, is attempting to make its appearance on the scene. Where is it to dwell? The ordinary man is not constructed to contain it; the superman does not exist to house it. Might it not, then, for lack of a suitable single vehicle, inform a group – rather like an encyclopedia grown too large for one volume? I don't know. But if it were so, then two super-spirits, residing in two groups, is no less probable.'

He paused, looking out of the open windows, watching a bumble-bee fly from one lavender-head to another, then he added reflectively:

'I have wondered about these two groups quite a lot. I have even felt that there ought to be names for these two super-spirits. One would imagine there were plenty of names to choose from, and yet I find just two, out of them all, persistently invading my mind. Somehow, I keep on thinking of – Adam – and Eve.'

*

Two or three days later I had a letter telling me that the job I had been angling for in Canada could be mine if I sailed without delay. I did, leaving Janet to clear things up, and follow me.

When she arrived she had little more news of Midwich except on a rather one-sided feud which had broken out between the Freemans and Zellaby.

Zellaby, it appeared, had told Bernard Westcott of his findings. An inquiry for further particulars had reached the Freemans to whom the whole idea came as a novelty, and one which they instinctively opposed. They at once instituted tests of their own, and were seen to be growing gloomier as they proceeded.

'But at least I imagine they'll stop short of Adam and Eve,' she added. 'Really, old Zellaby! The thing I shall never cease to be thankful for was that we happened to go to London when we did. Just fancy if I'd become the mother of a thirty-first part of an Adam, or a twenty-ninth part of an Eve. It's been bad enough as it is, and thank goodness we're out of it. I've had enough of Midwich, and I don't care if I never hear of the place again.'

Part Two

CHAPTER 16

Now We Are Nine

DURING the next few years, such visits home as we managed were brief and hurried, spent entirely in dashing from one lot of relatives to another, with interludes to improve business contacts. I never went anywhere near Midwich, nor indeed thought much about it. But, in the eighth summer after we had left, I managed a six-week spell, and at the end of the first week I ran into Bernard Wescott one day, in Piccadilly.

We went to the In and Out for a drink. In the course of a chat I asked him about Midwich. I think I expected to hear that the whole thing had fizzled out, for on the few occasions I had recalled the place lately, it and its inhabitants had the improbability of a tale once realistic, but now thoroughly unconvincing. I was more than half-ready to hear that the Children no longer trailed clouds of anything unconventional, that, as so often with suspected genius, expectations had never flowered, and that, for all their beginnings and indications, they had become an ordinary gang of village children, with only their looks to distinguish them.

Bernard considered for a moment, then he said:

'As it happens, I have to go down there tomorrow. Would you care to come for the run, renew old acquaintance, and so on?'

Janet had gone north to stay with an old school friend for a week leaving me on my own, with nothing particular to do.

'So you do still keep an eye on the place? Yes, I'd like to come and have a few words with them. Zellaby's still alive and well?'

'Oh, yes. He's that rather dry-stick type that seems set to go on for ever, unchanged.'

'The last time I saw him – apart from our farewell – he was off on a weird tack about composite personality,' I recalled. 'An old spellbinder. He manages to make the most exotic conceptions sound feasible while he's talking. Something about Adam and Eve, I remember.'

'You won't find much difference,' Bernard told me, but did not pursue that line. Instead, he went on: 'My own business there is a bit morbid I'm afraid – an inquest, but that needn't interfere with you.'

'One of the Children?' I asked.

'No,' he shook his head. 'A motor accident to a local boy called Pawle.'

'Pawle,' I repeated. 'Oh, yes, I remember. They've a farm a bit outside, nearer to Oppley.'

'That's it. Dacre Farm. Tragic business.'

It seemed intrusive to ask what interest he could have in the inquest, so I let him switch the conversation to my Canadian experiences.

The next morning, with a fine summer's day already well begun, we set off soon after breakfast. In the car he apparently felt at liberty to talk more freely than he had at the club.

'You'll find a few changes in Midwich,' he warned me. 'Your old cottage is now occupied by a couple called Welton – he etches, and his wife throws pots. I can't remember who is in Crimm's place at the moment – there's been quite a succession of people since the Freemans. But what's going to surprise you most is The Grange. The board outside has been repainted; it now reads: "Midwich Grange – Special School – Ministry of Education." '

'Oh? The Children?' I asked.

'Exactly.' He nodded. 'Zellaby's "exotic conception" was a lot less exotic than it seemed. In fact, it was a bull – to the great discomfiture of the Freemans. It showed them up so thoroughly that they had to clear out to hide their faces.'

'You mean his Adam and Eve stuff?' I said incredulously.

'Not that exactly. I meant the two mental groups. It was soon proved that there was this rapport – everything supported that – and it continued. At just over two years old one of the boys learnt to read simple words –'

'At two!' I exclaimed.

'Quite the equivalent of any other child's four,' he reminded me. 'And the next day it was found that any of the boys could read them. From then on, the progress was amazing. It was weeks later before one of the girls learnt to read, but when she did, all the rest of them could, too. Later on, one boy learnt to ride a bicycle; right away any of them could do it competently, first shot. Mrs Brinkman taught her girl to swim; all the rest of the girls were immediately able to swim; but the boys could not until one of them got the trick of it, then the rest could. Oh, from the moment Zellaby pointed it out, there was no doubt about it. The thing there has been – and still is – a whole series of rows about, on all levels, is his deduction that each group represents an individual. Not many people will wear that one. A form of thought transmission, possibly; a high degree of mutual sensitivity, perhaps; a number of units with a form of communication not yet clearly understood, feasible; but a single unit informing physically independent parts, no. There's precious little support for that.'

I was not greatly surprised to hear it, but he was going on:

'Anyway, the arguments are chiefly academic. The point is that, however it happens, they *do* have this rapport within the groups. Well, sending them to any ordinary school was obviously out of the question – there'd be tales about them all over the place in a few days if they'd just turned up at Oppley or Stouch schools. So that brought in the Ministry of Education, as well as the Ministry of Health, with the result that The Grange was opened up as a kind of school-cum-welfare-centre-cum-social-observatory for them.

'That has worked better than we expected. Even when you were here it was pretty obvious they were going to be a problem later on. They have a different sense of community – their pattern is not, and cannot by their nature, be the same as ours. Their ties to one another are far more important to them than any feeling for ordinary homes. Some of the homes resented them pretty much, too – they can't really become one of the family, they're too different; they were little good as company for the true children of the family, and the difficulties looked like growing. Somebody at The Grange had the idea of starting dormitories there for them. There was no pressure, no persuasion – they could just move in if they wanted to, and a dozen or more did, quite soon. Then others gradually joined them. It was rather as if they were beginning to learn that they could not have a great deal in common with the rest of the village, and so gravitated naturally towards a group of their own kind.'

'An odd arrangement. What did the village people think of it?' I asked.

'There was disapproval from some, of course – more from convention than conviction, really. A lot of them were relieved to lose a responsibility that had rather scared them, though they didn't feel it proper to admit it. A few were genuinely fond of them, still are, and have found it distressing. But in general they have just accepted. Nobody really tried to stop any of them shifting to The Grange, of course – it wouldn't have been any use. Where the mothers feel affectionately for them the Children keep on good terms, and are in and out of the houses as they like. Some others of the Children have made a complete break.'

'It sounds the queerest set-up I ever heard of,' I said.

Bernard smiled.

'Well, if you'll throw your mind back you'll recall that it had a somewhat queer beginning,' he reminded me.

'What do they do at The Grange?' I asked.

'Primarily it is a school, as it says. They have teaching and welfare staff, as well as social psychologists, and so on. They also have quite eminent teachers visiting and giving short courses in various subjects. At first they used to hold classes like an ordinary school, until it occurred to somebody that that wasn't necessary. So now any lesson is attended by one boy and one girl, and all the rest know what those two have been taught. And it doesn't have to be one lesson at a time, either. Teach six couples different subjects simultaneously, and they somehow sort it out so that it works the same way.'

'But, good heavens, they must be mopping up knowledge like blotting-paper, at that rate.'

'They are indeed. It seems to give some of the teachers a touch of jitters.'

'And yet you still manage to keep their existence quiet?'

'On the popular level, yes. There is still an understanding with the Press – and, anyway, the story hasn't nearly the possibilities now that it would have had in the early stages, from their point of view. As for the surrounding district, that has involved a certain amount of undercover work. The local reputation of Midwich was never very high – an ingenuous neighbourhood is perhaps the kindest way of putting it. Well, with a little helping-on, we've got it still lower. It is now regarded by the neighbouring villages, so Zellaby assures me, as a kind of mental home without bars. Everybody there, it is known, was affected by the Dayout; particularly the Children, who are spoken of as "daytouched" – an almost exact synonym of "moonstruck" – and are retarded to such an extent that a humane government has found it necessary to provide a special school for them. Oh, yes, we've got it pretty well established as a local deficiency area. It is in the same class of toleration as a dotty relative. There is occasional gossip; but it is accepted as an unfortunate affliction, and not a matter to be advertised to the outside world. Even protestations occasionally made by some of the Midwich people are not taken seriously, for, after all, the whole village had the same experience, so that all must be, in greater or lesser degree, "daytouched".'

'It must,' I said, 'have involved quite a deal of engineering and maintenance. What I never understood, and still don't understand, is why you were, and apparently are, so concerned to keep the matter quiet. Security at the time of the Dayout is understandable – something made an unauthorized landing; that was a Service concern. But now . . . ? All this trouble to keep the Children hidden away still. This queer arrangement at The Grange. A special school like that couldn't be run for a few pounds a year.'

'You don't think that the Welfare State should show so much concern for its responsibilities?' he suggested.

'Come off it, Bernard,' I told him.

But he did not. Though he went on talking of the Children, and the state of affairs in Midwich, he continued to avoid any answer to the question I had raised.

We lunched early at Trayne, and ran into Midwich a little after two. I found the place looking utterly unchanged. It might have been a week that had passed instead of eight years since I last saw it. Already there was quite a crowd waiting on the Green, outside the Hall where the inquest was to be held.

'It looks,' Bernard said as he parked the car, 'it looks as if you had better postpone your calls until later. Practically the whole place seems to be here.'

'Will it take long, do you think?' I inquired.

'Should be purely formal – I hope. Probably all over in half an hour.'

'Are you giving evidence?' I asked, wondering why, if it were to be so formal, he should bother to come all the way from London for it.

'No. Just keeping an eye on things,' he said.

I decided that he had been right about postponing my calls, and followed him into the hall. As the place filled up, and I watched familiar figures trooping in and finding seats, there could be no doubt that almost every mobile person in the place had chosen to attend. I did not quite understand why. Young Jim Pawle, the casualty, would be known to them all, of course, but that did not seem quite to account for it, and certainly did not account for the feeling of tension which inescapably pervaded the hall. I could not, after a few minutes, believe that the proceedings were going to be as formal as Bernard had predicted. I had a sense of waiting for an outburst of some kind from someone in the crowd.

But none came. The proceedings *were* formal, and brief, too. It was all over inside half an hour.

I noticed Zellaby slip out quickly as the meeting closed.

We found him standing by the steps outside watching us emerge. He greeted me as if we had last met a couple of days ago, and then said:

'How do you come into this? I thought you were in India.'

'Canada,' I said. 'It's accidental.' And explained that Bernard had brought me down.

Zellaby turned to look at Bernard.

'Satisfied?' he asked.

Bernard shrugged slightly. 'What else?' he asked.

At that moment a boy and a girl passed us, and walked up the road among the dispersing crowd. I had only time for a glimpse of their faces, and stared after them in astonishment.

'Surely, they can't be – ?' I began.

'They are,' Zellaby said. 'Didn't you see their eyes?'

'But it's preposterous! Why, they're only nine years old!'

'By the calendar,' Zellaby agreed.

I gazed after them as they strode along.

'But it's – it's unbelievable!'

'The unbelievable is, as you will recall, rather more prone to realization in Midwich than in some other places,' Zellaby observed. 'The improbable we can now assimilate at once; the incredible takes a little longer, but we have learnt to achieve it. Didn't the Colonel warn you?'

'In a way,' I admitted. 'But those two! They look fully sixteen or seventeen.'

'Physically, I am assured, they are.'

I kept my eyes on them, still unwilling to accept it.

'If you are in no hurry, come up to the house and have tea,' Zellaby suggested.

Bernard, after a glance at me, offered the use of his car.

'All right,' said Zellaby, 'but take it carefully, after what you've just heard.'

'I'm not a dangerous driver,' said Bernard.

'Nor was young Pawle – he was a *good* driver, too,' replied Zellaby.

A little way up the drive we came in sight of Kyle Manor at rest in the afternoon sun. I said:

'The first time I saw it it was looking just like this. I remember thinking that when I got a little closer I should hear it purring, and that's been the way I've seen it ever since.'

Zellaby nodded.

'When I saw it first it seemed to me a good place to end one's days in tranquillity – but now the tranquillity is, I think, questionable.'

I let that go. We ran past the front of the house, and parked round the side by the stables. Zellaby led the way to the veranda, and waved us to cushioned cane chairs.

'Angela's out at the moment, but she promised to be back for tea,' he said.

He leant back, gazing across the lawn for some moments. The nine years since the Midwich Dayout had treated him not unkindly. The fine silver hair was still as thick, and still as lucent in the August sunshine. The wrinkles about his eyes were just a little more numerous, perhaps; the face very slightly thinner, the lines on it faintly deeper, but if his lanky figure had become any sparser, it could not have been by a matter of more than four or five pounds.

Presently he turned to Bernard.

'So you're satisfied. You think it will end there?'

'I hope so. Nothing could be undone. The wise course was to accept the verdict, and they did,' Bernard told him.

'H'm,' said Zellaby. He turned to me. 'What, as a detached observer, did you think of our little charade this afternoon?'

'I don't – oh, the inquest, you mean. There seemed to be a bit of an atmosphere, but the proceedings appeared to me to be in good enough order. The boy was driving carelessly. He hit a pedestrian. Then, very foolishly, he got the wind up, and tried to make a getaway. He was accelerating too fast to take the corner by the church, and as a result he piled up against the wall. Are you suggesting that "accidental death" doesn't cover it – one might call it misadventure, but it comes to the same thing.'

'There was misadventure all right,' Zellaby said, 'but it scarcely comes to the same thing, and it occurred slightly before the fact. Let me tell you what happened – I've only been able to give the Colonel a brief account yet. . . .'

*

Zellaby had been returning, by way of the Oppley road, from his usual afternoon stroll. As he neared the turn to Hickham Lane four of the Children emerged from it, and turned towards the village, walking strung out in a line ahead of him.

They were three of the boys, and a girl. Zellaby studied them with an interest that had never lessened. The boys were so closely alike that he could not have identified them if he had tried, but he did not try; for some time he had regarded it as a waste of effort. Most of the village – except for a few of the women who seemed genuinely to be seldom in doubt – shared his inability to distinguish between them, and the Children were accustomed to it.

As always, he marvelled that they could have crammed so much development into so short a time. That alone set them right apart as a different species – it was not simply a matter of maturing early; it was development at almost twice normal speed. Perhaps they were a little light in structure compared with normal children of the same apparent age and height, but it was lightness of type, without the least suggestion of weediness, or overgrowth.

As always, too, he found himself wishing he could know them better, and learn more of them. It was not for lack of trying that he had made so little headway. He had tried, patiently and persistently, ever since they were small. They accepted him as much as they accepted anyone, and he, for his part, probably understood them quite as well as, if not better than, any of their mentors at The Grange. Superficially they were friendly with him – which they were not with many – they were willing to talk with him, and to listen, to be amused, and to learn; but it never went further than the superficial, and he had a feeling that it never would. Always, quite close under the surface, there was a barrier. What he saw and heard from them was their adaptation to their circumstances; their true selves and real nature lay beneath the barrier. Such understanding as passed between himself and them was curiously partial and impersonal; it lacked the dimension of feeling and sympathy. Their real lives seemed to be lived in a world of their own, as shut off from the main current as those of any Amazonian tribe with its utterly different standards and ethics. They were interested, they learnt, but one had the feeling that they were simply collecting knowledge – somewhat, perhaps, as a juggler acquires a useful skill which, however he may excel with it, has no influence whatever upon him, as a person. Zellaby wondered if anyone would get closer to them. The people up at The Grange were an unforthcoming lot, but, from what he had been able to discover, even the most assiduous had been held back by the same barrier.

Watching the Children walking ahead, talking between themselves, he suddenly found himself thinking of Ferrelyn. She did not come home as much as he could have wished, nowadays; the sight of the Children still disturbed her, so he did not try to persuade her; he made the best he could of the knowledge that she was happy at home with her own two boys.

It was odd to think that if Ferrelyn's Dayout boy had survived he would probably be no more able now to distinguish him from those walking ahead, than he was to distinguish them from one another – rather humiliating, too, for it seemed to bracket one with Miss Ogle, only she got round the difficulty by taking it for granted that any of the boys she chanced to meet was her son – and, curiously, none of them ever disillusioned her.

Presently, the quartet in front rounded a corner and passed out of his sight. He had just reached the corner himself when a car overtook him, and he had, therefore, a clear view of all that followed.

The car, a small, open two-seater, was not travelling fast, but it happened that just round the corner, and shielded from sight by it, the Children had stopped. They appeared, still strung out across the road, to be debating which way they should go.

The car's driver did his best. He pulled hard over to the right in an attempt to avoid them, and all but succeeded. Another two inches, and he would have missed them entirely. But he could not make the extra inches. The tip of his left wing caught the outermost boy on the hip, and flung him across the road against the fence of a cottage garden.

There was a moment of tableau which remained quite static in Zellaby's mind. The boy against the fence, the three other Children frozen where they stood, the young man in the car in the act of straightening his wheels again, still braking.

Whether the car actually came to a stop Zellaby could never be sure; if it did it was for the barest instant, then the engine roared.

The car sprang forward. The driver changed up, and put his foot down again, keeping straight ahead. He made no attempt whatever to take the corner to the left. The car was still accelerating when it hit the churchyard wall. It smashed to smithereens, and hurled the driver headlong against the wall.

People shouted, and the few who were near started running towards the wreckage. Zellaby did not move. He stood half-stunned as he watched the yellow flames leap out, and the black smoke start upwards. Then, with a stiff-seeming movement, he turned to look at the Children. They, too, were staring at the wreck, a similar tense expression on each face. He had only a glimpse of it before it passed off, and the three of them turned to the boy who lay by the fence, groaning.

Zellaby became aware that he was trembling. He walked on a few yards, unsteadily, until he reached a seat by the edge of the Green. There he sat down and leant back, pale in the face, feeling ill.

The rest of this incident reached me not from Zellaby

himself, but from Mrs Williams, of The Scythe and Stone, somewhat later on:

'I heard the car go tearing by, then a loud bang, and I looked out of the window and saw people running,' she said. 'Then I noticed Mr Zellaby go to the bench on the Green, walking very unsteadily. He sat down, and leaned back, but then his head fell forward, like he might be passing out. So I ran across the road to him, and when I got to him I found he *was* passed out, very near. Not quite, though. He managed to say something about "pills" and "pocket" in a sort of funny whisper. I found them in his pocket. It said two, on the bottle, but he was looking that bad I gave him four.

'Nobody else was taking any notice. They'd all gone up where the accident was. Well, the pills did him good, and after about five minutes I helped him into the house, and let him lay on the couch in the bar-parlour. He said he'd be all right there, just resting a bit, so I went to ask about the car.

'When I came back, his face wasn't so grey any more, but he was still lying like he was tired right out.

' "Sorry to be a nuisance, Mrs Williams. Rather a shock," he said.

' "I'd better get the doctor to you, Mr Zellaby," I said. But he shook his head.

' "No. Don't do that. I'll be all right in a few minutes," he told me.

' "I think you'd better see him," I said. "Fair put the wind up me, you did."

' "I'm sorry about that," he said. And then after a bit of a pause he went on: "Mrs Williams, I'm sure you can keep a secret?"

' "As well as the next, I reckon," I told him.

' "Well, I'd be very grateful if you'd not mention this – lapse of mine to anyone."

' "I don't know," I said. "To my way of thinking you *ought* to see the doctor."

'He shook his head at that.

' "I've seen a number of doctors, Mrs Williams, expensive

and important ones. But one just can't help growing old, you see, and as one does, the machinery begins to wear out, that's all."

' "Oh, Mr Zellaby, sir – " I began.

' "Don't distress yourself, Mrs Williams. I'm still quite tough in a lot of ways, so it may not come for some little time yet. But, in the meantime, I think it is rather important that one should not trouble the people one loves any more than can be helped, don't you think? It is an unkindness to cause them useless distress, I'm sure you'll agree?"

' "Well, yes, sir, if you're sure that there's nothing – ?"

' "I am. Quite sure. I am already in your debt, Mrs Williams, but you will have done me no service unless I can rely on you not to mention it. Can I?"

' "Very well. If that's the way you want it, Mr Zellaby," I told him.

' "Thank you, Mrs Williams. Thank you very much," he said.

'Then, after a bit, I asked him:

' "You saw it all happen, then, sir? Enough to give anyone a shock, it must've been."

' "Yes," he said. "I saw it – but I didn't see who it was in the car."

' "Young Jim Pawle," I told him, "from Dacre Farm."

'He shook his head.

' "I remember him – nice lad."

' "Yes, sir. A good boy, Jim. Not one of the wild ones. Can't think how he'd come to be driving mad in the village. Not like him at all."

'Then there was quite a pause till he said in a funny sort of voice:

' "Before that, he hit one of the Children – one of the boys. Not badly, I think, but he knocked him across the road."

' "One of the Children – " I said. Then I suddenly saw what he was meaning. "Oh no, sir! My God, they couldn't've –" but then I stopped again, because of the way he was looking at me.

' "Other people saw it, too," he told me. "Healthier – or, possibly less shockable people – Perhaps I myself should have found it less upsetting if, at some previous stage of my quite long life, I had already had the experience of witnessing deliberate murder. . . ." '

*

The account that Zellaby himself gave us, however, ended at the point where he had sat shakily down on the bench. When he finished, I looked from him to Bernard. There was no lead at all in Bernard's expression, so I said:

'You're suggesting that the Children did it – that they *made* him drive into that wall?'

'I'm not suggesting,' said Zellaby with a regretful shake of his head, 'I'm stating. They *did* it, just as surely as they *made* their mothers bring them back here.'

'But the witnesses – the ones who gave evidence . . . ?'

'They're perfectly well aware of what happened. They only had to say what they actually *saw*.'

'But if they know it's as you claim – ?'

'Well, what then? What would you have said if you had known, and happened to be called as a witness? In an affair such as this there has to be a verdict acceptable to authority – acceptable, that means, to our well-known figment, the reasonable man. Suppose that they had somehow managed to get a verdict that the boy was willed to kill himself – do you imagine that would stand? Of course it wouldn't. There'd have to be a second inquest, called to bring in a "reasonable" verdict, which would be the verdict we now have, so why should the witnesses run the risk of being thought unreliable, or superstitious, for nothing?

'If you want evidence that they would be, take a look at your own attitude now. You know that I have some little reputation through my books, and you know me personally, but how much is that worth against the thought-habits of the "reasonable man"? So little that when I tell you what actually occurred, your immediate reaction is to try to find ways in which what appeared to me to have occurred could not in actual fact have done so. You really ought to have more sense, my dear fellow. After all you were here when those Children forced their mothers to come back.'

'That wasn't quite on a level with what you are telling me now,' I objected.

'No? Would you care to explain the essential difference between being forced into the distasteful, and being forced into the fatal? Come, come, my dear fellow, since you've been away you have lost touch with improbability. You've been blunted by rationality. Here, the unorthodox is to be found on one's doorstep almost every morning.'

I took an opportunity to lead away from the topic of the inquest.

'To an extent which has caused Willers to abandon his championship of hysteria?' I asked.

'He abandoned that some little time before he died,' Zellaby replied.

I was taken aback. I had meant to ask Bernard about the doctor, but the intention had been mislaid in our talk.

'I'd no idea he was dead. He wasn't much over fifty, was he? How did it happen?'

'He took an overdose of some barbiturate drug.'

'He – you don't mean – ? But Willers wasn't that sort....'

'I agree,' said Zellaby. 'The official verdict was that "the balance of his mind was disturbed". A kindly-meant phrase, no doubt, but not explanatory. Indeed, one can think of minds so steady that disturbance would be a positive benefit. The truth is, of course, that nobody had the least idea why he did it. Certainly not poor Mrs Willers. But it had to suffice.' He paused, and then added: 'It was not until I realized what the verdict on young Pawle would have to be that I began to wonder about that on Willers.'

'Surely you don't really think that?' I said.

'I don't know. You yourself said Willers was not that sort. Now it has suddenly been revealed that we live much more precariously here than we had thought. That is a shock.

'One has, you see, to realize that, though it was the Pawle boy who came round the corner at that fatal moment, it might as easily have been Angela, or anyone else. . . . It suddenly becomes clear that she, or I, or any of us, may accidentally do something to harm or anger the Children at any moment. . . . There's no blame attached to that poor boy. He tried his very best to avoid hitting any of them, but he couldn't – And in a flare of anger and revenge they killed him for it.

'So one is faced with a decision. For myself – well, this is by far the most interesting thing that has ever come my way. I want very much to see how it goes. But Angela is still quite a young woman, and Michael is still dependent on her, too. . . . We have sent him away already. I am wondering whether I should try to persuade her to go, too. I don't want to do it until I must, but I can't quite decide whether the moment has arrived.

'These last few years have been like living on the slopes of an active volcano. Reason tells one that a force is building up inside, and that sooner or later there must be an eruption. But time passes, with no more than an occasional tremor, so that one begins to tell oneself that the eruption which appeared inevitable may, perhaps, not come after all. One becomes uncertain. I ask myself – is this business of the Pawle boy just a bigger tremor, or is it the first sign of the eruption? – and I do not know.

'One was more acutely aware of the presence of danger years ago, and made plans which came to seem unnecessary; now one is abruptly reminded of it, but is this where it changes to an active danger which justifies the breaking up of my home, or is it still only potential?'

He was obviously, and very genuinely, worried, nor was there any trace of scepticism in Bernard's manner. I felt impelled to say, apologetically:

'I suppose I have let the whole business of the Dayout fade in my mind – it needs a bit of adjustment when one's brought up against it once more. That's the subconscious for you –

trying to pass off the uncomfortable by telling me that the peculiarities would diminish as the Children grew older.'

'We all tried to think that,' said Zellaby. 'We used to show one another evidence that it was happening – but it wasn't.'

'But you're still no nearer to knowing *how* it is done – the compulsion, I mean?'

'No. It seems just to amount to asking how any personality dominates another. We all know individuals who seem to dominate any assembly they attend; it would appear that the Children have this quality greatly developed by cooperation, and can direct it as they wish. But that tells us nothing about *how* it is done.'

*

Angela Zellaby, looking very little changed since I had last seen her, emerged from the house on to the veranda a few minutes later. She was so clearly preoccupied that her attention was only brought to bear on us with a visible effort, and after a brief lobbing back and forth of civilities it showed signs of wavering again. A touch of awkwardness was relieved by the arrival of the tea tray. Zellaby bestirred himself to prevent the situation congealing.

'Richard and the Colonel were at the inquest, too,' he said. 'It was the expected verdict, of course. I suppose you've heard?'

Angela nodded. 'Yes, I was at Dacre Farm, with Mrs Pawle. Mr Pawle brought the news. The poor woman's quite beside herself. She adored Jim. It was difficult to keep her from going to the inquest herself. She wanted to go there and denounce the Children – make a public accusation. Mr Leebody and I managed between us to persuade her not to, and that she'd only get herself and her family into a lot of trouble, and do no good to anybody. So we stayed to keep her company while it was on.'

'The other Pawle boy, David, was there,' Zellaby told her.

'He looked as if he were on the point of coming out with it more than once, but his father stopped him.'

'Now I'm wondering whether it wouldn't have been better if someone had, after all,' Angela said. 'It *ought* to come out. It will have to some time. It isn't just a matter of a dog, or a bull, any more.'

'A dog and a bull. I've not heard of them,' I put in.

'The dog bit one of them on the hand; a minute or two later it dashed in front of a tractor, and was killed. The bull chased a party of them; then it suddenly turned aside, charged through two fences, and got itself drowned in the mill pond,' Zellaby explained, with unusual economy.

'But this,' said Angela, 'is murder.'

'Oh, I don't say they *meant* it that way. Very likely they were frightened and angry, and it was their way of hitting out blindly when one of them was hurt. But it was murder, all the same. The whole village knows it, and now everybody can see that they are going to get away with it. We simply can't afford to let it rest there. They don't even show any sign of compunction. None at all. That's what frightens me most. They just *did* it, and that's that. And now, after this afternoon, they know that, as far as they are concerned, murder carries no penalty. What is going to happen to anyone who seriously opposes them later on?'

Zellaby sipped his tea thoughtfully.

'You know, my dear, while it's proper for us to be concerned, the responsibility for a remedy isn't ours. If it ever was, and that is highly questionable, the authorities took it away from us a long time ago. Here's the Colonel representing some of them – for heaven knows what reason. And The Grange staff cannot be ignorant of what all the village knows. They will have made their report, so, in spite of the verdict, the authorities are aware of the true state of affairs – though just what they will be able to do about it, within the law and hampered by "the reasonable man", I'm bothered if I know. We must wait and see how they move.

'Above all, my dear, I do implore you most seriously not to

do anything that will bring you into conflict with the Children.'

'I shan't, dear,' Angela shook her head. 'I've a cowardly respect for them.'

'The dove is not a coward to fear the hawk; it is simply wise,' said Zellaby, and proceeded to steer the conversation on to more general lines.

*

My intention had been to look in on the Leebodys and one or two others, but by the time we got up to leave it was clear that, unless we were going to be back in London much later than we had intended, any further calls would have to be postponed until another visit.

I did not know how Bernard felt when we had made our farewells and were running down the drive – he had, in fact, talked very little since we had reached the village, and revealed scarcely anything of his own views – but, for my part, I had a pleasantly relaxing sensation of being on my way back to the normal world. Midwich values gave a feeling of having only a finger-tip touch with reality. One had a sense of being several stages in the rear. While I was back at the difficulties of reconciling myself to the Children's existence, and boggling at what I was told of them, the Zellabys had long ago left all that behind. For them, the improbable element had become submerged. They accepted the Children, and that, for good or ill, they were on their hands; their anxieties now were of a social nature over whether such a *modus vivendi* as had been contrived was going to collapse. The sense of uneasiness which I had caught from the tension in the Village Hall had been with me ever since.

Nor, I think, was Bernard unaffected by it. I had the impression that he drove with more than usual caution through the village and past the scene of the Pawle boy's accident. He began to increase his speed a little as we rounded the corner on to the Oppley Road, and then we caught sight of four figures approaching. Even at a distance they were unmistakably a quartet of the Children. On an impulse I said:

'Will you pull up, Bernard? I'd like the chance of a better look at them.'

He slowed again, and we came to a stop almost at the foot of Hickham Lane.

The Children came on towards us. There was a touch of institutionalism in their dress – the boys in blue cotton shirts and grey flannel trousers, the girls in short, pleated grey skirts and pale yellow shirts. So far I had only set eyes on the pair outside the Hall, and seen little of them but a glimpse of their faces, and then their backs.

As they approached I found the likeness between them even greater than I had expected. All four had the same browned complexions. The curious lucency of the skin that had been noticeable in them as babies had been greatly subdued by the sunburn, yet enough trace of it remained to attract one's notice. They shared the same dark-golden hair, straight, narrow noses, and rather small mouths. The way the eyes were set was perhaps more responsible than anything for a suggestion of 'foreigners', but it was an abstract foreignness, not calling to mind any particular race, or region. I could not see anything to distinguish one boy from the other; and, indeed, I doubted whether, had it not been for the cut of the hair, I could have told the boys' faces from the girls', with certainty.

Soon I was able to see the eyes themselves. I had forgotten how striking they were in the babies, and remembered them as yellow. But they were more than that: they had a quality of glowing gold. Strange indeed, but, if one could disregard the strangeness, with a singular beauty. They looked like living, semi-precious stones.

I went on watching, fascinated, as they drew level with us. They took no more notice of us than to give the car a brief, unembarrassed glance, and then turned into Hickham Lane.

At close quarters I found them disturbing in a way I could not quite account for, but it became less surprising to me that a number of the village homes had been unprotestingly willing for them to go and live at The Grange.

We watched them a few yards up the lane, then Bernard reached for the starter.

A sudden explosion close by made us both jump. I jerked my head round just in time to see one of the boys collapse, and fall face down on the road. The other three Children stood petrified. . . .

Bernard opened the door, and started to get out. The standing boy turned, and looked at us. His golden eyes were hard, and bright. I felt as if a sudden gust of confusion and weakness were sweeping through me. . . . Then the boy's eyes left ours, and his head turned further.

From behind the hedge opposite, came the sound of a second explosion, more muffled than the first – then, and further away, a scream. . . .

Bernard got out of the car, and I shifted across to follow him. One of the girls knelt down beside the fallen boy. As she made to touch him he groaned, and writhed where he lay. The standing boy's face was anguished. He groaned, too, as if in agony himself. The two girls began to cry.

Then, eerily down the lane, out of the trees that hid The Grange, swept a moan like a magnified echo, and, mingled with it, a threnody of young voices, weeping. . . .

Bernard stopped. I could feel my scalp prickling, and my hair beginning to rise. . . .

The sound came again; and ululation of many voices blended in pain, with the higher note of crying piercing through. . . . Then the sound of feet running down the lane. . . .

Neither of us tried to go on. For myself, I was held for the moment by sheer fright.

We stood there watching while half a dozen boys, all disconcertingly alike, came running to the fallen one, and lifted him between them. Not until they had started to carry him away did I become aware of a quite different sound of sobbing coming from behind the hedge to the left of the lane.

I clambered up the bank, and looked through the hedge there. A few yards away a girl in a summer frock was kneeling on the grass. Her hands were clenched to her face, and her whole body was shaking with her sobs.

Bernard scrambled up beside me, and together we pushed our way through the hedge. Standing up in the field now, I could see a man lying prone at the girl's knees, with the butt of a gun protruding from beneath his body.

As we stepped closer, she heard us. Her sobs stopped momentarily as she looked up with an expression of terror. Then when she saw us it faded, and she went on weeping, helplessly.

Bernard walked closer to her, and lifted her up. I looked down at the body. It was a very nasty sight indeed. I bent over it and pulled the jacket up, trying to make it hide what was left of the head. Bernard led the girl away, half supporting her.

There was a sound of voices on the road. As we neared the hedge a couple of men there looked up and saw us.

'Was that you shootin'?' one of them asked.

We shook our heads.

'There's a dead man up here,' Bernard said.

The girl beside him shivered, and whimpered.

' 'Oo is it?' asked the same man.

The girl said hysterically:

'It's David. They've killed him. They killed Jim; now they've killed David, too,' and choked in a fresh burst of grief.

One of the men scrambled up the bank.

'Oh, it's you, Elsa, lass,' he exclaimed.

'I tried to stop him, Joe. I tried to stop him, but he wouldn't listen,' she said through her sobs. 'I knew they'd kill him, but he wouldn't listen. . . . ' She became incoherent, and clung to Bernard, shaking violently.

'We must get her away,' I said. 'Do you know where she lives?'

'Aye,' said the man, and decisively picked the girl up, as though she were a child. He scrambled down the bank, and carried her, crying and shivering, to the car. Bernard turned to the other man.

'Will you stand by and keep anyone off till the police come?'

'Aye – It'll be young David Pawle?' the man said, climbing the bank.

'She said David. A young man,' Bernard told him.

'That'll be him – the bastards.' The man pushed through the hedge. 'Better call the coppers at Trayne, guv'nor. They got a car there.' He glanced towards the body. 'Murderin' young bastards!' he said.

*

They dropped me off at Kyle Manor, and I used Zellaby's phone to call the police. When I put the receiver down I found him at my elbow with a glass in his hand.

'You look as if you could do with it,' he said.

'I could,' I agreed. 'Very unexpected. Very messy.'

'Just how did it occur?' he inquired.

I gave him an account of our rather narrow angle on the affair. Twenty minutes later Bernard returned, able to tell more of it.

'The Pawle brothers were apparently very much attached,' he began. Zellaby nodded agreement. 'Well, it seems that the younger one, David, found the inquest the last straw, and decided that if nobody else was going to see justice done over his brother, he'd do it himself.

'This girl Elsa – his girl – called at Dacre Farm just as he was leaving. When she saw him carrying the gun she guessed what was happening, and tried to stop him. He wouldn't listen, and to get rid of her he locked her in a shed, and then went off.

'It took her a bit of time to break out, but she judged he would be making for The Grange, and followed across the fields. When she got to *the* field she thought she'd made a mistake because she didn't see him at first. Possibly he was lying down to take cover. Anyway, she doesn't seem to have spotted him until after the first shot. When she did, he was standing up, with the gun still pointed into the lane. Then while she was running towards him he reversed the gun, and put his thumb on the trigger....'

Zellaby remained silently thoughtful for some moments, then he said:

'It'll be a clear enough case from the police view. David considers the Children to be responsible for his brother's death, kills one of them in revenge and then, to escape the penalty, commits suicide. Obviously unbalanced. What else could a "reasonable man" think?'

'I may have been a bit sceptical before,' I admitted, 'but I'm not now. The way that boy looked at us! I believe that for a moment he thought one of us had done it – fired that shot, I mean – just for an instant, until he saw it was impossible. The sensation was indescribable, but it was frightening for the moment it lasted. Did you feel that, too?' I added, to Bernard.

He nodded. 'A queer, weak, and watery feeling,' he agreed. 'Very bleak.'

'It was just – ' I broke off, suddenly remembering. 'My God, I was so taken up with other business I forgot to tell the police anything about the wounded boy. Ought we to call an ambulance for The Grange?'

Zellaby shook his head.

'They've got a doctor of their own on the staff there,' he told us.

He reflected in silence for fully a minute, then he sighed, and shook his head. 'I don't much like this development, Colonel. I don't like it at all. Am I mistaken, do you think, in seeing here the very pattern of the way a blood feud starts ... ?'

CHAPTER 17

Midwich Protests

DINNER at Kyle Manor was postponed to allow Bernard and me to make our statements to the police, and by the time that was over I was feeling the need of it. I was grateful, too, for the Zellabys' offer to put both of us up for the night. The shooting had caused Bernard to change his mind about returning to London; he had decided to be on hand, if not in Midwich itself, then no further away than Trayne, leaving me with the alternative of keeping him company, or making a slow journey by railway. Moreover, I had a feeling that my sceptical attitude towards Zellaby in the afternoon had verged upon the discourteous, and I was not sorry for the chance to make amends.

I sipped my sherry, feeling a little ashamed.

'You cannot,' I told myself, 'you cannot protest or argue these Children and their qualities out of existence. And since they do exist, there must be some explanation of that existence. None of your accepted views explain it. Therefore, that explanation is going to be found, however uncomfortable it may be for you, in views that you do not at present accept. Whatever it is, it is going to arouse your prejudices. Just remember that, and clout your instinctive prejudices with it when they bob up.'

At dinner, however, I had no need to be vigilant for clouting. The Zellabys, feeling no doubt that we had passed through disquietment enough for the present, took pains to keep the conversation on subjects unrelated to Midwich and its troubles. Bernard remained somewhat abstracted, but I appreciated the effort, and ended the meal listening to Zellaby discoursing on the wave-motion of form and style, and the desirability of intermittent periods of social rigidity for the purpose of curbing the subversive energies of a new generation, in a far more equable frame of mind than I had started it.

Not long after we had withdrawn to the sitting-room, however, the peculiar problems of Midwich were back with us, re-entering with a visit by Mr Leebody. The Reverend Hubert was a badly troubled man, and looking, I thought, a lot older than the passage of eight years fully warranted.

Angela Zellaby sent for another cup and poured him some coffee. His attempts at small talk while he sipped it were valiant if erratic, but when he finally set down his empty cup, it was with an air of holding back no longer.

'Something,' he announced to us all, 'something will have to be done.'

Zellaby looked at him thoughtfully for a moment.

'My dear Vicar,' he reminded him gently, 'each of us has been saying that for years.'

'I mean done *soon*, and decisively. We've done our best to find a place for the Children, to preserve some kind of balance – and, considering everything, I don't think we have done too badly – but all along it has been makeshift, impromptu, empiric, and it can't go on like that any longer. We must have a code which includes the Children, some means by which the law can be brought to bear on them, as it does on the rest of us. If the law is seen to be incapable of ensuring that justice is done, it falls into contempt, and men feel that there is no resort and no protection but private revenge. That is what happened this afternoon, and even if we get through this crisis without serious trouble, there is bound to be another before long. It is useless for the authorities to employ the forms of law to produce verdicts which everyone knows to be false. This afternoon's verdict was a farce; and there is no doubt in the village that the inquest on the younger Pawle will be just as much of a farce. It is absolutely necessary that steps should be taken at once to bring the Children within the control of the law before worse trouble occurs.'

'We foresaw possible difficulty of the kind, you will

remember,' Zellaby reminded him. 'We even sent a memorandum on the subject to the Colonel here. I must admit that we did not envisage any such serious matters as have occurred – but we did point out the desirability of having some means of ensuring that the Children should conform to normal social and legal rules. And what happened? You, Colonel, passed it on to higher authorities, and eventually we received a reply appreciating our concern, but assuring us that the Department concerned had every confidence in the social psychologists who had been appointed to instruct and guide the Children. In other words they saw no way in which they could exert control over them, and simply were hoping that under suitable training no critical situation would arise. – And there, I must confess, I sympathize with the Department, for I am still quite unable to see how the Children can be compelled to obey rules of any kind, if they do not choose to.'

Mr Leebody entwined his fingers, looking miserably helpless.

'But something *must* be done,' he reiterated. 'It only needed an occurrence of this kind to bring it all to a head, now I'm afraid of it boiling over any minute. It isn't a matter of reasoning, it's more primitive. Almost every man in the village is at The Scythe and Stone tonight. Nobody called a meeting; they've just gravitated there, and most of the women are fluttering round to one another's houses, and whispering in groups. It's the kind of excuse the men have always wanted – or it might be.'

'Excuse?' I put in. 'I don't quite see – ?'

'Cuckoos,' explained Zellaby. 'You don't think the men have ever honestly *liked* these Children do you? The fair face they've put on it has been mostly for their wives' sakes. Considering the sense of outrage that must be abiding in their subconsciouses, it does them great credit – a little mitigated perhaps by one or two examples like Harriman's which made them scared to touch the Children.

'The women – most of them, at any rate – don't feel like

that. They all *know* well enough now that, biologically speaking, they are not even their own children, but they did have the trouble and pain of bearing them – and that, even if they resent the imposition deeply, which some of them do, still isn't the kind of link they can just snip and forget. Then there are others who – well, take Miss Ogle, for instance. If they had horns, tails, and cloven hooves Miss Ogle, Miss Lamb, and a number of others would still dote on them. But the most one can expect of the best of the men is toleration.'

'It has been very difficult,' added Mr Leebody. 'It cuts right across a proper family relationship. There's scarcely a man who doesn't resent their existence. We've kept on smoothing over the consequences, but that is the best we've been able to do. It's been like something always smouldering. . . .'

'And you think this Pawle business will supply the fatal draught?' Bernard asked.

'It could do. If not, something else will,' Mr Leebody said forlornly. 'If only there were something one could *do*, before it's too late.'

'There isn't, my dear fellow,' Zellaby said decisively. 'I've told you that before, and it's time you began to believe me. You've done marvels of patching-up and pacifying, but there's nothing fundamental that you or any of us can *do* because the initiative is not ours; it lies with the Children themselves. I suppose I know them as well as anybody. I've been teaching them, and doing my best to get to know them since they were babies, and I've got practically nowhere – nor have The Grange people done any better, however pompously they may cover it up. We can't even anticipate the Children because we don't understand, on any but the broadest lines, what they want, or how they think. What's happened to that boy who was shot, by the way? His condition could have some effect on developments.'

'The rest of them wouldn't let him go. They sent the ambulance away. Dr Anderby up there is looking after him.

There are quite a number of pellets to be removed, but he thinks he'll be all right,' said the Vicar.

'I hope he's right. If not, I can see us having a real feud on our hands,' said Zellaby.

'It is my impression that we already have,' Mr Leebody remarked unhappily.

'Not yet,' Zellaby maintained. 'It takes two parties to make a feud. So far the aggression has been by the village.'

'You're not going to deny that the Children murdered the two Pawle boys?'

'No, but it wasn't aggressive. I do have some experience of the Children. In the first case their action was a spontaneous hitting-back when one of them was hurt; in the second, too, it was defensive – don't forget there was a second barrel, loaded, and ready to be fired at someone. In both cases the response was over-drastic, I'll grant that, but in intent it was manslaughter, rather than murder. Both times they were the provoked, not the provokers. In fact, the one deliberate attempt at murder was by David Pawle.'

'If someone hits you with a car, and you kill him for it,' said the Vicar, 'it seems to me to be murder, and *that* seems to me to be provocation. And to David Pawle it *was* provocation. He waited for the law to administer justice, and the law failed him, so he took the matter into his own hands. Was that intended murder? – or was it intended justice?'

'The one thing it certainly was not, was justice,' Zellaby said firmly. 'It was feuding. He attempted to kill one of the Children, chosen at random, for an act they had committed collectively. What these incidents really make clear, my dear fellow, is that the laws evolved by one particular species, for the convenience of that species, are, by their nature, concerned only with the capacities of that species – against a species with different capacities they simply become inapplicable.'

The Vicar shook his head despondently.

'I don't know, Zellaby.... I simply don't know.... I'm in a

morass. I don't even know for certain whether these Children are imputable for murder.'

Zellaby raised his eyebrows.

' "And God said," ' quoted Mr Leebody, ' "Let us make man in our image, after our likeness." Very well, then, *what* are these Children? What *are* they? The image does not mean the outer image, or every statue would be man. It means the *inner* image, the spirit and the soul. But you have told me, and, on the evidence, I came to believe it, that the Children do not have individual spirits – that they have one man-spirit, and one woman-spirit, each far more powerful than we understand, that they share between them. What, then, are they? They cannot be what we know as man, for this inner image is on a *different* pattern – its likeness is to something else. They have the *look* of the *genus homo*, but not the nature. And since they are of *another* kind, and murder is, by definition, the killing of one of one's *own* kind, can the killing of one of them by us be, in fact, murder? It would appear not.

'And from that one must go further. For, since they do not come under the prohibition of murder, what is our attitude to them to be? At present, we are conceding them all the privileges of the true *homo sapiens*. Are we right to do this? Since they are another species, are we not fully entitled – indeed, have we not perhaps a duty? – to fight them in order to protect our own species? After all, if we were to discover dangerous wild animals in our midst our duty would be clear. I don't know.... I am, as I said, in a morass....'

'You are, my dear fellow, you are indeed,' agreed Zellaby. 'Only a few minutes ago you were telling me, with some heat, that the Children had murdered both the Pawle boys. Taking that in conjunction with your later proposition, it would appear that if they kill us it is murder, but if we were to kill them it would be something else. One cannot help feeling that a jurist, lay or ecclesiastical, would find such a proposition ethically unsatisfactory.

'Nor do I altogether follow your argument concerning the

"likeness". If your God is a purely terrestrial God, you are no doubt right – for in spite of one's opposition to the idea it can no longer be denied that the Children have in some way been introduced among us from "outside"; there is nowhere else they can have come from. But, as I understand it, your God is a universal God; He is God on all suns and all planets. Surely, then, He must have universal form? Would it not be a staggering vanity to imagine that He can manifest Himself only in the form that is appropriate to this particular, not very important planet?

'Our two approaches to such a problem are bound to differ greatly, but – '

He broke off at the sound of raised voices in the hall outside, and looked questioningly at his wife. Before either could move, however, the door was abruptly thrust open, and Mrs Brant appeared on the threshold. With a perfunctory 'Scuse me' to the Zellabys, she made for Mr Leebody, and grasped his sleeve.

'Oh, sir. You must come quick,' she told him breathlessly.

'My dear Mrs Brant – ' he began.

'You must come, sir,' she repeated. 'They're all going up to The Grange. They're going to burn it down. You must come and stop them.'

Mr Leebody stared at her while she continued to pull at his sleeve.

'They're starting now,' she said desperately. 'You can stop them, Vicar. You must. They want to burn the Children. Oh, hurry. Please. Please hurry!'

Mr Leebody got up. He turned to Angela Zellaby.

'I'm sorry. I think I'd better – ' he began, but his apology was cut short by Mrs Brant's tugging.

'Has anyone told the police?' Zellaby inquired.

'Yes – no. I don't know. They couldn't get here in time. Oh, Vicar, please *hurry*!' said Mrs Brant, dragging him forcibly through the doorway.

The four of us were left looking at one another. Angela crossed the room swiftly, and closed the door.

'I'd better go and back him up, I think,' said Bernard.

'We might be able to help,' agreed Zellaby, turning, and I moved to join them.

Angela was standing resolutely with her back to the door.

'No!' she said, decisively. 'If you want to do something useful, call the police.'

'You could do that, my dear, while we go and – '

'Gordon,' she said, in a severe voice, as if reprimanding a child. 'Stop and think. Colonel Westcott, you would do more harm than good. You are identified with the Children's interest.'

We all stood in front of her surprised, and a little sheepish.

'What are you afraid of, Angela?' Zellaby asked.

'I don't know. How can I possibly tell? – Except that the Colonel might be lynched.'

'But it will be important,' protested Zellaby. 'We know what the Children can do with individuals, I want to see how they handle a crowd. If they run true to form they'll only have to will the whole crowd to turn round and go away. It will be most interesting to see whether – '

'Nonsense,' said Angela flatly, and with a firmness which made Zellaby blink. 'That is *not* their "form", and you know it. If it were, they'd simply have made Jim Pawle *stop* his car; and they'd have made David Pawle fire his second barrel into the air. But they didn't. They're never content with repulsing – they always counter-attack.'

Zellaby blinked again.

'You're right, Angela,' he said, in surprise. 'I never thought of that. The reprisal *is* always too drastic for the occasion.'

'It is. And however they handle a crowd, I don't want you handled with it. Nor you, Colonel,' she added, to Bernard. 'You're going to be needed to get us out of the trouble you've helped to cause. I'm glad you're here – at least there's someone on the spot who will be listened to.'

'I might observe – from a distance, perhaps,' I suggested meekly.

'If you've any sense you'll stay here out of harm's way,'

Angela replied bluntly, and turned again to her husband. 'Gordon, we're wasting time. Will you ring up Trayne, and see whether anyone has told the police there, and ask for ambulances as well.'

'Ambulances! Isn't that a bit – er – premature?' Zellaby protested.

'You introduced this "true to form" consideration – but you don't seem to have considered it,' Angela replied. 'I have. I say ambulances, and if you don't, I will.'

Zellaby, with rather the air of a small boy subdued, picked up the telephone. To me he remarked:

'We don't even know – I mean, we've only Mrs Brant's word for any of it. . . .'

'As I recall Mrs Brant, she was one of the reliable pillars,' I said.

'That's true,' he admitted. 'Well, I'd better risk it.'

When he had finished he returned the telephone thoughtfully to the rest, and regarded it for a moment. He decided to make one more attempt.

'Angela, my dear, don't you think that if one were to keep at a discreet distance . . . ? After all, I am one of the people the Children trust, they're my friends, and –'

But Angela cut him short, with unweakened decision.

'Gordon, it's no good trying to get round me with that nonsense. You're just inquisitive. You know perfectly well that the Children have *no* friends.'

CHAPTER 18

Interview With a Child

THE Chief Constable of Winshire looked in at Kyle Manor the next morning, just at the right time for a glass of Madeira and a biscuit.

'Sorry to trouble you over this affair, Zellaby. Ghastly business – perfectly horrible. Can't make any sense of it. Nobody in your village quite on target, seems to me. Thought you might be able to put up a picture a fellow can understand.'

Angela leant forward.

'What are the real figures, Sir John? We've heard nothing officially yet.'

'Bad, I'm afraid.' He shook his head. 'One woman and three men dead. Eight men and five women in hospital. Two of the men and one woman in a pretty bad way. Several men who aren't in hospital look as if they ought to be. Regular riot by all accounts – everybody fighting everybody else. But why? That's what I can't get at. No sense out of anybody.' He turned back to Zellaby. 'Seeing that you called the police, and told them there was going to be trouble, it'd help us to know what put you on to it.'

'Well,' Zellaby began cautiously, 'it's a curious situation –'

His wife cut him short by breaking in:

'It was Mrs Brant, the blacksmith's wife,' she said, and went on to describe the vicar's departure. 'I'm sure Mr Leebody will be able to tell you more than we can. He was there, you see; we weren't.'

'He was there all right, and got home somehow, but now he's in Trayne hospital,' said the Chief Constable.

'Oh, poor Mr Leebody. Is he badly hurt?'

'I'm afraid I don't know. The doctor there tells me he's not to be disturbed for a bit. Now.' He turned back to Zellaby once more, 'you told my people that a crowd was marching on The Grange with the intention of setting fire to it. What was your source of information?'

Zellaby looked surprised.

'Why, Mrs Brant. My wife just told you.'

'Is that all! You didn't go out to see for yourself what was going on?'

'Er – no,' Zellaby admitted.

'You mean that, on the unsupported word of a woman in a semi-hysterical condition, you called out the police, in force, and told them that ambulances would be needed?'

'I insisted on it,' Angela told him, with a touch of chill. 'And I was perfectly right. They *were* needed.'

'But simply on this woman's word – '

'I've known Mrs Brant for years. She's a sensible woman.'

Bernard put in:

'If Mrs Zellaby had not advised us against going to see for ourselves, I'm quite sure we should now be either in hospital, or worse.'

The Chief Constable looked at us.

'I've had an exhausting night,' he said, at last. 'Perhaps I haven't got this straight. What you seem to be saying is that this Mrs Brant came here and told you that the villagers – perfectly ordinary English men and women, and good Winshire stock, were intending to march on a school full of children, their own children, too, and – '

'Not quite, Sir John. The men were going to march, and perhaps some of the women, but I think most of the women would be against it,' Angela objected.

'Very well. These men, then, ordinary, decent, country chaps, were going to set fire to a school full of children. You didn't question it. You accepted an incredible thing like that at once. You did not try to check up, or see for yourselves what was happening. You just called in the police – because Mrs Brant is a sensible woman?'

'Yes,' Angela said icily.

'Sir John,' Zellaby said, with equal coolness. 'I realize you have been busy all night, and I appreciate your official position, but I think that if this interview is to continue, it must be upon different lines.'

The Chief Constable went a little pink. His gaze dropped. Presently he massaged his forehead vigorously with a large fist. He apologized, first to Angela, and then to Zellaby. Almost pathetically he said:

'But there's nothing to get hold of. I've been asking questions for hours, and I can't make head or tail of anything. There's no sign that these people *were* trying to burn The Grange: they never touched it. They were simply fighting one another, men, and a few women, too – but they were doing it in The Grange grounds. Why? It wasn't just the women trying to stop the men – or, it seems, some of the men trying to stop the rest. No, it appears they all went up from the pub to The Grange together, with nobody trying to stop anybody, except the parson, whom they wouldn't listen to, and a few women who backed him up. And what was it all about? Something, apparently, to do with the children at the school – but what sort of a reason is that for a riot like this? It just doesn't make sense, any of it.' He shook his head, and ruminated a moment. 'I remember my predecessor, old Bodger, saying there was something deuced funny about Midwich. And, by God, he was right. But what *is* it?'

'It seems to me that the best we can do is to refer you to Colonel Westcott,' suggested Zellaby, indicating Bernard. With a slightly malicious touch, he added: 'His Department, for a reason which has continued to elude me for nine years, preserves a continuing interest in Midwich, so that he probably knows more about us than we do ourselves.'

Sir John turned his attention to Bernard.

'And what *is* your Department, sir?' he inquired.

At Bernard's reply his eyes bulged slightly. He looked like a man wishing to be given strength.

'Did you say Military Intelligence?' he inquired flatly.

'Yes, sir,' said Bernard.

The Chief Constable shook his head. 'I give up.' He looked

back at Zellaby, with the expression of one only two or three straws from the end. 'And now Military Intelligence,' he muttered.

*

About the same time that the Chief Constable had arrived at Kyle Manor, one of the Children – a boy – came walking unhurriedly down the drive of The Grange. The two policemen who were chatting at the gate broke off their conversation. One of them turned and strolled to meet the boy.

'And where'll you be off to, son?' he inquired amiably enough.

The boy looked at the policeman without expression, though the curious golden eyes were alert.

'Into the village,' he said.

'Better if you didn't,' advised the policeman. 'They're not feeling too friendly there about your lot – not after last night, they're not.'

But the boy neither answered, nor checked his walk. He simply kept on. The policeman turned and walked back towards the gate. His colleague looked at him curiously.

'Lumme,' he said. 'Didn't make much of a job of that, did you? Thought the idea was to persuade 'em to keep out of harm's way.'

The first policeman looked after the boy, going on down the lane, with a puzzled expression. He shook his head.

'Funny, that,' he said uneasily. 'I don't get it. If there's another, you have a try, Bert.'

A minute or two later one of the girls appeared. She, too, was walking in a casually confident way.

'Right,' said the second policeman. 'Just a bit of advice – fatherly-like, see?'

He began to stroll towards the girl.

After perhaps four steps he turned round, and came back again. The two policemen standing side by side watched her walk past them, and into the lane. She never even glanced at them.

'What the hell – ?' asked the second policeman, in a baffled voice.

'Bit off, isn't it?' said the other. 'You go to do something, and then you do something else instead. I don't reckon I like it much. Hey!' he called after the girl. 'Hey! you, missie!'

The girl did not look back. He started in pursuit, covered half a dozen yards, and then stopped dead. The girl passed out of sight, round the corner of the lane. The policeman relaxed, turned round, and came back. He was breathing rather fast, and had an uneasy look on his face.

'I definitely *don't* like it,' he said unhappily. 'There's something kind of funny about this place....'

*

The bus from Oppley, on its way to Trayne via Stouch, stopped in Midwich, opposite Mrs Welt's shop. The ten or a dozen women waiting for it allowed the two off-loading passengers to descend, and then moved forward in a ragged queue. Miss Latterly, at its head, took hold of the rail, and made to step aboard. Nothing further happened. Both her feet appeared to be glued to the ground.

'Hurry along there, please!' said the conductor.

Miss Latterly tried again; with no better success. She looked up helplessly at the conductor.

'Just you stand aside, and let 'em get on, mum. I'll give you a hand in a minute,' he advised her.

Miss Latterly, looking bewildered, took his advice. Mrs Dorry moved up to take her place, and grasped the rail. She, too, failed to get any further. The conductor reached down to take her arm and pull her up, but her foot would not lift to the step. She moved beside Miss Latterly, and they both watched the next in turn make an equally fruitless attempt to get aboard.

'What's this? Some kind of joke?' inquired the conductor. Then he saw the expression on the faces of the three. 'Sorry, ladies. No offence. But what's the trouble?'

It was Miss Latterly who, turning her attention from the

fourth woman's ineffective approach to the bus, noticed one of the Children. He was sitting casually on the mounting-block opposite The Scythe and Stone, with his face turned towards them, and one leg idly swinging. She detached herself from the group by the bus, and walked towards him. She studied him carefully as she approached. Even so, it was with a touch of uncertainty she said:

'You're not Joseph, are you?'

The boy shook his head. She went on:

'I want to go to Trayne to see Miss Foresham, Joseph's mother. She was hurt last night. She's in the hospital there.'

The boy kept on looking at her. He shook his head very slightly. Tears of anger came into Miss Latterly's eyes.

'Haven't you done enough harm? You're monsters. All we want to do is to go and see our friends who've been hurt – hurt because of what you did.'

The boy said nothing. Miss Latterly took an impulsive half-step towards him, and then checked herself.

'Don't you understand? Haven't you any human feelings?' she said, in a shaking voice.

Behind her, the conductor, half-puzzled, half-jocular was saying:

'Come along now, ladies. Make up your minds. The old bus don't bite, you know. Can't wait 'ere all day.'

The group of women stood irresolute, some of them looking frightened. Mrs Dorry made one more attempt to board the bus. It was no use. Two of the women turned to glare angrily at the boy who looked back at them unmoved.

Miss Latterly turned helplessly, and began to walk away. The conductor's temper shortened.

'Well, if you're not coming, we're off. Got our times to keep, you know.'

None of the group made any move. He hit the bell decisively, and the bus moved on. The conductor gazed at them as they dwindled forlornly behind, and shook his head. As he ambled forward to exchange comments with the driver he muttered to himself the local adage:

'In Oppley they're smart, and in Stouch they're smarmy, but Midwich folk are just plain barmy.'

*

Polly Rushton, her uncle's invaluable right hand in the parish ever since she had fled across the unmended breach between the two families, was driving Mrs Leebody into Trayne to see the vicar. His injuries in the fracas, the hospital had telephoned reassuringly, were uncomfortable, but not serious, only a fracture of the left radius, a broken right clavicle, and a number of contusions, but he was in need of rest and quiet. He would be glad of a visit in order to make some arrangements to cover his absence.

Two hundred yards out of Midwich, however, Polly braked abruptly, and started to turn the car about.

'What have we forgotten?' inquired Mrs Leebody, in surprise.

'Nothing,' Polly told her. 'I just can't go on, that's all.'

'Can't?' repeated Mrs Leebody.

'Can't,' said Polly.

'Well, really,' said Mrs Leebody. 'I should have thought that at a time like this. . . . '

'Aunt Dora, I said "can't", not "won't".'

'I don't understand what you're talking about,' said Mrs Leebody.

'All right,' said Polly. She drove on a few yards, and turned the car again so that it faced away from the village once more. 'Now change places, and *you* try,' she told her.

Unwillingly Mrs Leebody took the driving seat. She didn't care for driving, but accepted the challenge. They moved forward again, and at precisely the spot where Polly had braked, Mrs Leebody braked. There came the sound of a horn behind them, and a tradesman's van with a Trayne address on it squeezed by. They watched it vanish round the corner ahead. Mrs Leebody attempted to reach the accelerator-pedal, but her foot stopped short of it. She tried again. Her foot still could not get to it.

Polly looked round and saw one of the Children sitting half-hidden in the hedge, watching them. She looked harder at the girl, making sure which one it was.

'Judy,' Polly said, with sudden misgiving. 'Is it you doing this?'

The girl's nod was barely perceptible.

'But you mustn't,' Polly protested. 'We want to go to Trayne to see Uncle Hubert. He was hurt. He's in hospital.'

'You can't go,' the girl told her, with a faintly apologetic inflection.

'But, Judy. He has to arrange lots of things with me for the time he'll have to be away.'

The girl simply shook her head, slowly. Polly felt her temper rising. She drew breath to speak again, but Mrs Leebody cut in, nervously:

'Don't annoy her, Polly. Wasn't last night enough of a lesson for all of us?'

Her advice went home. Polly said no more. She sat glaring at the Child in the hedge, with a muddle of frustrated emotion that brought tears of resentment to her eyes.

Mrs Leebody succeeded in finding reverse, and moved the lever into it. She tentatively put her right foot forward and found that it now reached the accelerator without any difficulty. They backed a few yards, and changed seats again. Polly drove them back to the Vicarage, in silence.

*

At Kyle Manor we were still having difficulty with the Chief Constable.

'But,' he protested, from under corrugated brows, 'our information supports your original statement that the villagers were marching on The Grange to burn the place.'

'So they were,' agreed Zellaby.

'But you also say, and Colonel Westcott agrees, that the children at The Grange were the real culprits – they provoked it.'

'That's true,' Bernard agreed. 'But I'm afraid there's nothing we can do about that.'

'No evidence, you mean? Well, finding evidence is our job.'

'I don't mean no evidence. I mean no imputability under the law.'

'Look,' said the Chief Constable, with conscientious patience. 'Four people have been killed – I repeat *killed*; thirteen are in hospital; a number more have been badly knocked about. It is not the sort of thing we can just say "what a pity" about, and leave it at that. We have to bring the whole thing into the open, decide where responsibility lies, and draw up charges. You must see that.'

'These are very unusual Children – ' Bernard began.

'I know. I know. Lot of wrong-side-of-the-blanket stuff in these parts. Old Bodger told me about that when I took over. Not quite firing on all cylinders, either – special school for them, and so on.'

Bernard repressed a sigh.

'Sir John, it's *not* that they are backward. The special school was opened because they are *different*. They *are* morally responsible for last night's trouble, but that isn't the same as being *legally* responsible. There's nothing you can charge them with.'

'Minors can be charged – or somebody responsible for them can. You're not going to tell me that a gang of nine-year-old children can somehow – though I'm blest if I can see how – promote a riot in which people get killed, and then just get away with it scot free! It's fantastic!'

'But I've pointed out several times that these Children are *different*. Their years have no relevance – except in so far as they *are* children, which may mean that they are crueller in their acts than in their intentions. The law cannot touch them – and my Department doesn't want them publicized.'

'Ridiculous,' retorted the Chief Constable. 'I've heard of those fancy schools. Children mustn't be what-do-you-call it? – frustrated. Self-expression, co-education, wholemeal bread, and all the rest of it. Damned nonsense! More frustrated by being different about things than they would be if they were normal. But if some Departments think that because a school of that kind happens to be a government-run institution the children there are in a different position as regards the law, and can be – er – uninhibited as they like – well, they'll soon learn differently.'

Zellaby and Bernard exchanged hopeless glances. Bernard decided to try once more.

'These Children, Sir John, have strong willpower – quite remarkably strong – strong enough, when they exert it, to be considered a form of duress. Now, the law has not, so far, encountered this particular form of duress; consequently, having no knowledge of it, it cannot recognize it. Since, therefore, the form of duress has no legal existence, the Children cannot in law be said to be capable of exerting it. Therefore, in the eyes of the law, the crimes attributed by popular opinion to its exercise must (a) never have taken place at all, or (b) be attributable to other persons, or means. There cannot, within the knowledge of the law, be any connexion between the Children and the crimes.'

'Except that they did 'em, or so you all tell me,' said Sir John.

'As far as the law is concerned they've done nothing at all. And, what is more, if you could find a formula to charge them under you'd not get anywhere. They would bring this duress to bear on your officers. You can neither arrest them, nor hold them, if you try to.'

'We can leave those finer points to the lawyer fellows – that's their job. All we need is enough evidence to justify a warrant,' the Chief Constable assured him.

Zellaby gazed with innocent thoughtfulness at a corner of the ceiling. Bernard had the withdrawn air of a man who might be counting ten, not too quickly. I found myself troubled by a slight cough.

'This schoolmaster fellow at The Grange – what's his name – Torrance?' the Chief Constable went on. 'Director of the place. He must hold the official responsibility for these children, if anyone does. Saw the chap last night. Struck me as evasive. Everybody round here's evasive, of course.' He studiedly met no eye. 'But he definitely wasn't helpful.'

'Dr Torrance is an eminent psychiatrist, rather than a schoolmaster,' Bernard explained. 'I think he may be in considerable doubt as to his right course in the matter until he can take advice.'

'Psychiatrist?' repeated Sir John, suspiciously. 'I thought you said this is not a place for backward children?'

'It isn't,' Bernard repeated, patiently.

'Don't see what he has to be doubtful about. Nothing doubtful about the truth, is there? That's all you've got to tell when the police make inquiries: if you don't, you're in for trouble – and so you ought to be.'

'It's not quite as simple as that,' Bernard responded. 'He may not have felt himself at liberty to disclose some aspects of his work. I think that if you will let me come along with you and see him again he might be more willing to talk – and much better able to explain the situation than I am.'

He got to his feet as he finished. The rest of us rose, too. The Chief Constable's leave-taking was gruff. There was a barely perceptible flicker to Bernard's right eye as he said *au revoir* to the rest of us, and escorted him out of the room.

Zellaby collapsed into an easy chair, and sighed deeply. He searched absent-mindedly for his cigarette case.

'I've not met Dr Torrance,' I said, 'but I already feel quite sorry for him.'

'Unnecessary,' said Zellaby. 'Colonel Westcott's discretion has been irritating, but passive. Torrance's has always had an aggressive quality. If he has now got to make the situation lucid enough for Sir John, it's simply poetic justice.

'But what interests me more at the moment is your Colonel Westcott's attitude. The barrier there is down quite a bit. If he could have got as far as a mutually understandable vocabulary with Sir John, I do believe he might have told us all something. I wonder why? This seems to me just the kind of situation that he has been trying so hard to avoid all along. The Midwich bag is now very nearly too small for the cat. Why, then, doesn't he appear more concerned?' He lapsed into a reverie, tattooing gently on the chair-arm.

Presently Angela reappeared. Zellaby became aware of her from the far-off. It took him a moment or two to re-establish himself in the here and now, and observe her expression.

'What's the matter, my dear?' he inquired, and added in recollection: 'I thought you were bound for Trayne hospital, with a cornucopia.'

'I started,' she said. 'Now I've come back. It seems that we're not allowed to leave the village.'

Zellaby sat up.

'That's absurd. The old fool can't put the whole place under arrest. As a J.P. – ' he began indignantly.

'It's not Sir John. It's the Children. They're picketing all the roads, and won't let us out.'

'Are they indeed!' exclaimed Zellaby. 'That's extremely interesting. I wonder if – '

'Interesting be damned,' said his wife. 'It's very unpleasant, and quite outrageous. It's also rather alarming,' she added, 'because one can't see just what's behind it.'

Zellaby inquired how it was being done. She explained, concluding:

'And it's only us, you see – people who live in the village, I mean. They're letting other people come and go as they like.'

'But no violence?' asked Zellaby, with a touch of anxiety.

'No. You simply have to stop. Several people have appealed to the police, and they've looked into it. Hopeless, of course. The Children didn't stop *them*, or bother them, so naturally they can't understand what the fuss is about. The only result is that those who had merely heard that Midwich is half-witted are now sure of it.'

'They must have some reason for it – the Children, I mean,' said Zellaby.

Angela eyed him resentfully.

'I daresay, and possibly it will be of great sociological interest, but that isn't the point at the moment. What I want to know is what is to be done about it?'

'My dear,' said Zellaby soothingly. 'One appreciates your feelings, but we've known for some time now that if it should suit the Children to interfere with us we have no way of stopping them. Well, now, for some reason that I confess I do not perceive, it evidently does suit them.'

'But, Gordon, there are these people seriously hurt, in Trayne hospital. Their relatives want to visit them.'

'My dear, I don't see that there is anything you can do but find one of them, and put it to him on humane grounds. They *might* consider that, but it really depends on what their reason for doing it is, don't you think?'

Angela regarded her husband with a frown of dissatisfaction. She started to reply, thought better of it, and took herself off with an air of reproof. Zellaby shook his head as the door closed.

'Man's arrogance is boastful,' he observed, 'woman's is something in the fibre. We do occasionally contemplate the once lordly dinosaurs, and wonder when, and how, our little day will reach its end. But not she. Her eternity is an article of her faith. Great wars and disasters can ebb and flow, races rise and fall, empires wither with suffering and death, but these are superficialities: she, woman, is perpetual, essential; she will go on for ever. She doesn't believe in the dinosaurs: she doesn't really believe the world ever existed until she was upon it. Men may build and destroy and play with all their toys; they are uncomfortable nuisances, ephemeral conveniences, mere scamperers-about, while woman, in mystical umbilical connexion with the great tree of life itself, *knows* that she is indispensable. One wonders whether the female dinosaur in her day was blessed with the same comfortable certainty.'

He paused, in such obvious need of prompting that I said: 'And the relevance to the present?'

'Is that while man finds the thought of his supersession

abominable, she simply finds it unthinkable. And since she cannot think it, she must regard the hypothesis as frivolous.'

It seemed to be my service again.

'If you are implying that we see something which Mrs Zellaby fails to see, I'm afraid I – '

'But, my dear fellow, if one is not blinded by a sense of indispensability, one must take it that we, like the other lords of creation before us, will one day be replaced. There are two ways in which it can happen: either through ourselves, by our self-destruction, or by the incursion of some species which we lack the equipment to subdue. Well, here we are now, face to face with a superior will and mind. And what are we able to bring against it?'

'That,' I told him, 'sounds defeatist. If, as I assume, you do mean it quite seriously, isn't it rather a large conclusion from rather a small instance?'

'Very much what my wife said to me when the instance was considerably smaller, and younger,' Zellaby admitted. 'She also went on to scout the proposition that such a remarkable thing could happen here, in a prosaic English village. In vain did I try to convince her that it would be no less remarkable wherever it should happen. She felt that it was decidedly a thing that would be *less* remarkable in more exotic places – a Balinese village, perhaps, or a Mexican pueblo; that it was essentially one of those sorts of things that happens to other people. Unfortunately, however, the instance has developed here – and with melancholy logic.'

'It isn't the locality that troubles me,' I said. 'It's your assumptions. More particularly, your taking it for granted that the Children can do what they like, and there's no way of stopping them.'

'It would be foolish to be quite so didactic as that. It *may* be possible, but it will not be easy. Physically we are poor weak creatures compared with many animals, but we overcome them because we have better brains. The only thing that can beat us is something with a still better brain. That has scarcely seemed a threat: for one thing, its occurrence appeared to be improbable, and, for another, it seemed even more improbable that we should allow it to survive to become a menace.

'Yet here it is - another little gimmick out of Pandora's infinite evolutionary box: the contesserate mind - two mosaics, one of thirty, the other of twenty-eight, tiles. What can we, with our separate brains only in clumsily fumbling touch with one another, expect to do against thirty brains working almost as one?'

I protested that, even so, the Children could scarcely have accumulated enough knowledge in a mere nine years to oppose successfully the whole mass of human knowledge, but Zellaby shook his head.

'The government has for reasons of its own provided them with some excellent teachers, so that the sum of their knowledge should be considerable - indeed, I know it is, for I lecture to them myself sometimes, you know - that has importance, but it is not the source of the threat. One is not unaware that Francis Bacon wrote: *nam et ipsa scientia potestas est* - knowledge itself is power - and one must regret that so eminent a scholar should, at times, talk through his hat. The encyclopedia is crammed full of knowledge, and can do nothing with it; we all know of people who have amazing memories for facts, with no ability to use them; a computing-engine can roll out knowledge by the ream in multiplicate; but none of this knowledge is of the least use until it is informed by understanding. Knowledge is simply a kind of fuel; it needs the motor of understanding to convert it into power.

'Now, what frightens me is the thought of the power producible by an understanding working on even a small quantity of knowledge-fuel when it has an extraction-efficiency thirty times that of our own. What it may produce when the Children are mature I cannot begin to imagine.'

I frowned. As always, I was a little unsure of Zellaby.

'You are quite seriously maintaining that we have no means of preventing this group of fifty-eight Children from taking what course they choose?' I insisted.

'I am.' He nodded. 'What do you suggest we could do? You know what happened to that crowd last night; they intended to attack the Children – instead, they were induced to fight one another. Send police, and they would do the same. Send soldiers against them, and they would be induced to shoot one another.'

'Possibly,' I conceded. 'But there must be other ways of tackling them. From what you've told me, nobody knows nearly enough about them. They appear to have detached themselves emotionally from their host-mothers quite early – if, indeed, they ever had the emotions we normally expect. Most of them chose to adopt progressive segregation as soon as it was offered. As a result the village knows extremely little of them. In quite a short time most people seem scarcely to have thought of them as individuals. They found them difficult to tell apart, got into the habit of regarding them collectively so that they have tended to become two-dimensional figures with only a limited kind of reality.'

Zellaby looked appreciative of the point.

'You're perfectly right, my dear fellow. There is a lack of normal contacts and sympathies. But that is not entirely our shortcoming. I have myself kept as close to them as I can, but I am still at a distance. In spite of all my efforts I still find them, as you excellently put it, two-dimensional. And it is strongly my impression that the people at The Grange have done no better.'

'Then the question remains,' I said, 'how do we get more data?'

We contemplated that for a while until Zellaby emerged from his reverie to say:

'Has it occurred to you to wonder what your own status here is, my dear fellow? If you were thinking of leaving today it might be as well to find out whether the Children regard you as one of us, or not?'

That was an aspect that had not occurred to me, and I found it a little startling. I decided to find out.

Bernard had, it appeared, gone off in the Chief Constable's car, so I borrowed his for the test.

I found the answer a little way along the Oppley road. A very odd sensation. My hand and foot were guided to bring the car to a halt by no volition of my own. One of the girl Children was sitting by the roadside, nibbling at a stalk of grass, and looking at me without expression. I tried to put the gear in again. My hand wouldn't do it. Nor could I bring my foot on the clutch pedal. I looked at the girl, and told her that I did not live in Midwich, and wanted to get home. She simply shook her head. I tried the gear lever again, and found that the only way I could move it was into reverse.

'H'm,' said Zellaby, on my return. 'So you are an honorary villager, are you? I rather thought you might be. Just remind me to tell Angela to let the cook know, there's a good fellow.'

*

At the same time that Zellaby and I were talking at Kyle Manor, more talk, similar in matter but different in manner, was going on at The Grange. Dr Torrance, feeling some sanction in the presence of Colonel Westcott, had endeavoured to answer the Chief Constable's questions more explicitly than before. A stage had been reached, however, when lack of coordination between the parties could no longer be disguised, and a noticeably off-beat query caused the doctor to say, a little forlornly:

'I am afraid I cannot have made the situation quite clear to you, Sir John.'

The Chief Constable grunted impatiently.

'Everybody keeps on telling me that, and I'm not denying it; nobody round here seems to be capable of making anything clear. Everybody keeps on telling me, too – and without producing a scrap of evidence that I can understand – that these infernal children are in some way responsible for last night's affair – even you, who I am given to understand are in charge of them. I agree that I do not understand a situation in which young children are allowed to get so thoroughly out of hand that they can cause a breach of the peace amounting to a riot. I don't see why I should be expected to understand it. It is as a Constable that I wish to see one of the ringleaders, and find out what he has to say about it.'

'But, Sir John, I have already explained to you that there are no ringleaders. . . .'

'I know – I know. I heard you. Everyone is equal here, and all that – all very well perhaps in theory, but you know as well as I do that in every group there are fellers that stand out, and that those are the chaps you've got to get hold of. Manage them, and you can manage the rest.' He paused expectantly.

Dr Torrance exchanged a helpless look with Colonel Westcott. Bernard gave a slight shrug, and the faintest of nods. Dr Torrance's look of unhappiness increased. He said uneasily:

'Very well, Sir John, since you make it virtually a police order I have no alternative, but I must ask you to watch your words carefully. The Children are very – er – sensitive.'

His choice of the final word was unfortunate. In his own vocabulary it had a somewhat technical meaning; in the Chief Constable's it was a word used by doting mothers about spoilt sons, and did nothing to make him feel more sympathetically disposed towards the Children. He made a vowelless sound of disapproval as Dr Torrance got up and left the room. Bernard half opened his mouth to reinforce the Doctor's warning, and then decided that it would only increase the Chief Constable's irritation, thus doing more harm than good. The cussedness of commonsense, Bernard reflected, was that, invaluable as it might be in the right soils, it could turn into a pestiferous kind of bind-weed in others. So the two waited in silence until the Doctor presently returned, bringing one of the boy-Children with him.

'This is Eric,' he said, by way of introduction. To the boy he added, 'Sir John Tenby wishes to ask you some questions. It is his duty as Chief Constable, you see, to make a report on the trouble last night.'

The boy nodded, and turned to look at Sir John. Dr Torrance resumed his seat at his desk, and watched the two of them intently, and uneasily.

The boy's regard was steady, careful, but quite neutral; it gave no trace of feeling. Sir John met it with equal steadiness. A healthy-looking boy, he thought. A bit thin – well, not exactly thin in the sense of being scraggy, slight would be a better word. It was difficult to make much of a judgement from the features; the face was good-looking, though without weakness which often accompanies male good looks; on the other hand, it did not show strength – the mouth, indeed, was a little small, though not petulant. There was not a lot to be learnt from the face as a whole. The eyes, however, were even more remarkable than he had been led to expect. He had been told of the curious golden colour of the irises, but no one had succeeded in conveying to him their striking lambency, their strange effect of being softly lit from within. For a moment it disquieted him, then he took himself in hand; reminded himself that he had some kind of freak to deal with; a boy only nine years old, yet looking every bit of sixteen, brought up, moreover, on some of these fiddle-faddling theories of self-expression, non-inhibition, and so on. He decided to treat the boy as if he were the age he looked, and constrained himself into that man-to-boy attitude that is represented by its practitioners as man-to-man.

'Serious business last night,' he observed. 'Our job to clear it up and find out what really happened – who was responsible for the trouble, and so forth. People keep on telling me that you and the others here were – now, what do you say to that?'

'No,' said the boy promptly.

The Chief Constable nodded. One would scarcely expect an immediate admission, in any case.

'What happened, exactly?' he asked.

'The village people came here to burn The Grange down,' said the boy.

'You're sure of that?'

'It was what they said, and there was no other reason to bring them here at that time,' said the boy.

'All right, we'll not go into the whys and wherefores just now. Let's take it from there. You say some of them came intending to burn the place. Then I suppose others came to stop them doing it, and the fighting started?'

'Yes,' agreed the boy, but less definitely.

'Then, in point of fact, you and your friends had nothing to do with it. You were just spectators?'

'No,' said the boy. 'We had to defend ourselves. It was necessary, or they would have burnt the house.'

'You mean you called out to some of them to stop the rest, something like that?'

'No,' the boy told him patiently. 'We made them fight one another. We could simply have sent them away, but if we had they would very likely have come back some other time. Now they will not, they understand it is better for them to leave us alone.'

The Chief Constable paused, a little nonplussed.

'You say you "made" them fight one another. How did you do that?'

'It is too difficult to explain. I don't think you could understand,' said the boy, judicially.

Sir John pinked a little.

'Nevertheless, I'd like to hear,' he said, with an air of generous restraint that was wasted.

'It wouldn't be any use,' the boy told him. He spoke simply, and without innuendo, as one stating a fact.

The Chief Constable's face became a deeper pink. Dr Torrance put in hurriedly:

'This is an extremely abstruse matter, Sir John, and one which all of us here have been trying to understand, with very little headway, for some years now. One can really get little nearer to it than to say that the Children "willed" the people in the crowd to attack one another.'

Sir John looked at him and then at the boy. He muttered, but held himself in check. Presently, after two or three deep breaths, he spoke to the boy again, but now with his tone a little ruffled.

'However it was done – and we'll have to go into that later – you are admitting that you were responsible for what happened?'

'We are responsible for defending ourselves,' the boy said.

'To the extent of four lives and thirteen serious injuries – when you *could*, you say, have simply sent them away.'

'They wanted to kill us,' the boy told him, indifferently.

The Chief Constable looked lengthily at him.

'I don't understand *how* you can have done it, but I take your word for it that you did, for the present; also your word that it was unnecessary.'

'They would have come again. It would have been necessary then,' replied the boy.

'You can't be sure of that. Your whole attitude is monstrous. Don't you feel the least compunction for these unfortunate people?'

'No,' the boy told him. 'Why should we? Yesterday afternoon one of them shot one of us. Now we must protect ourselves.'

'But not by private vengeance. The law is for your protection, and for everyone's – '

'The law did not protect Wilfred from being shot; it would not have protected us last night. The law punishes the criminal *after* he has been successful: it is no use to us, we intend to stay alive.'

'But you don't mind being responsible – so you tell me – for the deaths of other people.'

'Do we have to go round in circles?' asked the boy. 'I have answered your questions because we thought it better that you should understand the situation. As you apparently have not grasped it, I will put it more plainly. It is that if there is any attempt to interfere with us or molest us, by anybody, we shall defend ourselves. We have shown that we can, and we hope that that will be warning enough to prevent further trouble.'

Sir John stared at the boy speechlessly while his knuckles whitened and his face empurpled. He half rose from his chair as if he meant to attack the boy, and then sank back, thinking better of it. Some seconds passed before he could trust himself to speak. Presently, in a half-choked voice he addressed the boy who was watching him with a kind of critically detached interest.

'You damned young blackguard! You insufferable little prig! How dare you speak to me like that! Do you understand that I represent the police force of this county? If you don't, it's time you learnt it, and I'll see that you do, b'God. Talking to your elders like that, you swollen-headed little upstart! So you're not to be "molested"; you'll defend yourselves, will you! Where do you think you are? You've got a lot to learn, m'lad, a whole –'

He broke off suddenly, and sat staring at the boy.

Dr Torrance leant forward over his desk.

'Eric –' he began in protest, but made no move to interfere.

Bernard Westcott remained carefully still in his chair, watching.

The Chief Constable's mouth went slack, his jaws fell a little, his eyes widened, and seemed to go on widening. His hair rose slightly. Sweat burst out on his forehead, at his temples, and came trickling down his face. Inarticulate gobblings came from his mouth. Tears ran down the sides of his nose. He began to tremble, but seemed unable to move. Then, after long rigid seconds, he did move. He lifted hands that fluttered, and fumbled them to his face. Behind them, he gave queer thin screams. He slid out of the chair to his knees on the floor, and fell forward. He lay there grovelling, and trembling, making high whinnying sounds as he clawed at the carpet, trying to dig himself into it. Suddenly he vomited.

The boy looked up. To Dr Torrance he said, as if answering a question:

'He is not hurt. He wanted to frighten us, so we have shown him what it means to be frightened. He'll understand better now. He will be all right when his glands are in balance again.'

Then he turned away and went out of the room, leaving the two men looking at one another.

Bernard pulled out a handkerchief, and dabbed at the sweat that stood in drops on his own forehead. Dr Torrance sat motionless, his face a sickly grey. They turned to look at the Chief Constable. Sir John was lying slackly now, seemingly unconscious, drawing long, greedy breaths, shaken occasionally by a violent tremor.

'My God!' exclaimed Bernard. He looked at Torrance again. 'And you have been here three years!'

'There's never been anything remotely like *this*,' the Doctor said. 'We've suspected many possibilities, but there's never been any enmity – and, after this, thank God for that!'

'Yes, you could well do worse than that,' Bernard told him. He looked at Sir John again.

'This chap ought to be got away before he pulls round. We'd be better out of the way, too – it's the sort of situation where a man can't forgive witnesses. Send in a couple of his men to collect him. Tell them he's had an attack of some kind.'

Five minutes later they stood on the steps and watched the Chief Constable driven off, still only semi-conscious.

' "All right when his glands are in balance"!' murmured Bernard. 'They seem better at physiology than at psychology. They've broken that man, for the rest of his life.'

CHAPTER 19

Impasse

AFTER a couple of strong whiskies Bernard began to lose some of the shaken look with which he had returned to Kyle Manor. When he had given us an account of the Chief Constable's disastrous interview at The Grange, he went on:

'You know, one of the few childlike things about the Children, it strikes me, is their inability to judge their own strength. Except, perhaps for the corralling of the village, everything they have done has been overdone. What might be excusable in intent they contrive to make unforgivable in practice. They wanted to scare Sir John in order to convince him that it would be unwise to interfere with them; but they did not do simply what was necessary for that; they went so much farther that they brought the poor man to a state of grovelling fear near the brink of imbecility. They induced a degree of personal degradation that was sickening, and utterly unpardonable.'

Zellaby asked, in his mild, reasonable tone:

'Are we not perhaps looking at this from too narrow an angle? You, Colonel, say "unpardonable", which assumes that they expect to be pardoned. But why should they? Do we concern ourselves whether jackals or wolves will pardon us for shooting them? We do not. We are concerned only to make them innocuous.

'In point of fact our ascendancy has been so complete that we are rarely called upon to kill wolves nowadays – in fact, most of us have quite forgotten what it means to have to fight in a personal way against another species. But, when the need arises we have no compunction in fully supporting those who slay the threat whether it is from wolves, insects, bacteria, or filterable viruses; we give no quarter, and certainly expect no pardon.

'The situation *vis-à-vis* the Children would seem to be that *we* have not grasped that they represent a danger to our species, while *they* are in no doubt that we are a danger to theirs. And they intend to survive. We might do well to remind ourselves what that intention implies. We can watch it any day in a garden; it is a fight that goes perpetually, bitterly, lawlessly, without trace of mercy or compassion. . . .'

His manner was quiet, but there was no doubt that his intention was pointed; and yet, somehow, as so often with Zellaby, the gap between theory and practical circumstances seemed too inadequately bridged to carry conviction.

Presently Bernard said:

'Surely this is quite a change of front by the Children. They've exerted persuasion and pressure from time to time, but, apart from a few early incidents, almost no violence. Now we have this outbreak. Can you point to the start of it, or has it been working up?'

'Decidedly,' said Zellaby. 'There was no sign whatever of anything in this category before the matter of Jimmy Pawle and his car.'

'And that was – let me see – last Wednesday, the third of July. I wonder – ' he was beginning, but broke off as the gong called us to luncheon.

*

'My experience, hitherto, of interplanetary invasion,' said Zellaby, as he concocted his own particular taste in salad-dressing, 'has been vicarious – indeed, one might even say hypothetically vicarious, or do I mean vicariously hypothetical – ?' He pondered that a moment, and resumed: 'At any rate it has been quite extensive. Yet, oddly enough, I cannot recall a single account of one that is of the least help in our present dilemma. They were, almost without exception, unpleasant; but, also, they were almost always forthright, rather than insidious.

'Take H. G. Wells' Martians, for instance. As the original exponents of the death-ray they were formidable, but their behaviour was quite conventional: they simply conducted a straightforward campaign with this weapon which outclassed anything that could be brought against it. But at least we could try to fight back, whereas in this case – '

'Not cayenne, dear,' said his wife.

'Not what?'

'Not cayenne. Hiccups,' Angela reminded him.

'So it does. Where is the sugar?'

'By your left hand, dear.'

'Oh, yes . . . where was I?'

'With H. G.'s Martians,' I told him.

'Of course. Well, there you have the prototype of innumerable invasions. A super-weapon which man fights valiantly with his own puny armoury until he is saved by one of several possible kinds of bell. Naturally, in America it is all rather bigger and better. Something descends, and something comes out of it. Within ten minutes, owing no doubt to the excellent communications in that country, there is a coast-to-coast panic, and all highways out of all cities are crammed, in all lanes, by the fleeing populace – except in Washington. There, by contrast, enormous crowds stretching as far as the eye can reach, stand grave and silent, white-faced but trusting, with their eyes upon the White House, while somewhere in the Catskills a hitherto ignored professor and his daughter, with their rugged young assistant strive like demented midwives to assist the birth of the *dea ex laboritoria* which will save the world at the last moment, minus one.

'Over here, one feels, the report of such an invasion would be received in at least some quarters with a tinge of preliminary scepticism, but we must allow the Americans to know their own people best.

'Yet, overall, what do we have? Just another war. The motivations are simplified, the armaments complicated, but the pattern is the same, and, as a result, not one of the prognostications, speculations, or extrapolations turns out to be of the least use to us when the thing actually happens. It really does seem a pity when one thinks of all the cerebration the prognosticators have spent on it, doesn't it?'

He busied himself with eating his salad.

'It is still one of my problems to know when you are to be taken literally, and when metaphorically,' I told him.

'This time you can take him literally, with assurance,' Bernard put in.

Zellaby cocked a sideways look at him.

'Just like that? Not even reflex opposition?' he inquired. 'Tell me, Colonel, how long have you accepted this invasion as a fact?'

'For about eight years,' Bernard told him. 'And you?'

'About the same time – perhaps a little before. I did not like it, I do not like it, I am probably going to like it even less. But I had to accept it. The old Holmes axiom, you know: "When you have eliminated the impossible, whatever remains, *however improbable*, must be the truth." I had not known, however, that that was recognized in official circles. What did you decide to do about it?'

'Well, we did our best to preserve their isolation here, and to see to their education.'

'And a fine, helpful thing that turns out to have been, if I may say so. Why?'

'Just a minute,' I put in, 'I'm in between the literal and figurative again. You are both of you seriously accepting as a fact that these Children are – a kind of invaders? That they do originate somewhere outside the Earth?'

'See?' said Zellaby. 'No coast-to-coast panic. Just scepticism. I told you.'

'We are,' Bernard told me. 'It is the only hypothesis that my department has not been forced to abandon – though, of course, there are some who still won't accept it, even though we had the help of a little more evidence than Mr Zellaby did.'

'Ah!' said Zellaby, brought to sudden attention, with a forkful of greenstuff in mid-air. 'Are we getting closer to the mysterious M.I. interest in us?'

'There's no longer any reason now, I think, why it should not have a restricted circulation,' Bernard admitted. 'I know that in the early stages you did quite a little inquiring into our interest on your own account, Zellaby, but I don't believe you ever discovered the clue.'

'Which was?' inquired Zellaby.

'Simply that Midwich was not the only, nor even the first place to have a Dayout. Also, that during the three weeks around that time there was a marked rise in the radar detection of unidentified flying objects.'

'Well, I'm damned!' said Zellaby. 'Oh, vanity, vanity... ! There are *other* groups of Children beside ours, then? Where?'

But Bernard was not to be hurried, he continued deliberately:

'One Dayout took place at a small township in the Northern Territory of Australia. Something apparently went badly wrong there. There were thirty-three pregnancies, but for some reason the Children all died; most of them a few hours after birth, the eldest at a week old.

'There was another Dayout at an Eskimo settlement on Victoria Island, north of Canada. The inhabitants are cagey about what happened there, but it is believed that they were so outraged, or perhaps alarmed, at the arrival of babies so unlike their own kind that they exposed them almost at once. At any rate, none survived. And that, by the way, taken in conjunction with the time of the Midwich babies' return here, suggests that the power of duress does not develop until they are a week or two old, and that they may be truly individuals until then. Still another Dayout – '

Zellaby held up his hand.

'Let me guess. There was one behind the Iron Curtain.'

'There were two *known* ones behind the Curtain,' Bernard corrected him. 'One of them was in the Irkutsk region, near the border of Outer Mongolia – a very grim affair. It was assumed that the women had been lying with devils, and they perished, as well as the Children. The other was right away to the east, a place called Gizhinsk, in the mountains north-east of Okhotsk. There may have been others that we didn't hear of. It's pretty certain it happened in some places in

South America and in Africa, too, but it's difficult to check. The inhabitants tend to be secretive. It's even possible that an isolated village would miss a day and not know it – in which case the babies would be even more of a puzzle. In most of the instances we do know of, the babies were regarded as freaks, and were killed, but we suspect that in some they may have been hidden away.'

'But not, I take it, in Gizhinsk?' put in Zellaby.

Bernard looked at him with a small twitch to the corner of his mouth.

'You don't miss much, do you, Zellaby? You're right – not in Gizhinsk. The Dayout there took place a week before the Midwich one. We had the report of it three or four days later. It worried the Russians quite a lot. That was at least some consolation to us when it happened here; we knew that they couldn't have been responsible. They, presumably, in due course found out about Midwich, and were also relieved. Meanwhile, our agent kept an eye on Gizhinsk, and in due course reported the curious fact that every woman there was simultaneously pregnant. We were a little slow in appreciating any significance in that – it sounded like useless, if peculiar, tittle-tattle – but presently we discovered the state of affairs in Midwich, and began to take more interest. Once the babies were born the situation was easier for the Russians than for us; they practically sealed off Gizhinsk – a place about twice the size of Midwich – and our information from there virtually ceased. We could not exactly seal off Midwich, so we had to work differently, and, in the circumstances, I don't think we did too badly.'

Zellaby nodded. 'I see. The War Office view being that it did not know quite what we had here, or what the Russians had there. But *if* it should turn out that the Russians had a flock of potential geniuses, it would be useful for us to have a similar flock to put up against them?'

'More or less that. It was quite quickly clear that they were something unusual.'

'I ought to have seen that,' said Zellaby. He shook his head sadly. 'It simply never crossed my mind that we in Midwich were not unique. It does, however, now cross my mind that something must have happened to cause you to admit it. I don't quite see why the events here should justify that, so it probably happened somewhere else, say in Gizhinsk? Has there been a new development there that our Children are likely to display shortly?'

Bernard put his knife and fork neatly together on his plate, regarded them for a moment, and then looked up.

'The Far-East Army,' he said slowly, 'has recently been equipped with a new medium-type atomic cannon, believed to have a range of between fifty and sixty miles. Last week they carried out the first live tests with it. The town of Gizhinsk no longer exists. . . .'

We stared at him. With a horrified expression, Angela leant forward.

'You mean – everybody there?' she said incredulously.

Bernard nodded. 'Everybody. The entire place. No one there could have been warned without the Children getting to know of it. Besides, the way it was done it could be officially attributed to an error in calculation – or, possibly to sabotage.'

He paused again.

'Officially,' he repeated, 'and for home and general consumption. We have, however, received a carefully channelled observation from Russian sources. It is rather guarded on details and particulars, but there is no doubt that it refers to Gizhinsk, and was probably released simultaneously with the action taken there. It doesn't refer directly to Midwich, either, but what it does do, is to put out a most forcefully expressed warning. After a description which fits the Children exactly, it speaks of them as groups which present not just a national danger, wherever they exist, but a racial danger of a most urgent kind. It calls upon all governments everywhere to "neutralize" any such known groups with the least possible delay. It does this most emphatically, with almost a note of panic, at times. It insists, over and over again, even with a touch of pleading, that this should be done swiftly, not just for the sake of nations, or of continents, but because these Children are a threat to the whole human race.'

Zellaby went on tracing the damask pattern on the table cloth for some time before he looked up. Then he said:

'And M.I.'s reaction to this? To wonder what fast one the Russians were trying to pull this time, I suppose?' And he returned to doodling on the damask.

'Most of us, yes – some of us, no,' admitted Bernard.

Presently Zellaby looked up again.

'They dealt with Gizhinsk last week, you say. Which day?'

'Tuesday, the second of July,' Bernard told him.

Zellaby nodded several times, slowly.

'Interesting,' he said. 'But how, I wonder, did ours know . . . ?'

*

Soon after luncheon, Bernard announced that he was going up to The Grange again.

'I didn't have a chance to talk to Torrance while Sir John was there – and after that, well, we both needed a bit of a break.'

'I suppose you can't give us any idea of what you intend to do about the Children?' Angela asked.

He shook his head. 'If I had any ideas I suppose they'd have to be official secrets. As it is, I'm going to see whether Torrance, from his knowledge of them, can make any suggestions. I hope to be back in an hour or so,' he added, as he left us.

Emerging from the front door, he made automatically towards his car, and then as he reached for the handle, changed his mind. A little exercise, he decided, would freshen him up, and he set off briskly down the drive, on foot.

Just outside the gate a small lady in a blue tweed suit looked at him, hesitated, and then advanced to meet him. Her face went a little pink, but she pushed resolutely on. Bernard raised his hat.

'You won't know me. I am Miss Lamb, but of course we all know who you are, Colonel Westcott.'

Bernard acknowledged the introduction with a small bow, wondering how much 'we all' (which presumably comprehended the whole of Midwich) knew about him, and for how long they had known it. He asked what he could do for her.

'It's about the Children, Colonel. What is going to be done?'

He told her, honestly enough, that no decision had yet been made. She listened, her eyes intently on his face, her gloved hands clasped together.

'It won't be anything severe, will it?' she asked. 'Oh, I know last night was dreadful, but it wasn't their fault. They don't really understand yet. They're so very young you see. I know they look twice their age, but even that's not very old, is it? They didn't really *mean* the harm they did. They were frightened. Wouldn't any of us be frightened if a crowd came to our house wanting to burn it down? Of course we should. We should have a right to defend ourselves, and nobody could blame us. Why, if the villagers came to my house like that I should defend it with whatever I could find – perhaps an axe.'

Bernard doubted it. The picture of this small lady setting about a crowd with an axe was one that did not easily come into focus.

'It was a very drastic remedy they took,' he reminded her, gently.

'I know. But when you are young and frightened it is very easy to be more violent than you mean to be. I know when I was a child there were injustices which positively made me burn inside. If I had had the strength to do what I wanted to do it would have been dreadful, really dreadful, I assure you.'

'Unfortunately,' he pointed out, 'the Children do have that strength, and you must agree that they can't be allowed to use it.'

'No,' she said. 'But they won't when they're old enough to

understand. I'm sure they won't. People are saying they must be sent away. But you won't do that, will you? They're so young. I know they're wilful, but they need us. They aren't wicked. It's just that lately they have been frightened. They weren't like this before. If they can stay here we can teach them love and gentleness, show them that people don't really mean them any harm. . . .'

She looked up into his face, her hands pressed anxiously together, her eyes pleading, with tears not far behind them.

Bernard looked back at her unhappily, marvelling at the devotion that was able to regard six deaths and a number of serious injuries as a kind of youthful peccadillo. He could almost see in her mind the adored slight figure with golden eyes which filled all her view. She would never blame, never cease to adore, never understand. . . . There had been just one wonderful, miraculous thing in all her life. . . . His heart ached for Miss Lamb. . . .

He could only explain that the decision did not lie in his hands, assure her, trying not to raise any false hopes, that what she had told him would be included in his report; and then detach himself as gently as possible to go on his way, conscious of her anxious, reproachful eyes at his back.

The village, as he passed through it, was wearing a sparse appearance and a subdued air. There must, he imagined, be strong feelings concerning the corralling measure, but the few people about, except for one or two chatting pairs, had a rather noticeable air of minding their own business. A single policeman on patrol round the Green was clearly bored with his job. Lesson One, from the Children – that there was danger in numbers – appeared to have been understood. An efficient step in dictatorship: no wonder the Russians had not cared for the look of things at Gizhinsk. . . .

Twenty yards up Hickham Lane he came upon two of the Children. They were sitting on the roadside bank, staring upward and westward with such concentration that they did not notice his approach.

Bernard stopped, and turned his head to follow their line

of sight, becoming aware at the same time of the sound of jet engines. The aircraft was easy to spot, a silver shape against the blue summer sky, approaching at about five thousand feet. Just as he found it, black dots appeared beneath it. White parachutes opened in quick succession, five of them, and began the long float down. The aircraft flew steadily on.

He glanced back at the Children just in time to see them exchange an unmistakable smile of satisfaction. He looked up again at the aircraft serenely pursuing its way, and at the five, gently sinking, white blobs behind it. His knowledge of aircraft was slight, but he was fairly certain that he was looking at a Carey light long-range bomber that normally carried a complement of five. He looked thoughtfully at the two Children again, and at the same moment they noticed him.

The three of them studied one another while the bomber droned on, right overhead now.

'That,' Bernard observed, 'was a very expensive machine. Someone is going to be very annoyed about losing it.'

'It's a warning. But they'll probably have to lose several more before they believe it,' said the boy.

'Probably. Yours is an unusual accomplishment,' he paused, still studying them. 'You don't care for the idea of aircraft flying over you, is that it?'

'Yes,' agreed the boy.

Bernard nodded. 'I can understand that. But, tell me, why do you always make your warnings so severe – why do you always carry them a stage further than necessary? Couldn't you simply have turned him back?'

'We *could* have made him crash,' said the girl.

'I suppose so. We must be grateful that you didn't, I'm sure. But it would have been no less effective to turn him back, wouldn't it? I don't see why you have to be so drastic.'

'It makes more of an impression. We should have to turn a lot of aircraft back before anyone would believe we were doing it. But if they lose an aircraft every time they come this way they'll take notice,' the boy told him.

'I see. The same argument applies to last night, I suppose.

If you had just sent the crowd away, it would not have been warning enough,' Bernard suggested.

'Do you think it would?' asked the boy.

'It seems to me to depend on how it was done. Surely there was no need to make them fight one another, murderously? I mean, isn't it, to put it on its most practical level, politically unsound always to take that extra step that simply increases anger and hatred?'

'Fear, too,' the boy pointed out.

'Oh, you *want* to instil fear, do you? Why?' inquired Bernard.

'Only to make you leave us alone,' said the boy. 'It is a means; not an end.' His golden eyes were turned towards Bernard, with a steady, earnest look. 'Sooner or later, you will try to kill us. However we behave, you will want to wipe us out. Our position can be made stronger only if we take the initiative.'

The boy spoke quite calmly, but somehow the words pierced right through the front that Bernard had adopted.

In one startling flash he was hearing an adult, seeing a sixteen-year-old, knowing that it was a nine-year-old who spoke.

'For a moment,' he said later, 'it bowled me right over. I was as near panic as I have ever been. The child-adult combination seemed to be full of a terrifying significance that knocked away all the props from the right order of things.... I know it seems a small thing now; but at the time it hit me like a revelation, and, by God, it frightened me. . . . I suddenly saw them double: individually, still children; collectively, adult; talking to me on my own level.... '

It took Bernard a few moments to pull himself together. As he did so, he recalled the scene with the Chief Constable which had been alarming, too, but in another, much more concrete, way, and he looked at the boy more closely.

'Are you Eric?' he asked him.

'No,' said the boy. 'Sometimes I am Joseph. But now I am all of us. You needn't be afraid of us; we want to talk to you.'

Bernard had himself under control again. He deliberately sat down on the bank beside them, and forced a reasonable tone.

'Wanting to kill you seems to me a very large assumption,' he said. 'Naturally, if you go on doing the kind of things you have been doing lately we *shall* hate you, and we shall take revenge – or perhaps one should say, we shall have to protect ourselves from you. But if you don't, well, we can see. Do *you* have such a great hatred of *us*? If you don't, then surely some kind of *modus vivendi* can be managed. . . ?'

He looked at the boy, still with a faint hope that he ought to have spoken more as one would to a child. The boy finally dispelled any illusion about that. He shook his head, and said:

'You're putting this on the wrong level. It isn't a matter of hates, or likes. They make no difference. Nor is it something that can be arranged by discussion. It is a biological obligation. You cannot afford *not* to kill us, for if you don't, you are finished. . . . ' He paused to give that weight, and then went on: 'There is a political obligation, but that takes a more immediate view, on a more conscious level. Already, some of your politicians who know about us must be wondering whether something like the Russian solution could not be managed here.'

'Oh, so you *do* know about them?'

'Yes, of course. As long as the Children of Gizhinsk were alive we did not need to look after ourselves, but when they died, two things happened: one was that the balance was destroyed, and the other was the realization that the Russians would not have destroyed the balance unless they were quite sure that a colony of the Children was more of a liability than a possible asset.

'The biological obligation will not be denied. The Russians fulfilled it from political motives, as, no doubt, you will try to do. The Eskimos did it by primitive instinct. But the result is the same.

'For you, however, it will be more difficult. To the Russians, once they had decided that the Children at Gizhinsk were not going to be useful, as they had hoped, the proper course was not in question. In Russia, the individual exists to serve the State; if he puts self above State, he is a traitor, and it is the duty of the community to protect itself from traitors whether they are individuals, or groups. In this case, then, biological duty and political duty coincided. And if it were inevitable that a number of innocently involved persons should perish too, well, that could not be helped; it was their duty to die, if necessary to serve the State.

'But for you, the issue is less clear. Not only has your will to survive been much more deeply submerged by convention, but you have the inconvenience here of the idea that the State exists to serve the individuals who compose it. Therefore your consciences will be troubled by the thought that we have "rights".

'Our first moment of real danger has passed. It occurred when you first heard of the Russian action against the Children. A decisive man might have arranged a quick "accident" here. It has suited you to keep us hidden away here, and it suited us to be hidden, so it might have been cunningly managed without too much trouble. Now, however, it cannot. Already, the people in Trayne hospital will have talked about us; in fact, after last night there must be talk and rumours spreading all round. The chance of making any convincing "accident" has gone. So what are you going to do to liquidate us?'

Bernard shook his head.

'Look,' he said, 'suppose we consider this thing from a more civilized standpoint – after all, this is a civilized country, and famous for its ability to find compromises. I'm not convinced by the sweeping way you assume there can be no agreement. History has shown us to be more tolerant of minorities than most.'

It was the girl who answered this time:

'This is not a civilized matter,' she said, 'it is a very primitive matter. If we exist, we shall dominate you – that is clear and inevitable. Will you agree to be superseded, and start on the way to extinction without a struggle? I do not think you are decadent enough for that. And then, politically, the question is: Can *any* State, however tolerant, afford to harbour an increasingly powerful minority which it has no power to control? Obviously the answer is again, no.

'So what will you do? We are very likely safe for a time while you talk about it. The more primitive of you, your masses, will let their instincts lead them – we saw the pattern in the village last night – they will want to hunt us down, and destroy us. Your more liberal, responsibly-minded, and religious people will be greatly troubled over the ethical position. Opposed to any form of drastic action at all, you will have your true idealists – and also your sham idealists: the quite large number of people who profess ideals as a form of premium for other-life insurance, and are content to lay up slavery and destitution for their descendants so long as they are enabled to produce personal copybooks of elevated views at the gate of heaven.

'Then, too, with your Government of the Right reluctantly driven to consider drastic action against us, your politicians of the Left will see a chance of party capital, and possible dismissal of the Government. They will defend our rights as a threatened minority, and children, at that. Their leaders will glow with righteousness on our behalf. They will claim, without referendum, to be representing justice, compassion, and the great heart of the people. Then it will occur to some of them that there really *is* a serious problem, and that if they were to force an election there would very likely be a split between the promoters of the party's official Warm-heart policy, and the rank and file whose misgivings about us will make them a Cold-feet faction; so the display of abstract righteousness, and the plugging of well-tested, best-selling virtues will diminish.'

'You don't appear to think very highly of our institutions,' Bernard put in. The girl shrugged.

'As a securely dominant species you could afford to lose touch with reality, and amuse yourselves with abstractions,' she replied. Then she went on: 'While these people are wrangling, it will come home to a lot of them that the problem of dealing with a more advanced species than themselves is not going to be easy, and will become less easy with procrastination. There may be practical attempts to deal with us. But we have shown last night what is going to happen to soldiers if they are sent against us. If you send aircraft, they will crash. Very well then, you will think of artillery, as the Russians did, or of guided missiles whose electronics we cannot affect. But if you send them, you won't be able to kill only us, you will have to kill all the people in the village as well – it would take you a long time even to contemplate such an action, and if it *were* carried out, what government in this country could survive such a massacre of innocents on the grounds of expediency? Not only would the party that sanctioned it be finished for good, but, if they were successful in removing the danger, the leaders could then be safely lynched, by way of atonement and expiation.'

She stopped speaking, and the boy took up:

'The details may vary, but something of the sort will become inevitable as the threat of our existence is more widely understood. You might easily have a curious epoch when both parties are fighting to keep out of office rather than be the one that has to take action against us.' He paused, looking out thoughtfully across the fields for some moments, then he added:

'Well, there it is. Neither you, nor we, have wishes that count in the matter – or should one say that we both have been given the same wish – to survive? We are all, you see, toys of the life-force. It made you numerically strong, but mentally undeveloped; it made us mentally strong, but physically weak: now it has set us at one another, to see what will happen. A cruel sport, perhaps, from both our points of view, but a very, very old one. Cruelty is as old as life itself. There is some improvement: humour and compassion are the most important of human inventions; but they are not very firmly established yet, though promising well.' He paused, and smiled. 'A real bit of Zellaby, that – our first teacher,' he put in, and then went on. 'But the life force is a great deal stronger than they are; and it won't be denied its blood-sports.

'However, it has seemed possible to us that the serious stage of the combat might at least be postponed. And that is what we want to talk to you about. . . .'

CHAPTER 20

Ultimatum

'THIS,' Zellaby said reprovingly, to a golden-eyed girl who was sitting on the branch of a tree beside the path, 'this is a quite uncalled-for circumscription of my movements. You know perfectly well that I *always* take an afternoon stroll, and that I always return for tea. Tyranny easily becomes a very bad habit. Besides, you've got my wife as a hostage.'

The Child appeared to think it over, and presently pushed a large bullseye into one cheek.

'All right, Mr Zellaby,' she said.

Zellaby advanced a foot. This time it passed unobstructedly over an invisible barrier that had stopped it before.

'Thank you, my dear,' he said, with a polite inclination of his head. 'Come along, Gayford.'

We passed on into the woods, leaving the guardian of the path idly swinging her legs, and crunching her bullseye.

'A very interesting aspect of this affair is the demarcations between the individual and the collective,' Zellaby remarked. 'I've really made precious little progress in determining it. The Child's appreciation of her sweet is indubitably individual, it could scarcely be other; but her permission for us to go on was collective, as was the influence that stopped us. And since the mind is collective, what about the sensations it receives? Are the rest of the Children vicariously enjoying her bullseye, too? It would appear not, yet they must be aware of it, and perhaps of its flavour. A similar problem arises when I show them my films and lecture to them. In theory, if I had two of them only as my audience, all of them would share the experience – that's the way they learn their lessons, as I told you – but in practice I always have a full house when I go up to The Grange. As far as I can understand it, when I show a film they *could* get it from one representative of each sex, but, presumably, in the transmission of visual sensation something is lost, for they all very much prefer to see it with their own eyes. It is difficult to get them to talk about it much, but it does appear that individual experience of a picture is more satisfactory to them as, one must suppose, is individual experience of a bullseye. It is a reflection that sets off a whole train of questions.'

'I can believe that,' I agreed, 'but they are post-graduate questions. As far as I am concerned, the basic problem of their presence here at all gives me quite enough to be going on with.'

'Oh,' said Zellaby, 'I don't think there is much that's novel about that. Our presence here at all raises the same problem.'

'I don't see that. We evolved here – but where did the Children come from?'

'Aren't you taking a theory for an established fact, my dear fellow? It is widely *supposed* that we evolved here, and to support that supposition it is *supposed* that there once existed a creature who was the ancestor of ourselves, and of the apes – what our grandfathers used to call "the missing link". But there has never been any satisfactory proof that such a creature existed. And *the* missing link, why, bless my soul, the whole proposition is riddled with missing links – if that is an acceptable metaphor. Can you see the whole diversity of races evolving from this one link? I can't, however hard I try. Nor, at a later stage, can I see a nomadic creature segregating the strains which would give rise to such fixed and distinctive characteristics of race. On islands it is understandable, but not on the great land-masses. At first sight, climate might have some effect – until one considers the Mongolian characteristics apparently indigenous from the equator to the North Pole. Think, too, of the innumerable intermediary types there would have to be, and then of the few poor relics we have been able to find. Think of the number of generations we should have to go back to trace the blacks, the whites, the reds, and the yellows to a common ancestor, and consider that where there should be innumerable traces of this development left by millions of evolving ancestors there is practically nothing but a great blank. Why, we know more about the age of reptiles than we do about the age of supposedly evolving man. We had a complete evolutionary tree for the horse many years ago. If it were possible to do the same for man we should have done it by now. But what do we have? Just a few, remarkably few, isolated specimens. Nobody knows where, or if, they fit into an evolutionary picture because there is no picture – only supposition. The specimens are as unattached to us as we are to the Children. . . .'

For half an hour or so I listened to a discourse on the erratic and unsatisfactory phylogeny of mankind, which Zellaby concluded with an apology for his inadequate coverage of a subject which was not susceptible to a condensation into half a dozen sentences, as he had attempted.

'However,' he added, 'you will have gathered that the conventional assumption has more lacunae than substance.'

'But if you invalidate it, what then?' I inquired.

'I don't know,' Zellaby admitted, 'but I do refuse to accept a bad theory simply on the grounds that there is not a better, and I take the lack of evidence that ought, if it were valid, to be plentiful, as an argument for the opposition – whatever that may be. As a result I find the occurrence of the Children scarcely more startling, objectively, than that of the various other races of mankind that have apparently popped into existence fully formed, or at least with no clear line of ancestral development.'

So dissolute a conclusion seemed unlike Zellaby. I suggested that he probably had a theory of his own.

Zellaby shook his head.

'No,' he admitted modestly. Then he added: 'One has to speculate, of course. Not very satisfactorily, I'm afraid, and sometimes uncomfortably. It is, for instance, disquieting for a good rationalist, such as myself, to find himself wondering whether perhaps there is not some Outside Power arranging things here. When I look round the world, it does sometimes seem to hold a suggestion of a rather disorderly testing-ground. The sort of place where someone might let loose a new strain now and then, and see how it will make out in our rough and tumble. Fascinating for an inventor to watch his creations acquitting themselves, don't you think? To discover whether this time he has produced a successful tearer-to-pieces, or just another torn-to-pieces and, too, to observe the progress of the earlier models, and see which of them have proved really competent at making life a form of hell for others. . . . You don't think so? – Ah, well, as I told you, the speculations tend to be uncomfortable.'

I told him:

'As man to man, Zellaby, not only do you talk a great deal, but you talk a great deal of nonsense, and make *some* of it sound like sense. It is very confusing for a listener.'

Zellaby looked hurt.

'My dear fellow, I always talk sense. It is my primary social failing. One must distinguish between the content, and the container. Would you prefer me to talk with that monotonous dogmatic intensity which our simpler-minded brethren believe, God help them, to be a guarantee of sincerity? Even if I should, you would still have to evaluate the content.'

'What I want to know,' I said firmly, 'is whether, having disposed of human evolution, you have any serious hypothesis to put in its place?'

'You don't like my Inventor speculation? Nor do I, very much. But at least it has the merit of being no less improbable, and a lot more comprehensible than many religious suggestions. And when I say "Inventor", I don't necessarily mean an individual, of course. More probably a team. It seems to me that if a team of our own biologists and geneticists were to take a remote island for their testing-ground they would find great interest and instruction in observing their specimens there in ecological conflict. And, after all, what is a planet but an island in space? But a speculation is, as I said, far from being a theory.'

Our circuit had taken us round to the Oppley road. As we were approaching the village a figure, deep in thought, emerged from Hickham Lane, and turned to walk ahead of us. Zellaby called to him. Bernard came out of his abstraction. He stopped and waited for us to catch up.

'You don't look,' remarked Zellaby, 'as though Torrance has been helpful.'

'I didn't get as far as Dr Torrance,' Bernard admitted. 'And now there seems to be little point in troubling him. I've been talking with a couple of your Children.'

'Not with a couple of them,' Zellaby protested gently. 'One talks with either the Composite Boy, or the Composite Girl, or with both.'

'All right. I accept the correction. I have been talking with *all* the Children – at least, I think so, though I seemed to detect what one might call a strong Zellaby flavour in the conversational style of both boy and girl.'

Zellaby looked pleased.

'Considering we are lion and lamb, our relations have usually been good. It is gratifying to have had some educational influence,' he observed. 'How did you get on?'

'I don't think "get on" quite expresses it,' Bernard told him. 'I was informed, lectured, and instructed. And, finally, I have been charged with bearing an ultimatum.'

'Indeed – and to whom?' asked Zellaby.

'I am really not quite sure. Roughly, I think, to anyone who is in a position to supply them with air transport.'

Zellaby raised his brows. 'Where to?'

'They didn't say. Somewhere, I imagine, where they will be able to live unmolested.'

He gave us a brief version of the Children's arguments.

'So it really amounts to this,' he summed up. 'In their view, their existence here constitutes a challenge to authority which cannot be evaded for long. They cannot be ignored, but any government that tries to deal with them will bring immense political trouble down on itself if it is not successful, and very little less if it is. The Children themselves have no wish to attack, or to be forced to defend themselves – '

'Naturally,' murmured Zellaby. 'Their immediate concern is to survive, in order, eventually, to dominate.'

'– therefore it is in the best interests of all parties that they should be provided with the means of removing themselves.'

'Which would mean, game to the Children,' Zellaby commented, and withdrew into thought.

'It sounds risky – from their point of view, I mean. All conveniently in one aircraft,' I suggested.

'Oh, trust them to think of that. They've considered quite a lot of details. There are to be several aircraft. A squad is to be put at their disposal to check the aircraft, and search for time-bombs, or any such devices. Parachutes are to be provided, some of which, picked out by themselves, are to be tested. There are quite a number of similar provisos. They've been quicker to grasp the full implications of the Gizhinsk business than our own people here, and they aren't leaving much scope for sharp practice.'

'H'm,' I said. 'I can't say I envy you the job of pushing a proposition like that through the red tape. What's their alternative?'

Bernard shook his head.

'There isn't one. Perhaps ultimatum wasn't quite the right word. Demand would be better. I told the Children I could see very little hope of getting anyone to listen to me seriously. They said they would prefer to try it that way first – there'd be less trouble all round if it could be put through quietly. If I can't put it across – and it is pretty obvious I shall not be able to by myself – then they propose that two of them shall accompany me on a second approach.

'After seeing what their "duress" could do to the Chief Constable, it isn't a pleasant prospect. I can see no reason why they should not apply pressure at one level after another until they reach the very top, if necessary. What's to stop them?'

'One has, for some time, seen this coming, as inevitably as the change of the seasons,' Zellaby said, emerging from his reflections. 'But I did not expect it so soon – nor do I think it would have come for years yet if the Russians had not precipitated it. I would guess it has come earlier than the Children themselves would wish, too. They know they are not ready to face it. That is why they want to get away to some place where they can reach maturity unmolested.

'We are presented with a moral dilemma of some niceness. On the one hand, it is our duty to our race and culture to liquidate the Children, for it is clear that if we do not we shall, at best, be completely dominated by them, and their culture, whatever it may turn out to be, will extinguish ours.

'On the other hand, it is our culture that gives us scruples about the ruthless liquidation of unarmed minorities, not to mention the practical obstacles to such a solution.

'On the – oh dear, how difficult – on the third hand, to enable the Children to shift the problem they represent to the territory of a people even more ill equipped to deal with it is a form of evasive procrastination which lacks any moral courage at all.

'It makes one long for H. G.'s straightforward Martians. This would seem to be one of those unfortunate situations where no solution is morally defensible.'

Bernard and I received that in silence. Presently I felt compelled to say:

'That sounds to me the kind of masterly summing-up that has landed philosophers in sticky situations throughout the ages.'

'Oh, surely not,' Zellaby protested. 'In a quandary where every course is immoral, there still remains the ability to act for the greatest good of the greatest number. Ergo, the Children *ought* to be eliminated at the least possible cost, with the least possible delay. I am sorry to have to arrive at that conclusion. In nine years I have grown rather fond of them. And, in spite of what my wife says, I think I have come as near friendship with them as possible.'

He allowed another, and longer, pause, and shook his head.

'It is the right step,' he repeated. 'But, of course, our authorities will not be able to bring themselves to take it – for which I am personally thankful because I can see no practical course open to them which would not involve the destruction of all of us in the village, as well.' He stopped and looked about him at Midwich resting quietly in the afternoon sun. 'I am getting to be an old man, and I shall not live much longer in any case, but I have a younger wife, and a young son; and I should like to think, too, that all this will go on as long as it may. No, the authorities will argue, no doubt; but if the Children want to go, they'll go. Humanitarianism will triumph over biological duty – is that probity, would you say? Or is it decadence? But so the evil day will be put off – for how long, I wonder . . . ?'

Back at Kyle Manor tea was ready, but after one cup Bernard rose, and made his farewells to the Zellabys.

'I shan't learn any more by staying longer,' he said. 'The sooner I present the Children's demands to my incredulous superiors, the sooner we shall get things moving. I have no doubt your arguments are right, on their plane, Mr Zellaby, but I personally shall work to get the Children anywhere out of this country, and quickly. I have seen a number of unpleasant sights in my life, but none that has ever been such a clear warning as the degradation of your Chief Constable. I'll keep you informed how it goes, of course.'

He looked at me.

'Coming with me, Richard?'

I hesitated. Janet was still in Scotland, and not due back for a couple of days yet. There was nothing that needed my presence in London, and I was finding the problem of the Midwich Children far more fascinating than anything I was likely to encounter there. Angela noticed.

'Do stay if you would like to,' she said. 'I think we'd both be rather glad of some company just now.'

I judged that she meant it, and accepted.

'Anyway,' I added, to Bernard. 'We don't even know that your new courier status includes a companion. If I were to try to come with you we'd probably find that I am still under the ban.'

'Oh, yes, that ridiculous ban,' said Zellaby. 'I must talk to them seriously about that – a quite absurd panic measure on their part.'

We accompanied Bernard to the door, and watched him set off down the drive, with a wave of his hand.

'Yes. Game to the Children, I think,' Zellaby said again, as the car turned out into the road. 'And set, too . . . later on . . . ?' He shrugged faintly, and shook his head.

CHAPTER 21

Zellaby of Macedon

'MY DEAR,' said Zellaby, looking along the breakfast table at his wife, 'if you happen to be going into Trayne this morning, will you get one of those large jars of bullseyes?'

Angela switched her attention from the toaster to her husband.

'Darling,' she said, though without endearment, 'in the first place, if you recall yesterday, you will remember that there is no question of going to Trayne. In the second, I have no inclination to provide the Children with sweets. In the third, if this means that you are proposing to go and show them films at The Grange this evening, I strongly protest.'

'The ban,' said Zellaby, 'is raised. I pointed out to them last night that it was really rather silly and ill-considered. Their hostages cannot make a concerted flight without word reaching them, if only through Miss Lamb, or Miss Ogle. Everybody is inconvenienced to no purpose; only half, or a quarter, of the village makes as good a shield for them as the whole of it. And furthermore, that I proposed to cancel my lecture on the Aegean Islands this evening if half of them were going to be out making a nuisance of themselves on the roads and paths.'

'And they just agreed?' asked Angela.

'Of course. They're not stupid, you know. They are very susceptible to reasoned argument.'

'Well, really! After all we've been through – '

'But they are,' protested Zellaby. 'When they are jittery, or startled, they do foolish things, but don't we all? And because they are young they over-reach themselves, but don't all the young? Also, they are anxious and nervous – and shouldn't *we* be nervous if the threat of what happened at Gizhinsk were hanging over us?'

'Gordon,' his wife said, 'I don't understand you. The

Children are responsible for the loss of six lives. They have *killed* these six people whom we knew well, and hurt a lot more, some of them badly. At any time the same thing may happen to any of us. Are you *defending* that?'

'Of course not, my dear. I am simply explaining that they can make mistakes when they are alarmed, just as we can. One day they will have to fight us for their lives; they know that, and out of nervousness they made the mistake of thinking that the time had come.'

'So now all we have to do is to say: "We're so sorry you killed six people by mistake. Let's forget all about it." '

'What else do you suggest? Would you prefer to antagonize them?' asked Zellaby.

'Of course not, but if the law can't touch them as you say it can't – though I really don't see what good the law is if it can't admit what everybody knows – but even if it can't, it doesn't mean we've got to take no notice and pretend it never happened. There are social sanctions, as well as legal ones.'

'I should be careful, my dear. We have just been shown that the sanction of power can override both,' Zellaby told her seriously.

Angela looked at him with a puzzled expression.

'Gordon, I *don't* understand you,' she repeated. 'We think alike about so many things. We share the same principles, but now I seem to have lost you. We *can't* just ignore what has happened: it would be as bad as condoning it.'

'You and I, my dear, are using different yardsticks. You are judging by social rules, and finding crime. I am considering an elemental struggle, and finding no crime – just grim, primeval danger.' The tone in which he said the last words was so different from his usual manner that it startled both of us into staring at him. For the first time in my knowledge I saw another Zellaby – the one whose incisive hints of his existence made the Works more than they seemed – showing clearly through, and seeming younger than, the familiar, dilettante spinner of words. Then he slipped back to his usual style. 'The wise lamb does not enrage the lion,' he said. 'It placates him, plays for time, and hopes for the best. The Children like bullseyes, and will be expecting them.'

His eyes and Angela's held for some seconds. I watched the puzzlement and hurt fade out of hers, and give place to a look of trust so naked that I was embarrassed.

Zellaby turned to me.

'I'm afraid there is some business that needs my attention this morning, my dear fellow. Perhaps you would care to celebrate the lifting of our siege by escorting Angela into Trayne?'

*

When we got back to Kyle Manor, a little before lunchtime, I found Zellaby in a canvas chair on the bricks in front of the veranda. He did not hear me at first, and as I looked at him I was struck by the contrasts in him. At breakfast there had been a glimpse of a younger, stronger man; now he looked old and tired, older than I had ever thought him; showing, too, something of the withdrawal of age as he sat with the light wind stirring his silky white hair, and his gaze on things far, far away.

Then my foot gritted on the bricks, and he changed. The air of lassitude left him, the vacancy went out of his eyes, and the face he turned to me was the Zellaby countenance I had known for ten years.

I took a chair beside him, and set down the large bottle of bullseyes on the bricks. His eyes rested on it a moment.

'Good,' he said. 'They're very fond of those. After all, they are still children – with a small "c" – too.'

'Look,' I said, 'I don't want to be intrusive, but – well, do you think it's wise of you to go up there this evening? After all, one can't really put the clock back. Things have changed. There is acknowledged enmity now, between them and the village, if not between them and all of us. They must suspect that there will be moves against them. Their ultimatum to Bernard isn't going to be accepted right away, if it is at all.

You said they were nervous, well, they must still be nervous – and, therefore, still dangerous.'

Zellaby shook his head.

'Not to me, my dear fellow. I began to teach them before the authorities took any hand in it, and I've gone on teaching them. I wouldn't say I understand them, but I think I know them better than anyone else does. The most important thing is that they trust me. . . .'

He lapsed into silence, leaning back in his chair, watching the poplars sway with the wind.

'Trust – ' he was beginning when Angela came out with the sherry decanter and glasses, and he broke off to ask what they were saying about us in Trayne.

At lunch he talked less than usual, and afterwards disappeared into the study. A little later I saw him setting off down the drive on his habitual afternoon walk, but as he had not invited me to join him I made myself comfortable in a deck-chair in the garden. He was back for tea – at which he warned me to eat well as dinner was replaced by a late supper on the evenings that he lectured to the Children.

Angela put in, though not very hopefully:

'Darling, don't you think – ? I mean, they've seen all your films. I know you've shown them the Aegean one twice before, at least. Couldn't you put it off, and perhaps hire a film that will be new to them?'

'My dear, it's a good film; it will stand seeing more than once or twice,' Zellaby explained, a little hurt. 'Besides, I don't give the same talk every time – there's always something more to say about the Isles of Greece.'

At half past six we started loading his gear into the car. There seemed to be a great deal of it. Numerous cases containing projector, resistance, amplifier, loud-speaker, a case of films, a tape-recorder so that his words should not be lost, all of them very heavy. By the time we had the lot in, and a stand microphone on top, it began to look as if he were starting on a lengthy safari rather than an evening's talk.

Zellaby himself hovered round while we were at work,

inspected, counted everything over, including the jar of bullseyes, and finally approved. He turned to Angela.

'I've asked Gayford if he'll drive me up there and help to unload the stuff,' he said. 'There's nothing to worry about.' He drew her to him, and kissed her.

'Gordon – ' she began. 'Gordon – '

Still with his left arm round her he caressed her face with his right hand, looking into her eyes. He shook his head, in gentle reproof.

'But, Gordon, I'm afraid of the Children now. . . . Suppose they – ?'

'You don't need to be anxious, my dear. I know what I'm doing,' he told her.

Then he turned and got into the car, and we drove down the drive, with Angela standing on the steps, looking after us unhappily.

*

It was not entirely without misgiving that I drove up to the front door of The Grange. Nothing in its appearance, however, justified alarm. It was simply a large, rather ugly Victorian house, incongruously flanked by the new, industrial-looking wings that had been built as laboratories in Mr Crimm's time. The lawn in front of it showed little sign of the battle of a couple of nights before, and though a number of the surrounding bushes had suffered, it was difficult to believe in what had actually taken place.

We had not arrived unobserved. Before I could open the car door to get out, the front door of the house was pulled violently back, and a dozen or more of the Children ran excitedly down the steps with a scattered chorus of 'Hullo, Mr Zellaby.' They had the rear doors open in a moment, and two of the boys began to hand things out for the others to carry. Two girls dashed back up the steps with the microphone, and the roller screen, another pounced with a cry of triumph on the jar of bullseyes, and hurried after them.

'Hi, there,' said Zellaby anxiously, as they came to the heavier cases, 'that's delicate stuff. Go gently with it.'

A boy grinned at him, and lifted out one of the black cases with exaggerated care to hand to another. There was nothing odd or mysterious about the Children now unless it was the suggestion of musical-comedy chorus work given by their similarity. For the first time since my return I was able to appreciate that the Children had 'a small "c", too'. Nor was there any doubt at all that Zellaby's visit was a popular event. I watched him as he stood watching them with a kindly, half-wistful smile. It was impossible to associate the Children, as I saw them now, with danger. I had a confused feeling that these could not be *the* Children, at all; that the theories, fears, and threats we had discussed must have to do with some other group of Children. It was hard indeed to credit them with the deliquium of the vigorous Chief Constable that had shaken Bernard so badly. All but impossible to believe that they could have issued an ultimatum which was being taken seriously enough to be carried to the highest levels.

'I hope there'll be a good attendance,' Zellaby said, in half-question.

'Oh, yes, Mr Zellaby,' one of the boys assured him. 'Everybody – except Wilfred, of course. He's in the sick-room.'

'Oh, yes. How is he?' Zellaby asked.

'His back hurts still, but they've got all the pellets out, and the doctor says he'll be quite all right,' said the boy.

My feeling of schism went on increasing. I was finding it harder every moment to believe that we had not all of us been somehow deluded by a sweeping misunderstanding about the Children, and incredible that the Zellaby who stood beside me could be the same Zellaby who had spoken that morning of 'grim, primeval danger'.

The last of the cases was lifted out of the car. I remembered that it had been in the car already when we loaded the rest. It was evidently heavy, because two of the boys carried it between them. Zellaby watched them up the steps a little anxiously, and then turned to me.

'Thank you very much for your help,' he said, as though dismissing me.

I was disappointed. This new aspect of the Children fascinated me; I had decided I would like to attend his talk, and study them when they were all relaxed, all together, and being children with a small 'c'. Zellaby caught my expression.

'I would ask you to join us,' he explained. 'But I must confess that Angela is considerably in my thoughts this evening. She is anxious, you know. She has always been uneasy about the Children, and these last few days have upset her more than she shows. She would, I think, be the better for company this evening. I was rather hoping that you, my dear fellow. . . . It would be a great kindness. . . .'

'But of course,' I told him. 'How inconsiderate of me not to have thought of it. Of course.' What else could one say?

He smiled, and held out his hand.

'Excellent. I am most grateful, my dear fellow. I'm sure I can rely on you.'

Then he turned to three or four of the Children who still hovered near, and beamed on them.

'They'll be getting impatient,' he remarked. 'Lead on, Priscilla.'

'I'm Helen, Mr Zellaby,' she told him.

'Ah, well. Never mind. Come along, my dear,' said Zellaby, and they went up the steps together.

*

I got back into the car and drove off unhurriedly. On the way through the village I noticed that The Scythe and Stone seemed to be doing well, and was tempted to pause there to find out how local feeling was running now, but, with Zellaby's request in mind, I resisted, and kept going. In the Kyle Manor drive I turned the car round and left it standing, ready to fetch him back later on, and went in.

In the main sitting-room Angela was sitting in front of the

open windows, with the radio playing a Haydn quartet. She turned her head as I came in, and at the sight of her face I was glad Zellaby had asked me to come back.

'An enthusiastic welcome,' I told her, in answer to her unspoken question. 'For all I could tell they might – apart from the bewildering feeling that one was seeing multiple – have been a crowd of decent schoolchildren anywhere. I've no doubt he's right when he says they trust him.'

'Perhaps,' she allowed, 'but *I* don't trust *them*. I don't think I have, ever since the time they forced their mothers back here. I managed not to let it worry me much until they killed Jim Pawle, but ever since then I've been afraid of them. Thank goodness I packed Michael off at once. . . . There's no telling what they might do at any time. Even Gordon admits that they are nervous and panicky. It's nonsense for us to go on staying here, with our lives at the mercy of any childish fright or temper that comes over them. . . .

'Can you see anybody taking Colonel Westcott's "ultimatum" seriously? I can't. That means that the Children will have to do something to show that they *must* be listened to; they've got to convince important, hard-headed, and thick-headed people, and goodness knows how they may decide to do that. After what's happened already, I'm frightened – I really am. . . . They just don't care what becomes of any of us. . . .'

'It wouldn't do much good their making their demonstration here,' I tried to console her. 'They'll have to do it where it counts. Go up to London with Bernard, as they threatened. If they treat a few big-wigs there as they treated the Chief Constable –'

I broke off, interrupted by a bright flash, like lightning, and a sharp tremor that shook the house.

'What – ?' I began. But I got no further.

The blast that blew in through the open window almost carried me off my feet. The noise came, too, in a great, turbulent, shattering breaker of sound, while the house seemed to rock about us.

The overwhelming crash was followed by a clatter and tinkle of things falling, and then by an utter silence.

Without any conscious purpose I ran past Angela, huddled in her chair, through the open french windows, out on to the lawn. The sky was full of leaves torn from the trees, and still fluttering down. I turned, and looked at the house. Two great swatches of creeper had been pulled from the wall, and hung raggedly down. Every window in the west front gaped blankly back at me, without a pane of glass left. I looked the other way again, and through and above the trees there was a white and red glare. I had not a moment's doubt what it meant....

Turning again I ran back to the sitting-room, but Angela had gone, and the chair was empty.... I called to her, but there was no answer....

I found her at last, in Zellaby's study. The room was littered with broken glass. One curtain had been torn from its hangings and was draped half across the sofa. A part of the Zellaby family record had been swept from the mantel-shelf and now lay shattered in the hearth. Angela herself was sitting in Zellaby's working chair, lying forward across his desk, with her head on her bare arms. She did not move nor make any sound as I came in.

The opening of the door brought a draught through the empty window-frames. It caught a piece of paper lying on the desk beside her, slid it to the edge, and sent it fluttering to the floor.

I picked it up. A letter in Zellaby's pointed handwriting. I did not need to read it. The whole thing had been clear the moment I saw the red-white glow in the direction of The Grange, and recalled in the same instant the heavy cases which I had supposed to contain his recording-machine, and other gear. Nor was the letter mine to read, but as I put it back on the desk beside the motionless Angela, I caught sight of a few lines in the middle:

'... doctor will tell you, a matter of a few weeks, or months, at best. So no bitterness, my own love.

'As to this – well, we have lived so long in a garden that we have all but forgotten the commonplaces of survival. It was said: *Si fueris Romae, Romani vivito more*, and quite sensibly, too. But it is a more fundamental expression of the same sentiment to say: If you want to keep alive in the jungle, you must live as the jungle does. . . .'